ON HONEYMAN BALD

A novel

On Honeyman Bald

On Honeyman Bald

On Honeyman Bald is a work of fiction. All characters and situations are fictitious, and any resemblance to actual persons, events, or locales is purely coincidental. Although if there were a place like Honeyman Bald in the Smokies, it would be named a "bald," which is the local name for a mountain whose top is devoid of forests or other vegetation.

ISBN 978-0-9826576-5-2

By Tom Blackburn:
>   Fiction:
>>   The Cello Francesca, or, Balderdash
>>   Surviving Mozart
>>   Thanks to Mister Merrydown
>>   Roots of Evil
>>   On Honeyman Bald
>>   Dancing with Granny
>>   Assisted Living
>   Nonfiction:
>>   Equilibrium: A Chemistry of Solutions
>>   Getting Science Grants

On Honeyman Bald

My sweet Lesbia, let us live and love,
And though the wiser sort our ways reprove,
We need not hear them; the air's great lights may dive
Into the west, and soon again revive,
But, soon as once is set our little light,
Then must we sleep one everlasting night.

- Gaius Valerius Catullus,
trans. Ezra Pound

On Honeyman Bald

Prologue: The Old Man's Tale

Here is the story the old man told us up there, while the sun sank through a hundred miles of air, and we fidgeted and sneaked looks at each other, and the old man's son kept his eyes on nothing in particular, but on the women in general. The old man ignored him, and sat himself with many a creak and sigh against a boulder that commanded a good view of the sunset.

Long time ago,
the old man said, in a hazy, far-off voice that made that time seem long ago indeed,
at a time when the Cherokees and the Seminoles were having trouble ironing out a trade matter – to the point that insults had been exchanged and one or two fools had killed and been killed over it on each side – the Seminoles sent a runner all the way from what is now Florida to this very place, to what would be called Honeyman Bald when white men put names on places, but was called The Snake Mountain by the Cherokees. The Seminole runner, who went by the name of Looks Far, was the son of a chief, and it was a sign of the great seriousness with which the Seminoles took this dispute, that they sent him. He was met by a party of Cherokee elders at the top of this cliff, right up where we set this minute. Recognizing that he had run the hundreds of miles from his lowland elders to The Snake Mountain, the Cherokees gave him a brief time to catch his breath before speaking, so that he would neither betray weakness by puffing and sweating, nor insult the Cherokees by speaking unclearly.

On Honeyman Bald

Thing is, the run from Florida had gone badly from the start. Looks Far set out in good time and full of pride at being picked for this important mission, with two companions who were supposed to know the way. But the most experienced of these broke his ankle two days out, and the other tried to persuade Looks Far to turn back after leading them astray the next afternoon. It had been necessary in the end for the boy to rise from a restless midnight sleep and kill the false guide, and to strike out for the northwest alone, relying on the stars and the sun for navigation.

But navigation in this country was not a matter of position and direction only; in following the direct line toward his destination, the boy missed any number of easy trails and passes, plunged through swamps he could have skirted in half the time on firm ground, and in the end been forced to go without sleep in order to run almost without stopping through the piedmont country, higher and higher into the Great Smokies and at last to the east side of The Snake Mountain, only hours short of the time - before sunset on that very day - when he was charged with delivering a message of peace to the Cherokees.

Wavering with exhaustion in the afternoon shadow of mountain, Looks Far felt that he would be lucky indeed to live through the next hours of effort; he had not eaten for a full day, and he was bruised by falls and ripped by briars. His clothing had gone, except for the briefest of loincloths, and that was wet and filthy. But he did it. His dogged run up the east slope of Honeyman Bald, just where y'all come up today, was done in the time it took the sun to sink through the last quarter of the sky. As he ran toward the Cherokee elders on the edge of the cliff, their shadows stretched past him across the summit of this very mountain, and pitched off its eastern edge to fly at the speed of light all the way back to Florida.

The boy pulled the packet of gifts and the message, all of them soaked with sweat, from his loincloth and presented them to him who seemed to be the principal among the Cherokees. Then his eyes rolled back in his head, and he fell into the Cherokee's unwilling arms. But the war was averted because Looks Far was the son of a chief, and because the Cherokees could see that he had sacrificed so much of himself to deliver the needed words and gifts in time. They offered him the hospitality of their village for a few days to recover from his mighty struggle.

But that was not to say that the Cherokees had much love for Seminoles. They sent Looks Far to a lodge of women to be cleaned up and outfitted with expendable clothing for his return trip, more or less as you might send a mongrel dog to the vet to be clipped and wormed. Among Indians in those days, being turned over to the women was not necessarily a soft landing; most men would as soon take their chances against a war party. Those women had themselves a time with Looks Far, stripping him naked and scrubbing him down with pine cones and holly branches to the point that he bled. Looks Far didn't dare insult the Cherokees by objecting to it, so he pretended not to notice.

The old man leaned forward with a twinkle in his eye. Now y'all listen up, he said. We're about to come to the good part.

One of them Cherokee women had a daughter named Windshadow, a girl about the same age of Looks Far; and Windshadow thought he was just about the bravest, most handsome fella that had ever come through this part of the Blue

On Honeyman Bald

Ridge. By the time Looks Far had got his wits back from being cleaned up, he come to feel similarly about Windshadow. They exchanged glances, and blushes, and little notes and tokens. And in the long run, a good deal more than that.

Of course, none of this could be done in what would pass for privacy. The Cherokee elders and women put a quick stop to it, once they saw what was going on, and they sent Looks Far on his way back down the mountain with persuasive advice to keep headed southeast and forget about Windshadow. Windshadow's daddy was particularly strong on the subject, and told Looks Far if he ever laid eyes on him again he'd make Looks Far wish them women had rubbed him down to a skeleton right then and been done with it.

Naturally, Looks Far ignored their advice; he ran without stopping down the slope of the mountain, leaving behind the warriors Windshadow's pa had sent with him to make sure he didn't try to sneak back and kidnap Windshadow. When he got back to the valley, Looks Far bushwhacked through the laurel and creepers around toward the west, until he got to the foot of this here cliff, and he started creeping up the sheer face with his fingers and toes, figuring nobody would expect him to come up the hard way.

For a while, it went pretty good. In the afternoon, which it was, and when there's a west wind, which there was, there's a hell of an updraft along that cliff, that seemed to lift him over the hard spots just like he had a friend below him giving him a boost. He made pretty short work of about a thousand feet of almost sheer rock face, just the tiniest little handholds so you can get a grip.

Trouble is, there's a overhang just below the summit, that nobody's ever figured out how to skirt or to climb over. Don't matter how brave or clever you are, there's flat no way in hell

On Honeyman Bald

to climb the west face of Honeyman Bald without you've got somebody already up top, belaying lines for you. Been tried, been the death of six-eight smart fellas, thought they could use these pitons and carabiners, all that. Looks Far was just finding this out along late afternoon, and he slumps himself onto a ledge, down not more'n twenty feet below where we sit at this minute, to cry his heart out.

After a while, though, he chirks up. He figures when he gets the strength, he'll go back down and see about sneaking up the easy way, on flanks of the east side. He concludes there's no great shame in that, 'specially in view of the Cherokee fellas he'd left behind there, big mean suckers with long knives and hard eyes, that he might have to kill to get by 'em. But about the time he's ready to work his way back down the cliff, he hears a lady's voice, singing the blues, standing out of sight on the edge of the cliff just spitting distance above him. He listens for a bit, and he hears it's Windshadow, watching the sun go down on the last day she'd ever see Looks Far. He's kinda gratified she feels so strong, and he calls her name, meaning to let her know things ain't all that bad.

Well, it backfires. Windshadow hears his voice, but she can't see him, or tell what he's saying; it sounds like he's calling out to her from nowhere, like a miracle. She can only figure he's dead; that the mean guys with the long knives had special instructions about seeing to it that Looks Far will never come back, that he's laying in some gully down the east side of The Snake Mountain with his throat slit, calling her from the spirit world.

I'm coming, Looks Far, she calls. I'm coming to you. And she throws herself off the cliff. Looks Far sees her pitch past, and with a scream of "Windshadow", he throws himself off his little ledge, out over a thousand feet of air, to join her in death.

On Honeyman Bald

The old man hitched himself a little straighter against his rock, and winked at Bethany and Suellen.

Here comes the good part, though, see. That updraft along the cliff face, it caught them two lovers, just as gentle as a momma's arms, and it stopped 'em from falling. Fact is, once they hit terminal velocity, Windshadow's skirt flared out like a parachute, and, why, it blew her, and him hanging on to her, right back onto the top of Honeyman Bald again. When most of the Cherokees seen that, they like to fall in a heap, talking miracle.

But Windshadow's daddy was fit to be tied, and says he knows the secret of that updraft. And to demonstrate, he steps off the edge himself. And sure enough there he sits, out there in empty space, scowling at Looks Far and whacking his hand with the flat of his long knife. But he forgot it's sundown, and the wind dies off in the evening, as you can see right here as we speak. Slowly, and then a little faster, Windshadow's pa sinks down toward the valley, and he falls out of where the updraft is strongest, and then he's flat-out falling, and the last they see of him is a little speck and a spash, way down at the very bottom, where that crick runs.

After that, the rest of the Cherokees figured them two deserve each other, and they didn't raise no further objection. Looks Far and Windshadow went back to his country in Florida. After a lot of feasting and celebration about the great job he'd done, and the great gal he'd brought back, they got hitched and had about forty kids, which wore her out. She turned just as mean, and him just as hard-ass and shiftless, as any other married folks in them times.

The old man heaved himself to his feet, walked to the

edge of the cliff, and spat, taking care to avoid the dying updraft.

And that's the true story of the doomed lovers of Honeyman Bald.

On Honeyman Bald

1.

Already in May, it was hot that year. A sun twice life size blared through pale haze, copying itself on everything of glass or metal. The brass handle on the post office door, dingy where it wasn't skin-polished, prickled as I went in to mail tax returns. Ellis Reed, the postmaster, nodded as I crossed the lobby.

"Hot one," Ellis allowed.

"Already," I said. I wasn't feeling wordy.

Ellis slanted his face at the pair of fat envelopes. "Kinda complex this year, I guess. They <u>Lord</u>, not that a fella needs no extra complexities to tangle it up anyways. How's Lee?"

"Coming along," I lied. "Up and around now. We think she'll be on stage when Commencement comes along."

I expect he thought I was being terse. I didn't owe Ellis Reed a rundown on my late tax returns, any more than I owed him a medical bulletin.

The two subjects were the same thing, or rather different faces of one certain thing, the life-wrecking monster that had come to live with us. Lee Morgan Maryland, my wife and my life for twenty years, had damn near died of a brain tumor six months before. The headaches started after Labor Day, the little slips of speech at Hallowe'en, and the tremor three weeks after that. The surgery that neither quite killed, nor quite cured her, took place on Thanksgiving morning while Bethany and I stood like a pair of corpses in the waiting

11

room, praying for just one blessing to count. Bethany is Lee's daughter, my stepdaughter, at that time in her first year at Chapel Hill.

After two weeks of intensive, and one of perfunctory, care at Duke, Lee came home to Gabbro on December 18th, so light it broke my heart to carry her upstairs. She was listless and private, and immune to cheerful talk of when she would be feeling better; she was barely able to hear anything about how she would be feeling this or any future morning, for a good month. Bethany came home a week early for Christmas break, laden with books, to help look after her.

All through Christmas, Bethany and I crept through the dimmed house, muffling our voices, sleeping in shifts, breathing shallowly. Students and neighbors and colleagues sent so many flowers and casseroles that you just about couldn't tell whether Lee was merely desperately sick, or had died last week.

We got a visit from representatives of the Ministerial Alliance, which was the social improvement cabal of the ordained in Gabbro County. It consisted of Sam Wainright, the pastor of Gabbro Presbyterian, where I'd once had the infernal gall to pose as an Elder; Father Conor from St. Ann's; The Reverend Farnell Hastie of True Foundation AME Zion in East Gabbro; and Pastor Plummer Baley of the Indian Girl Swamp Pentecostal Tabernacle. I'd had dealings off and on with the first three, but Baley was a new one. The Baleys are a sort of outcaste family around Gabbro, of the sort you can only get in the rural South; sallow, skinny, maybe a little inbred, and very much in a world of their own making, since their share of the public world tends to be the short end.

Pastor Plummer stayed pretty much in the background, peeking shyly at Bethany while Sam and the others wrung their hands, prayed over us and spoke of doing anything they could do. After they left, Bethany rolled her eyes and took up a station by Lee's side with a pile of books, reading quietly while Lee slept, and reciting telling passages from John McPhee, Steven Gould, and Derwood Barnes Cather when Lee was awake.

For another month, while the chemo and radiation kept her gaunt and bald, Lee slept, and vomited, and lay back again to gather the strength to vomit again. She smelled musty and abandoned, as if she already belonged in another life, in another place and time. When she spoke, it was of weariness, and of settling her affairs. Bethany, reduced to puddles of sorrow and frustration by it, would respond with uplifting, take-the-long-view poetry from Cather, whom she had met at Chapel Hill.

Bethany had changed surprisingly at Chapel Hill. She'd grown up a tomboy, running with neighborhood boys in the fields and woods around our street. When her childhood buddy Crystal Sue hit fourteen and began painting her face and batting her eyes at boys, Bethany boycotted for a few months - earning abrupt ostracism from Crystal Sue and her mall pack - and then chummed up with the dorkiest boys, either to keep sex unthinkable or to show she didn't care what Crystal Sue's circle thought.

At seventeen, she segued from the asocial to the unsuitable, bringing home a lineup of punks-of-the-month who either slouched into the house and sneered at everyone from parents to our little dog Covington, or sat out in the driveway revving their engines while Bethany did whatever unavoidable thing had brought her home. For a year, I scarcely dared hope she might end up the First Lady of a Jiffy-Lube. That phase climaxed with her being released to her parents' recognizance and reimbursing the County for the cost of repainting the water tower, after she spent a Hallowe'en with one of her thugs revising the Chamber of Commerce slogan on it to *GABBRO COUNTY: A Great Place to Love and Jerk.*

Then, with the abruptness that only the very young can achieve, she'd become dreamy and idealistic at Chapel Hill, given to self-immersion in greater realities than she'd encountered at Gabbro Consolidated. Apparently, the catalyst had been a seminar on Sustainable Citizenship, or some such, in which she had met a series of the leading lights of Earth stewardship, each of them more saintly, amusing, provocative, and admirable than the last. After a semester of it, she was ready to dedicate her life to harmony with Gaiea and Her footstool the Earth. In another age, I suppose she might have been talking about holy orders.

"Listen to this, Mom," she would say, and if Lee looked receptive would launch into stuff like, *"When I walk through the granite of my dooryard, when I touch the sunwarmed gneiss, my hand skates across the reworked corpses of my Archean ancestors, the crystalline iron and silicon that framed them; and I know that the trivial leavings of my own life will frame the dooryards of creatures as remote from me as I from the trilobites, the aeons-distant heirs of this fleeting millennium."*

Lee roused herself. "Who was that, hon?"

"Derwood Barnes Cather. He lives in the wilderness, out in the Smoky Mountains. Doesn't he just make your hair stand up?"

Lee smiled faintly. "If I had any. He writes a long

sentence."

Maybe it was the uplift of all that. Maybe just Lee's native vitality, responding to constant care and love. But as the hours of daylight lengthened, as late sunshine dawdled on her windowsill until five and six in the afternoon, Lee came back from her peek over the edge of the world. She started eating, and her jaw firmed up and her eyes opened wide and smiled on things. Birds caroled and bred in the live oak by her window, and it was as if the Angel of Death had morphed into Saint Cecilia, and turned a gracious hand to the organ to improvise a few little paeans. The lustrous black hair she'd lost grew back in, and it was curly and taffy-colored, just for a light-hearted change. Little by little, she started exercising, and taking an interest, and finally pestering me about the College.

Which presented a dilemma. One of the great virtues of Gabbro College was that it got along with an absolute minimum of administrators. In particular there was no Vice President, or obvious second-in-command after Lee, who was then in her tenth year as President. The Academic Dean, who would have been the logical choice for Acting President when Lee became unable to work, had resigned to take a job in California, and Lee had been doing his work on top of her own. The faculty, which was the owner and governing body of the place, finally asked me to fill in, on the grounds that I'd been acting President once before, knew where the executive washroom was, and hadn't actually wrecked the place back then.

The dilemma was that Gabbro College was ticking along just fine, in the black, with a healthy crop of students, and a nostalgic and growingly affluent body of alumni. Running it on a short-term basis was not taxing. And I did the smart thing and created the office of Executive Vice President. At Lee's suggestion, I asked a math professor named Tim Summerton to put down his chalk and follow me.

Tim was smart, helpful, and self-effacing. I could probably have handed him the whole portfolio a week or two after he started. Only two considerations held me back: first, we would need him in the classroom when Lee came back; and second, he'd once been a beau of Lee's, before we were married, and he was so manly and good-looking that it was a constant amazement to me that she'd passed him up for me. I know, that shouldn't have played the least role, but I'm being honest here. And besides, the College was in good enough shape that I could manage it just fine with only occasional consultations with Lee.

But it wasn't such a snap, either, that I wanted Lee to pick it up again while she was supposed to be devoting herself 100 percent to recuperation. I temporized, invented ongoing business with the State Department of Education, made up task forces whose reports were pending, spoke of planning a formal handing-back of the reins in a month or so.

By April, Lee had had all she could stomach of it. She demanded to see the financial reports, and when she'd read them through, mm-hm'ing and nodding, she admitted that matters were swimming. And when I said, smugly, See, she challenged me to an arm-wrestle that I didn't have to fake too hard letting her win - and that led to our first love-making since summer. And she woke up the next morning with a headache and an inability to pronounce the word "breakfast".

Oh, and then it was Duke all over again, another fearful trip home from Chapel Hill for Bethany, and MRIs and PETs and blood tests, and a lot of lip-pursing and head-scratching, while Bethany and I smiled over roaring pits of fear, and Lee shrugged and said, Nonsense, I'm as healthy as a torch. A whore. *A horse*, damn it.

In the end, the medics concluded that they couldn't find any obvious anomalies in any of their scans, and they offered a theory involving postoperative neural reintegration, or some such, and a choice of exploratory surgery, another round of chemo, or watchful waiting. Lee bristled.

"You want permission to go on a fishing expedition inside my head, see what else you can mess up, rooting around? Bring me your damn chemicals, and that's absolutely the last I'm going to do. After that it's in the Lord's lap."

And I looked at her, and she looked so mad and alive, and I reflected that she'd got that whole speech out without tangling her tongue, and I thought, Well, so be it.

So she let them drip poison into her veins again, and her hair fell out again, and she got sickly and nauseous, and when it was over, she fought her way back again. But it took longer than before, and her dalliance with death was more serious, and when the curls came back this time, they were shot with gray. And that's about where we were when I mailed in our tax returns, six weeks late.

*   *

The hot weather broke for about three days in May, around the time Lee walked up to a podium in front of a thousand cheering students, the boys whistling like banshees, the women sniffling and yelling Girl Power through their tears, to take back the helm of Gabbro College from my more-than-willing hands. She was thin and wobbly, but she got through a graceful and humble speech with no slips. At

On Honeyman Bald

Commencement, a week after that, she stood in blistering heat between me and Tim Summerton and handed out diplomas for an hour, enduring soulful handshakes and tearful hugs from about every one of the three hundred graduates, and from their parents ("Janey Anne just like to worship the ground you stand on, Dr. Maryland. Me and Purvis knows she got a fine education here. God bless you, Ma'am.") for another hour after that.

That, in a hundred variants, and the heat, and the endless flesh-pressing just about did her in. When I got her out of there, she was staggering, and when we got home, I had to carry her up to bed. But at least she was heavier than she'd been in December, and she'd begun to get back some muscle tone. So I tucked her in, chucked her chin, and went downstairs for a stiff one. The next morning, Lee had a headache, sore throat and sniffles, so I told her she'd caught something from the hordes who'd been inside her bubble all day.

Bethany got home from Chapel Hill about noon, announcing that she'd decided to major in Earth Stewardship And The Experience Of The Sacred. I opened my mouth to ask her about career structures, shut it again, and set her as guard to keep her mother down while I ran an errand. Bethany settled next to Lee with a book and the dog in her lap, and threatened to read Christian eco-poetry out loud, if Lee so much as budged. I figured that was enough to enforce the peace, and I went back to the College to pick up Suellen Ransom.

For those whose minds it may have slipped, Suellen was the daughter of Eddie Ransom, a militia demolitions unexpert, and his thugette wife Trudi, a racketeering topless

On Honeyman Bald

waitress and gentlewoman whore who in one 24-hour period
- before Lee and I were married - seduced me, bewitched my
son, and wounded Lee with a pistol. She hit the highway
with her then preadolescent daughter twenty minutes ahead
of the law. News of Trudi Ransom's death - I will grit my
teeth and call it untimely - in a Branson, Missouri bar brawl
followed by a few years her outright, selfish, screw-you
abandonment of Suellen to the tender parenting of a
Fayetteville off-duty cop named Wetmore Parsonage.

It was under Wet's doubtful aegis that Suellen came of
age and, just in time, to her senses after a childhood misspent
with her unlamented mother learning to lie, steal, and grift.
And it was because of Wet Parsonage - whom Lee and I
despised but also couldn't help sort of liking - that we agreed
to house Suellen for a summer, so she could apply her
research stipend as fully as possible toward next year's
tuition. After all, we assured each other, the girl isn't
responsible for the sins of her mother and father, or the
unletteredness, cynicism, and crudity of her guardian. Plus,
she and Bethany had become buddies the summer before,
when Bethany had just finished Gabbro Consolidated High,
and Suellen was working in town for tuition money.

Suellen was a sharp-featured golden girl with a mane
of blonde microcurls. She had inherited from her mother
some trick of effortless sexiness, a kind of Nordic felinity,
which she compounded by being smart, athletic, and - to the
amazement of anyone who knew her provenance - bookishly
inclined. She aced her feeble parochial high school in
Fayetteville, enrolled at Gabbro College as a pre-med
chemistry major, starred at softball, and knocked out of the
park every quiz, lab, and final exam the chemists could throw
at her. After two years of it the Gabbro chemistry

department, swooning, I guess, at her easy mastery of orbitals and the Ideal Gas Law, applied for grants that would keep her on campus and under their tutelage twelve months a year. Early training, though, is powerful; chatting about science with Suellen was sort of like hearing a Hay Street hooker mull macromolecules. She was slumped leggily against a duffel bag when I pulled up outside her dorm. "Christ, it's hot," she bitched. "You know how many days straight it's been over a hundred?"

"About two," I said. "Is that why you've hardly got any clothes on?"

"Nah." She stretched, letting her chest pull the halfie tee shirt up to give me about a yard of high-definition midriff. "That's to bug Coach Helms when I go turn in my softball gear. He pats my butt every chance he gets, even when I strike out. All those faculty guys are like that, and the married ones are worse than the bachelors. Doc Peters gave us a lecture on the Second Law this spring, and never took his eyes off my left knocker the whole time."

I popped the trunk. The backhand way she tossed her duffel in made it look light, but the car jolted and settled a little when it hit the floor of the trunk.

"I gotta say, he knows the stuff, though. Said everything the book did, and never looked at his notes once." She settled in the passenger seat, braced a grass-stained foot on the dash, cracked her gum, and winked at me.

"Yeah," I grunted. "Look, I'll give you the benefit of the doubt that you're kidding around here. If I thought for a second you had your mother's talents in that direction - "

Suellen squared around on the seat with a look that would have given a more sensitive guy pause. "Don't get on about my mother. And don't think of me as a sex threat. I had all that shit I could take before I was thirteen, and if I never feel another guy on my butt the rest of my life, it'll be too soon. You got no worries about me. Plus, far as I heard, you're devoted to Lee, which I am too."

"Thanks. I wasn't talking about me or Lee. I was talking about getting a coach hot and bothered, to where Lee'd have to get involved, and probably can the guy. It's the sort of thing your late Mom was a whiz at. I gotta say, dressed like that, you look kind of apt to - "

She skinned her face back. "Apt? On a scale of one to apt, I'd say I'm about a ten to the minus eighty. I'm not even on that metric. The only reason I want to shake him up is I don't like guys looking, and thinking, patting me on the butt and watching me move, wishing they could rub their ugly - "

She broke off and faced the street again. "Excuse me. I was about to say something coarse. Kindly do not worry about sex where I am concerned; it is extremely unlikely to involve yourself, or any of the Gabbro faculty. And if you are going to continue to bad-mouth my mother, you may wish to let me out of the car. Otherwise, you may please drive on. Sir." I drove on, corrected. And after a couple of blocks, she sighed. "Not that I'm sensitive on the subject."

"Actually, I was way out of line, and I owe you an apology. Just, I'm a little gun-shy on wiles in your family."

"Mommy told me about that, you know? Never guess you were such a stud, to look at you now."

"Are we finished?"

"If you are."

*   *

Lee got better and better all during the summer;

picking up the reins of College governance with sure hands - keeping Tim Summerton in place as insurance - and getting the idled faculty organized to think again about stiffening graduation requirements. She went to a couple of conclaves of higher ed bigwigs and knocked their socks off - I have this on independent testimony - with her clarity and calmness and rationality about the future of liberal arts colleges in the South. Once, late at night, she told me that she would never, ever, go through anything like that spring's slow undeath again, that I was to take her out and shoot her cleanly at the first sign of recurrence. I didn't promise, but I managed to make her feel enough better that she drifted to sleep on my shoulder. Lord, I thought, while I dealt with the pins and needles in my arm and listened to her treble snores, please do not give me that option.

Be careful what you pray for.

Bethany, after a week or so of stalling, allowed herself to take the summer job I'd found for her at the Gabbro *Intelligencer*, our thrice-weekly newsrag, to see if she maybe wanted to think about a career in journalism in case the job market in Earth Stewardship And The Experience Of The Sacred should tank. Once there, she was taken in hand by an ageing but still ferocious managing editor named Faye Bynum, about whom she complained in that tone of voice that's not far from hero-worship.

As for Suellen, reports I got second hand from the chemistry department bore out what I could pretty well read on her face every evening: that her summer research was going fine. And that after about three weeks, she began having better ideas about how to pursue it than Ed Peters, her alleged mentor, who was something of a holdover from the bad old days. So Lee had her hands full with Suellen, steering her into ways of doing a good job at her research without getting impatient with her slow-witted mentor. Thank God for the Internet, the great leveler of intellectual access.

I have to give Lee a lot of credit for taking the trouble. She fiercely hated Suellen's late mother, and distrusted Wet Parsonage, her guardian. For her part, Suellen had the patience and tact of any very bright late-adolescent woman, supplemented by a vocabulary learned while kicking would-be child molesters in the nuts. More than once during the summer, I had to intervene when Lee's no-nonsense approach to learning or home hygiene threatened to tip Suellen into gutter-fight mode. But in general, life seemed to have returned to something like blessed normal, and we were so liberated from life-and-death fears as to be free to suffer from the heat.

Which was ferocious, aggressive, sticky, smothering. We would go for weeks without rain, and then we'd get a rank 4:30 shower that would only jack the humidity back up from 95 to 99. Bankers mopped their brows and talked of the Thirties. The Intelligencer ran out of synonyms. Lawn-watering was restricted for the first time in Gabbro history, and then banned, and we began to enjoy brownouts because every structure in ten counties was air-conditioning itself around the clock. Covington who, at 11 people-years was getting a little elderly, confined herself to a shady spot in the back yard, where she dozed and panted. People dropped their pencils in the middle of writing their wills, and went to swim at Riverbend, where the fiercely chill Gabbro River snakes through perpetual shade. Neighbors who couldn't do that, greeted each other with that weary grin that says, Sure is, in't it, and for God's sake shut up about it.

But silence didn't save Faye Bynum, who had a heat stroke weeding her sun-blasted garden over the Fourth, which led to a real stroke and landed her in the "Total Care" wing of Gabbro General. Bethany was devastated, and took me and Suellen to visit her. Lee said she'd had her fill of hospitals, and to give Faye her love and best wishes.

The Total Care wing was a nursing home by another name. It was closed off from the rest of Gabbro General by a guarded airlock to keep the inmates from wandering off and depressing those who were only diseased or broken, and had not yet contracted the incurable sickness of age. Bright posters on the walls reminded them that today was <u>Tuesday</u>, that the season was <u>Summer</u>. This was illustrated by a picture of a sun beating down on a field of head-high corn. The Client of the Week was Mary-Claire MacFell, 92 years young on the 5th. Mary-Claire smiled from the poster, blowing mildly at a blazing eternity of candles.

Past the airlock, the things that hit you were the warmth, the smell of urine and the noise of dementia. The staff were plenty dedicated, I do not doubt, but stretched thin keeping up with just basic life needs. You get used to a certain base load of incontinence and incoherence.

We passed through a common room a-tangle with aluminum walkers and four-footed canes and wheelchairs and a piano on which a tightly permed lady played the first eight bars of The Merry Widow Waltz over and over. We walked past half-closed doors that allowed millisecond glimpses of inert heads on plump pillows, and a room in which a middle-aged man slammed his hand against the tray of his wheelchair, shouting in time to it, "Four-eight-nine!

On Honeyman Bald

Four-eight-nine!" The skin of his palm was bright red.

Faye Bynum lay in a big, comfy-looking bed, staring at the ceiling with the good side of her face, registering dismay with the bad side.

"Beffany," she said when we entered. "They Lord, honey, you bring the poison?"

"Ma'am?"

The good side of Faye's face sagged to match the other. "Honey, the poison. It's the only answer to this snakepit. I'm warning you, sweetheart. You show up here again without cyanide, I'm writing you such an evaluation, you'll never work in journalism again."

Bethany teared up and leaned over the bed to hug her. "You're going to be OK, Miz Bynum. I promise. You'll be out of here and drivin us nuts before we're ready for you."

"Stop," Faye said. "You're killing me. They brought me the paper this morning. Seven typos above the fold on the front page. I'm recommending they change the name to the *Stupefier*. Who's this young lady?"

Bethany introduced Suellen as a brilliant chemist-in-training, and Faye gave her a left-handed shake and an appraising sniff. She raised a quavering finger on her good side. "Pleased to meet you, Suellen. The rest of you, take a good look. I give you ten years, Hap. Twenty if you stop eating fried clams, but what's the point? I don't know Suellen yet, but she looks healthy. Kind of a looker, really. You wouldn't think for a minute I looked like that once, would you?"

So, what's the right answer to that? Or to the snakepit that waits for all who are lucky enough to live a long and healthy life? On the way out, the tray-banger had advanced to four-nine-one. The clean humidity outdoors felt like a

On Honeyman Bald

Divine gift, for five minutes.

By the first of August, Suellen and Bethany were agitating for a trip to the Smokies, to get out of the heat and, for Bethany at least, to commune with Nature. I consulted Lee, who was willing to take a break, having satisfied herself that the College was again springily flourishing. I asked around about borrowable camping gear, and got maps from the scoutmaster at Gabbro Presbyterian.

And on the dog day morning of Thursday, August 15, we transferred Covington to the care of a neighborhood kid and piled into the car, heading west and upwards for a four-day vacation in the Great Smokies. We couldn't wait to get up there, to breathe cool, clean air for a change.

On Honeyman Bald

2.

Lee held my shoulder and slapped at a bug on her ankle. Around us, gigantic hardwoods sighed and chattered at the wind that found us even here in a little draw in deep forest. I could feel the sweat drying on my back - as it never did in the lowlands, and worth a half-day drive to experience it - when I lifted the pack to get some breeze under it. Bethany dropped her pack and walked down to a stony little creek to poke around for minnows; Suellen clunked a boot onto a log, scratched her thigh, and cracked her gum.

"We gonna be down in the jungle the whole time?" she asked. "I was thinking we'd get some views, up here."

I showed her the tope sheet we'd picked up at Fontana. "Another mile, looks like, we'll come out on a little ledge over some clear area. Maybe we'll get a longer sightline from there."

Suellen shrugged, poutishly. She'd been on edge since we walked into the forest at eight this morning, not so much spooked at the woods, and certainly not thrashing around and talking as you might expect from pretty much a city girl; but uneasy. She'd quieted down if anything, and gone on what the military calls heightened alert. As if the squirrels and jays were agents for something creepy, or the earth would crumble beneath our boots, once we were out of sight of a paved road.

I have to think it was that; the lack of cars and traffic here, the humlessness that she, born and raised on

On Honeyman Bald

Interstates, had never experienced. Bethany, by contrast, was where she wanted to be, in one of the least populated, most Nature-fraught corners of North Carolina. She pulled a book from her pack and prepared to match an apt line to the local scenery.

"The narrowest rill will round a stone," she declaimed, planting a boot on either side of the creek. "As Earthen grace wears down the greedy heart."

I held out a hand for the book. This Most Fragile Footstool, by Derwood Barnes Cather, he whose leavings were destined to decorate rocky dooryards aeons hence. It was signed by the author, "For Bethany Morgan, whose voice will be heard in the future of Earth Stewardship," apparently on the occasion of Cather's having received an honorary DSc from Chapel Hill in June. The back cover bore an appreciation of the "eco-poet and pastor of the biosphere," from the pages of Gopherwood, the journal of the EcoDruid Siblinghood.

"Siblinghood?"

"It used to be less inclusive," Bethany sniffed.

I turned to Lee, looking for signs that the hike was being too much for her. It was Lee who'd insisted on getting away from cars and motels, renting gear, and finding a path into wilderness. I'd consulted the ranger at Fontana, waiting until Lee left to pee to tell him we had a convalescent with us, and to give us something not too strenuous.

The circular hike he'd recommended was high, off the beaten path, and more or less level, once we drove up to a startoff. Which didn't mean that it didn't have ups and downs, some of them pretty severe. I could see Lee's muscles - all her life strong, toned, and lithe - quivering a little when we stopped to puff after stiff climbs. But her color was good, she wasn't sweating any more than the rest of us, and she kept up a motivational commentary for the girls, pointing out short-range marvels like a rotten log adorned with a tiny garden of moss and microfungi, and a smartly colored millipede scuttling away when Suellen's boot kicked aside a leaf.

Bethany picked up her pack. "God, yes," she groaned. "Let's get up on that rise, it's only the 87th climb today. I wish I could fly."

"Keep reading that book," Suellen said.

Bethany stuck out a siblingly tongue, and if one can blow a razzberry fondly, she did.

I have said that Bethany had grown up a tomboy; and under the eco-aesthete she'd become, there was still an edgy athleticism. She had always favored Lee's looks, all the more so as she grew to young womanhood. Over the summer, I had begun to notice her mother's body language and mannerisms in her too, and of course her speech had always been pure Gabbro: soft but clipped, with the charming little vowel shifts ("wont" for "want", "sell" for "sale" and so on) that mark eastern North Carolina. Suellen teased her about it, but in two months she was doing it too.

On the way up the next rise, we ran into a family we'd heard coming for a while, kids clamoring, mother calling distantly and scolding about not racing ahead. The kids proved to be in what used to be called the "latent" stage, somewhere around 8 or 10, a boy and a girl brattishly dressed in fuck-you tee shirts and reversed ball caps, lightly loaded with fanny packs, followed after five minutes by a couple of adults wobbling under loads big enough to hold tents, bags, cookware, food, and a couple of playstations.

"Hi," they panted. "We getting there?"

On Honeyman Bald

"Couple hours, if that was your Cherokee parked in the jumpoff this morning." I decided not to add that they would find their passenger window broken, their hood up and their battery pilfered when they got there. I'd removed our battery and locked it in the trunk, and stripped the inside of the car clean, to minimize our chances of sharing their fate. Also, I kind of made it a point to exchange names and addresses with these folks, hoping they'd remember that, if they were tempted to solve their battery problem by taking ours. They were the Chesterfields, from High Point, if it matters.

"Yeah, well, I expect them hellions'll get there about a hour quicker'n we do," Mr. Chesterfield sighed, mopping his face.

"If you gave them more to carry, they'd go slower," Suellen said. "The family that schleps together, steps together." Mrs. Chesterfield looked at her like she was crazy.

"The family that strives together, arrives together," Bethany explained, trying to help out.

Mr. Chesterfield hitched his gigantic pack higher and started down the trail. "Givin them kids a little taste of natur' don't ya see," he grunted. "They'll get their loads soon enough. C'mon, Phyllis."

Suellen started up the trail. "Strives? she snorted. "That was lame."

"Yeah, and steps together, speaking of lame," Bethany shot back. "Steps in what? Doggie-doo?"

"The family that lugs together, hugs together," Lee said, and hitched her own pack into a forward lean, to motivate herself. "Let's see if we can get to your ledge without stopping eight times."

And up we went, slowly, Bethany and Suellen yelling inspirations at each other about families that sleep together

On Honeyman Bald

keeping together, and ones that screw together being easier to fix than the kind they used rivets on.

"Oh, my land," Lee said. "My stars. Will you look at that." She sat on a rock where she had tottered onto the ledge, and stared out across a mile of treetops at pure majesty.

"What is it, Daddy?"

"Hold on." I pulled out the tope sheet, and turned it to coincide with the territory. "Uh...Honeyman Bald. See? We're here." The map showed our piddling ledge as a minor aberration, a little bulge in the regular march of contour lines that traced the shoulder of the highlands. In the other direction, they spread downward across the space before us, and then dozens of them bunched drastically into a black mass no wider than a pencil line, showing us the cliff of gneiss and granite that soared over the valley, a vast wall of rock turned buttery by afternoon sun. It was as if a good-sized mountain had been chopped in two, half of it carted off for a massive road project somewhere, and the other half left to dream and weather in the sun. At higher altitude, the green smudge of vegetation thinned and died away, leaving the top bare. About halfway up the cliff, three or four motes circulated; hawks, riding updrafts and prospecting for snacks.

Bethany leaned on me and looked at the shining wall. "Now I really do wish I could fly. Wouldn't that be magic, to be up there?"

Suellen leaned in and nudged my arm with a breast, which she knew would make me let go of the map. "We could," she announced, taking it. "See here? Little trail takes offa ours, down below, and runs around behind that, and up to the top. What's that little triangle jigger?"

On Honeyman Bald

"A benchmark," I said, taking the map back. "5752 feet, up there. Pretty tough climb." I twitched my head microscopically in Lee's direction; the kind of hint Suellen would get in a flash if she was paying attention, and wanted to get it. She wasn't.

"Nah, look here, we're at almost 4000 feet already. It's not hardly a couple thousand feet." I think, now, that anything Bethany wanted, Suellen wanted for her.

I dragged my feet. "Sure, but you look where that trail goes, before it starts climbing, down to, lemme see.... down to under 3000 feet, over at the far side of the valley. Once we got down there, maybe an hour or two from now, we'd be looking at a 3000 foot climb, and tireder than we are now. Plus, it would knock our schedule to - " Bethany groaned at that.

"What schedule, Daddy? Nobody has to get back home before Monday, an' look, we can circle back to the car this way. Or, I guess we could split up, if you or Mom doesn't want to -"

"Uh uh. We're not splitting up so you two can go off in the wilderness by yourselves. Young women get ambushed out here every - well, every once in a while. Frankly, it isn't that, or anything but your mother's condition. She isn't - "

"My what, Harper F Maryland? I have no goddamn 'condition' that I know of." She blew her nose on a banner of toilet paper. "Other than the human one. Show me the map."

Knowing defeat when I suffered it, I let Suellen and Bethany show Lee the negligible dashed line that crossed ours a few hundred yards down the trail, meandered across the lowlands before us, and diagonaled up the southerly flank of Honeyman Bald. I went to the dropoff and looked out over it, imagining the journey, stewing about Lee's fitness to do it, fuming at Bethany and Suellen, who so plainly believed she could do anything they wanted to do.

*   *

We reached the far side of the valley at four in the afternoon, all of us hot, bug-bitten, and scratched by brambles. The cross-trail had been overgrown, little-used, and tough going. Where we'd seen little groups like the Chesterfields every half hour or so on the main trail, on this one we might have been the only humans in the forest. We encountered a lot of animals, including a smallish black bear rooting for a grubstake in a rotten log. We took a wide detour to avoid getting him as alarmed as we were, which added to the bushwhacking. When we came back to the trail, it was so brambled and overgrown that there was controversy whether it really was a trail, until Lee spotted one of the orange blazes that marked it, on the trunk of an ironwood. A little stream, that the map called Fall Creek, hugged the base of Honeyman Bald, following the lowest edge of the valley. When we reached it, we took off our boots and socks and soaked our feet.

We were still soaking, stiffening with tiredness and dried sweat a half hour later, so I suggested that we camp there, and start the climb in the morning when we were fresh. That piece of leadership was a lot more popular than my earlier plea for common sense. We found a clearing where the creek chuckled over a gravel bar, and dropped our packs gratefully. Lee opened hers and busied herself with supper prep. I fiddled with guy stuff like bear-resistant food stowage and firewood and a cautionary lecture about giardia; and Bethany and Suellen with air mattresses and tents, and with beautifying the area by means of aesthetically placed rocks.

Suellen picked a slick and pleasantly rounded one out of the water and gave it a fairly funny Meyers-Briggs greed inventory, which Bethany pretended to ignore.

"Got a ways to go, yet," Suellen said, tossing it back. "It still commutes to Knoxville in a SUV to do day trading."

Bethany spashed creek water on her, which Suellen returned, taunting Bethany with the information that almost all the rounding of rocks happens during flash floods, not from sitting in skinny rills, because as anyone but a Druid knows, hydrodynamic forces increase as the square of flow rate. The seminar degenerated somehow into a wet tee-shirt contest which in my opinion, not sought, Lee would have won if she'd entered.

The girls' choice of tent sites put Lee and me under an adolescent maple, and them out of sight upstream. I could have worried a little about it, but chose not to. By the time the beans and ham were hot, the sun was down, and we were shipshape. Suellen fished in her pack and came up with diaquiri mix and lab alcohol which, to keep from putting Lee in a legal bind, she claimed was vodka. After that, nobody thought much about Gabbro College, or its federal alcohol permit, or any other legal or civil matter.

We ate and drank, and while the sun set and matters cooled and dimmed, we worked up dessert appetites by arguing about why it was called Fall Creek, since the tope sheet made it plain that no waterfall broke its steady descent around the foot of Honeyman Bald. When that was talked to death, we passed time throwing rocks from the gravel bar, trying to hit a foot-wide triangular mini-cave in the cliff, for the pleasure of either hearing them rattle into the black depths, or bang against the gneiss and patter back into the creek. After four throws, I popped something in my shoulder, and graduated to cheerleader. Lee and Bethany threw like girls (forgive me; guys will know what I mean) but Suellen displayed an arm like a major league catcher. After a particularly feckless effort by Bethany, Suellen put her hands on her hips and spat into the creek.

"F'God's sake, Beffie," she snorted. "You throw like you were swatting flies. Keep your elbow in close and stride with the opposite foot, not the side you're throwing from. Here, c'mere."

Suellen picked up eight or ten walnut-sized rocks and kept feeding them to Bethany, standing behind her and tweaking and critiquing, and after 4 or 5 throws the speed and accuracy started to pick up, and after another half-dozen - Bethany now panting and slick with sweat - she started in with the Zen stuff.

"That rock <u>wants</u> to hit that little cave, Beff. Feel the space between you and the cave, and give it permission just before you release. Like this." And she winged one cleanly through the black triangle.

Bethany displayed a little pique at that, but after a pretty good effort, she lit up. "I <u>felt</u> it! It was like all one thing, me and the cliff ... " She scooped up another handful, and hit the cave three out of four times, with authority. On her last throw, the impact with something in the cave struck a pale spark in the gloom. We cheered, Suellen hugged Bethany and patted her butt like a high school coach, and Bethany looked flustered.

By then we were full, and dizzy with 160 proof diaquiris. We sorted ourselves out and bedded down. I don't remember my head hitting the sleeping bag.

On Honeyman Bald

*   *

I woke in perfect darkness when the slow leak in my mattress lowered me onto a root. The babble of little Fall Creek was loud, but it didn't overpower the mix of bug talk, hoots, and small-mammal death screams that rose around us like cocktail chatter. A minor windburst swept along the stream, following the foot of Honeyman Bald south, detouring to chasten our tree and whump the roof of our tent. It bore a faint flavor of autumn; I tried not to imagine Suellen and Bethany upwind, burning forbidden leaves.

The bugs quieted some, thinking maybe the sudden rustling wasn't wind, but the wings of bug-eaters. The liquid chatter of the creek became voices, and one of them sang of sorrow. I wiped the drool off my cheek and groped for Lee's butt, for almost twenty years my magnetic north in the landscape of sleep. And found it gone. After I thought about that for a minute or two, I found I needed a leak anyhow, so I extracted myself from the sleeping bag and crawled into the open.

Far above our clearing, the cliff-face of Honeyman Bald truncated the Milky Way in comprehensive blackness. There was no moon, but the stars made a faint illumination that you saw only because it was so much darker under the trees. By Saturnlight, I scanned our clearing for Lee. I saw her at the edge of the gravel bar, hunkered motionless. She looked like a small fogbank or a grieving watersprite. Stepping carefully, I found a downhill place to pee, and then storked toward the creek to see what held Lee so still.

Mistaken identity, was the answer. What I had taken for Lee was a weathered stump at the edge of the gravel. Lee herself was behind the stump, leaning against it, looking up at the dark cliff. I settled gingerly next to her.

"Done sleeping?"

She made an exasperated little sound. "You smelled the marijuana, I expect."

I admitted it. "Are you affronted as a mother, or as the president of Suellen's college?"

"Both. Which, I know, is a tricky mix. In fact, before I was halfway there to bust them, I thought better of it." She sighed impatiently. "Which is a good thing, I guess. It kept me from tripping over them."

A bolt of fear sat me straight upright. "What?"

"Yes," Lee said, evenly. "I wasn't going to tell you about this, but, honestly, Hap, I'm too... Well, I'm too tired to deal with it alone. They were out there under the stars on a sleeping bag, stark naked." She flipped a pebble into the creek. "Making love." She sighed again. "Doing sex, I mean."

I leaned back, breathing quietly, and let my line of vision climb up the cliff, looking for the boundary between blackness and sky. I'd been sure Lee meant they were unconscious, or dead. It didn't seem helpful to say that. After a minute or two, I thought of a useful thing to ask.

"Did they see you?"

"No. I don't think so. Our daughter is a lesbian. My daughter. What difference does it make whether she knows I know it?"

"Our daughter." It seemed like it made a big difference, in a way I couldn't think through at that hour, hung over and sleepy. "Well," I said finally. "It's a long ways between a little late-adolescent exploration, playing around, and - well, army boots and tattoos, and stuff. And things are starting to change about that, anyhow. Maybe, well ... "

On Honeyman Bald

Lee shuddered. "I respect everybody's freedom to express their stupid goddamn sexual orientation. Jesus, I wrote the rule on it for Gabbro College, back in Ted Billett's day, when it was worth your job to just vote Democratic." She was silent for a while. "Maybe I don't even blame Suellen, the life she's had. But Bethany."

Lee stood. "This place gives me the shivers. It seems like the water's trying to say something, that just isn't quite words."

When we were back in the tent, she curled herself against me and whispered, "Bethany is my girl. I so want her to live a happy, normal life, and have a family, after I'm gone. I don't want her moving to Washington, somewhere, and shacking up with a - a gym teacher. Surely you can see that."

On Honeyman Bald

3.

Once across Fall Creek, the trail became if anything more sketchy and wild. I think surely we must have been the first hikers that year to walk it.

And a silent group we were. Footsore, hung over, grouchy, severally uncommunicative. Suellen and Bethany had risen late and reluctantly, and I'd had to send Lee on a made-up errand to treat creek water with disinfectant pills while I stomped into their love nest, if that's what it was, snapping twigs with every step. I needn't have bothered. Suellen, sure enough, manifested as a spill of blonde at the mouth of a sleeping bag outside the tent; beside her was a flashlight and a face-down copy of Solids and Surfaces by Roald Hoffmann. Bethany was in the tent, coiled tightly around the same stuffed dog she'd slept with since age 3, and with her toothbrush stuffed into This Most Fragile Footstool. Neither showed the least discomfiture, except at the necessity to get a shine on and pack up their gear.

The woods were wet at first, which didn't improve the tone. But as we climbed, we also rounded the south flank of Honeyman Bald, and were greeted by light as yellow and multi-armed as the sun in a child's drawing. It dried the greenery, and loosened tongues. Bethany resumed her catalogue of nature marvels, and her poetry; Suellen began to sing something that could have been written in Icelandic, for all I could make of it. Bethany became solicitous of Lee's progress, giving her little warnings about trail hazards, counseling easy going, suggesting rest stops with a frequency she'd not shown before. I might have sworn she was conscious of a need to placate Lee, except that, as far as I could see, Lee was not giving out the appropriate signals. But then, I'm not a blood relative.

Bethany is. After the third "Why don't you take a break, Mom?" in an hour, Lee rounded on her.

"Well, my stars, Bethany. You think the old lady is some kind of cripple?"

"No, Mom, of course not. Just, well, maybe in your condition, it makes - "

"God damn it to hell, Bethany, I am not in a contention! *Contrition*! Oh, Jesus Christ."

Lee broke off and ran a little way up the trail; stopping then and pressing her temple against the trunk of a massive beech. A morning breeze rattled the dark leaves around her. Suellen looked after her like she was a bizarre exhibit at the zoo, but Bethany and I looked at each other, our eyes exchanging fear. We joined hands and walked toward Lee as carefully as if she might detonate. But she only turned toward us, her face as neutral as a diplomat's.

"Excuse me," she said. She smiled then, and it seemed genuine and relaxed. "I just got a little excited, that's all. Beffie, I twisted my ankle a bit. Come and give mommy a shoulder."

Beffie did. They walked together to a fallen log, and Lee took off her boot and a nested pair of socks. "Time to shed one pair of these anyhow," she enunciated. The crispness of her diction left nothing to be desired, and reassured me ... well, maybe a little. We went on, then, after Lee had treated her twisted ankle to a few minutes' worth of cool washcloth, dried it, and resumed her boots.

On Honeyman Bald

Lee seemed OK. She seemed OK. At one point, she spent a little more of our drinking water to soak a handkerchief and tie it over the top of her head. She smiled in relief as the cool water made little runnels down her neck.

"That's better," she said. "Anybody else that's hung over ought to try it." Bethany and Suellen adopted it immediately, and after a while, so did I.

"More of a high, for a bald guy, in't it?" Suellen snickered.

The trail took a generally optimistic path up the flank of Honeyman Bald, gaining altitude when it could, while it slowly traversed the south face, mooching around toward the east. There, according to the tope sheet, we would find a straight shot up a ravine until near the top, where the final steepness threw some zig-zags and switchbacks into it.

Around noon, we got to the easternmost point, which turned out to be a rocky ledge that featured a broken-down bench and a view of probably twenty miles of the Great Smoky Mountains. The bench was the first sign of humanity we'd seen since we left the main trail, almost a day ago. It looked like it hadn't been sat on since CCC days. Lee sat on the ground and leaned against it, looking out over the Smokes and letting a fitful little breeze dry her face. She looked so goddamn beautiful it brought a lump to my throat. And when she'd puffed herself back to normal breath, she began very quietly to sing.

"*A-amazing grace, how sweet the sound; that saved a wretch like me,*" she crooned; and her voice trailed out over the valley, mixing with the haze and the sunlight and the circling raptors.

And on the next line, Bethany and, amazingly, Suellen joined in. That Suellen Ransom, the nineteen-year-old science whiz, postgraduate grifter and, if Lee was to be believed, seducer of our daughter, even knew the hymn was miracle enough; but she also knew a silken strand of harmony that would have made a taxman cry, and she sang it in an angel's voice.

I didn't try to add a bass line. I have no musical ability whatsoever, and lately have lost even what sonority I used to have when I was belting hymns at Gabbro Presbyterian. I knew better than to wreck perfection. I just very quietly sat down, looking out over the forest so I could hide the tears. And when the three treble voices recapped the first verse, and wove a rope of harmony around

> "Wa-as blind;
> bu-u-ut now:
> I see;"

and when that last "see" had whispered out to a hyperpianissimo that became indistinguishable from the sibilance of the wind, we grinned at each other. And each of us, I guess, saw at the same time that the others were on the verge of tears. We rushed together to make a jumbled hug that sent the knot of us staggering toward the lip of the ledge.

"Whoa!" Suellen said, muscling us back from the brink. "The family that hums together, succumbs together." But even her eyes were a little shiny.

We ate some fig bars and tangerines and a handful of gorp each, and watched the play of cloud-shadow over the forest below us. When Lee was finished, she lay back and stared into the sky.

"What a very nice thing," she whispered, so quietly that

On Honeyman Bald

I don't think she was addressing it to anyone but herself, or possibly the breeze. "Damn, what a very nice gift."

"Where'd you learn the harmony?" Bethany asked Suellen; and Suellen shrugged, and said she and her Momma had been hooked up with an evangelist for a time, out in Wisconsin.

"He called us his Resurrection Angels," she smirked. "Had us come out of the congregation dressed in tank tops and microskirts like whores, crying for Jesus, but still kind of struttin it, to build interest, like. He'd pretend to be appalled at us, hold a cross out and have us kiss it to prove we weren't the Devil in disguise, before he'd touch us. Then he'd get one of the ladies in the crowd to wipe off the makeup, and ask us, were we truly sorry for our sin and ready to receive Jesus as our Lord and Father. We'd say yes, yes, Lord, take us.

"So he'd get us to put on white robes like hospital gowns, that were split up the back, and take off the whore clothes under there and drop 'em on the stage, the teeny little bras and the lacy red bikinis and all. And he'd dunk us in this big tank he trucked around, and we'd sing all these old hymns. People about went wild, partic'ly when we'd give the men a little flash of butt skin while we were changing."

She looked abashedly reminiscent. "We must of made a thousand bucks a week with that crazy bastard. We'd stand there naked under those skinny wet robes, and the old farmers squirming around in their camp chairs with their eyes just buggin. He'd always yell out, Stand up tall, darlins, the Lord wants to see his new brides. Then the folks'd start up either, like, Amazing Grace, or Old Rugged Cross, one of them, and we'd rise up out of that tank looking sanctified, standing up tall with our shoulders thrown back and those wet robes clinging to us, and I tell you, folks about passed out, how he'd saved these hookers, which they had to know was plants in the first place."

She stretched, and winked at me. "Specially the old goats that come back in the next town to see it again."

Our new ladies' trio sang one hymn after another for another hour, stopping every so often to rest and get their wind. After a few, I added a few little bum-bums of a bass line, which were neither derided nor applauded, unless you count another wink from Suellen and a brief hand-squeeze from Lee.

Most of the time we were in deep cover, following our little draw up through tight laurel thickets, darkening as the sun veered to the southwest and began to sink into the trees that lined the edge of the draw over our heads. At maybe 3 o'clock, we came out of tree cover into a rash of low shrubs, and then out of that to a rockpile that marked the head of the draw. Discouragingly, the orange blaze marks danced straight up the heap of boulders toward what appeared to be a vanishing point in the sky. Bethany sat down on one of the boulders.

"So," I said. "Here's where it gets tough. How's it going, everybody?"

The girls shrugged and fluttered their tee shirts to pump air in to where it would cool them off. "Headache's gone," Suellen grunted.

"Lee? Beffie?" I pulled out the map.

Lee looked like she was still hearing hymns, though they'd trailed off in favor of panting a half hour ago. "I'm just lovely, Hap," she said.

Bethany looked at me, and I looked back and shrugged.

"We're here," I said, pointing to a spot maybe three

quarters of the way to the top, where the green overlay that marked forest cover stopped. "Not far from the top, on the map, but we've got a lot of altitude to do, yet. I'd guess it'll be another hour, anyhow. There'd be no shame in turning back, maybe camp out on that overlook."

No takers for that piece of realism. Bethany rolled her eyes, and took a swig of water. She put a boot on the first boulder, and started looking overhead for handholds. "Let's go."

OK, but the rustle of the folding map was answered somewhere overhead. "Hold it," I yelled.

"What was that?"

"Take your hand off that rock, right now!"

Bethany did, and backed away. We all did. And when we were far enough back from the boulder, we could see the heads of two rattlesnakes coiled on the top of the rock Bethany had been ready to vault to the top of.

"Yee, shit," Suellen said.

"Anybody want to think again about turning back?" Still no takers. Suellen kicked a cobble against the foot of the boulder, bringing another crescendo of rattling.

"Thing to do," she said, "Is carry good-size sticks, and poke ahead of yourself, and not put a foot down where you can't see all around it." She picked a ten-foot length of silvery dead sapling out of a tangle of brush, broke it in half over her knee, handed half of it to Bethany, and started a circuitous route up the rockfall. Bethany followed, keeping a wary eye on the rattlers.

When she and Suellen were a pair of lithe rumps thirty feet up and going higher, I turned to Lee. "If you don't feel like you can do it, I should call them back now."

Lee shrugged herself into her pack and put a hand on

my cheek. "Just stay with me," she said. "I'll be fine."

It took us well over an hour. In spite of her state of grace, Lee had a struggle with it, since now it wasn't so much a matter of endurance as of the strength to heave herself again and again up rockpiles that ranged from knee to waist height. At first I went ahead to pull her up, but she said she felt better with me below, and promised to scream like a banshee at the least sign of a snake. So I pushed instead, and then pulled myself up, panting and rueing the months of deskbind that being acting president of Gabbro College had enforced. We saw more snakes, not all of them necessarily lethal-looking, but I'm no herpetologist. We gave them every courtesy. Not hearing screams, I had to believe that Bethany and Suellen were keeping a sharp eye out as well.

I'm also not a vertebrate anatomist, so I didn't say anything to Lee about the bone. It was lying in a little nest of twigs and debris, in a hollow where a small flash flood might leave it. It was fairly fresh, or a little weathered, but not dry and porous like it had been out there for years. Maybe two inches long, a quarter or three-eighths in diameter, flared at each end like a chicken's drumstick. I couldn't recall seeing any such bone in any chicken I'd ever eaten. And when I picked it up, I couldn't help noticing its kinship with the fingers that held it. Trying it here and there like a jigsaw piece, I found a match with the first joint of my right ring finger. Probably, I could have done the same thing with a bear cub skeleton, or a fox's tailbones. I put it in my pocket, meaning to ask one of the Gabbro pre-med faculty about it when we got back.

In due course, well before I could legitimately think about a coronary, a boot entered my field of view from above, and I found myself five feet below Suellen and Bethany. Lee, puffing hard and sweating, was settling next to them.

"You're almost there, Daddy," Bethany said.

"Yeah? Where, the Pearly Gates?"

"The top."

I nodded. "OK. Is it worth it?"

Suellen cleared her throat. "It's nice," she said. "It's super-nice. But we're not alone."

That seemed hard to believe. There'd been not a sign of anyone else all the way up, unless you count the bone. Not a gum wrapper or a boot scuff on the trail, before it degenerated into trackless boulders.

"Somebody else is up there?"

Suellen spat over the edge of the rocks. "Old dude that looks like Santy Claus on his day off. Lotta white hair, chubby, big ol' white mustache."

"And wait'll you hear who it is," Bethany said. Suellen grunted, dismissively.

"Well," Lee said. "We've had the mountain to ourselves all day. I expect there's room at the top for five people."

So up we went, and found that the top of Honeyman Bald was a smooth half-dome of granite, or gneiss, or something that looked unweatherable; that it did in fact end in a sheer pitch of cliff, the cliff at whose base we had camped. And that one could groin-tinglingly stand at the edge of that cliff as the August sun beat on it, feel the warm thermal updraft that powered the eagles and hawks that circled leagues below us in that vast whispering bowl of air, and look out over the tag ends of North Carolina, Tennessee, and seemed like half of the Great Southeast.

And finally, that Santy Claus had a helper.

On Honeyman Bald

"Heighdy, people" the old man greeted us. "You must be young Bethany's folks. My name's Derwood Barnes Cather. This here's my son and associate, Mister DB Cather. He don't like 'Junior', so we use the alternative ta distinguish between us."

4.

The biospheric pastor was a barrel of a guy, anywhere from 55 to 75 years old. If anybody remembers Burl Ives, you'd be close, but Santy Claus on his day off will answer as well. He was ruddy and lively, and he wore - on this warm day in the mountains - hiking boots, tan corduroy pants, and a long-sleeved flannel shirt with an ecclesiastical collar. He was bald, with a fringe of white hair that continued down his back in a two-foot pigtail, while it connected neatly in front with his white mustache, muttonchop style. His son and associate DB looked nothing like him at all.

DB had short, wavy grey hair, a pair of little brown eyes set close to a hawkish nose, and a mouth as wide as the slot on a toaster. He wore lederhosen over a tee shirt that said something about British Columbia, but the suspender superstructure got in the way of the message.

"It is a pleasure," he said. His narrow-gauge eyes seemed to have trouble moving past Bethany's chest as he shook hands all around. His shoulders were broad and hunched, and it wasn't immediately evident whether he was a brick or two shy of a load, or just a somewhat idiosyncratic guy.

"Where'd you pop up from?" Suellen asked him, bluntly enough. "You weren't here when we got up here."

DB looked a little flustered. "I was occupied in the middle distance," he said.

"DB suffers from a bladder condition," the old man

boomed. "Keeps him hoppin some days."

"Unfortunately..." DB looked parricide at the old guy, who sailed on unabashed.

"Don't know as I caught your names, Sir and Madam," he said. "Suellen and Bethany was good enough to share theirs right off. I always feel like folks are like to get on just fine if they know each other's Christian and family names right off. Saved a lot of awkwardness later on, more than once. And I can't stand this postmodern nonsense of introducing yourself by one name, like you was an apostle or something. 'Hi, my name's Mark,' my soul. Yeah, and I'm Revelations."

So we laughed, and shared our entire given and family names. Even Bethany, who'd kept her miscreant father's name of Morgan, explained that he'd died in a car crash before she was born, and that she and her mother had, as she put it, married me some time after that.

DB turned to Derwood, curving his big toaster-slot mouth into something that would have accommodated a banana sideways. "Poppa, you ever hear a child say anything half as nice as that about her stepfather? Most of the time, they can't stand the sight of 'em."

"Is there another way up here?" Suellen asked. "We thought we were just about alone on that trail, and we didn't see a sign of anybody ahead of us."

"There is at that," said DB said. "Poppa and me, we know quite a number of little manways all through these woods, you could look at from ten feet away and swear it was all as wild as Dick's mare. We ain't discouraged by steepness nor brambles, and we come and go among whole communities out here, bringing the comforts of the Wilderness Gospel where meek souls thirst for the Good

News."

Suellen rolled her eyes a little. "Were you planning to camp here? We don't want to bust in on you."

Derwood smiled. "No, no, child. DB is expected later on tonight at the home of a parishioner for a midnight vespers, over to Windy Notch, and I will serve as his acolyte. It's not but maybe an hour's walk. You can see it from here, know where to look. No, we'll leave this lovely site to y'all tonight, though we'd be more than happy for a little time yet in your company."

DB lit up and turned to Lee. "You must, you simply must, mustn't they, Poppa, sing us a hymn before we go, as the sun of this radiant day drops to rest. Poppa and me heard you earlier on, and when the strains first fell on our ears, Poppa said to me, DB, praise Jesus, it's the day of the Rapture. I can hear the angels singin. Ain't that so, Poppa?"

Derwood nodded. "I may not have put it so - well, spontaneously. But we were ready to join the company of the saints."

DB beamed. "Poppa and me spend the bulk of our time under God's heaven. We stand always ready for the Rapture, not like these pale and listless churchfolk in the no-account listless towns."

Derwood chuckled at this burst of eloquence from his awkward associate. "Well, well, you folks are splendid, if not the angels we thought we heard. We'd be honored to set up your tents and all, if you'd lubricate the work with the sweet oil of your voices. Y'all know 'Jesus Calls Us O'er the Tumult'?"

We declined help with the tents, but took their advice about safe and comfortable sites to set them up - no small thing on a rocky dome that would laugh at the notion of tent pegs. DB pointed out a pair of places where previous campers had driven pitons into cracks in the rock, and when we were set up, Suellen broke out the refreshments.

Apparently Temperance was not indispensible to ministers of the Wilderness Gospel; we sat in a circle in the late sun, sipping carefully at Suellen's white lightning while she and Bethany and Lee wove ribbons of harmony that flared and danced in the turbulent air, and Derwood and DB Cather and I basked in the beauty of the moment.

After we'd had eight or ten good old favorites and a snort or two each, Derwood wiped a tear of bliss from his cheek, and told them to stop before he became enchanted like Odysseus of old, and had to be tied to the mast to keep from jumping overboard to his eternal bondage.

"We will share the inspiration of this moment with them unto whom we minister tonight, Poppa and me," DB said, and Derwood chimed in, "As a tiny and entirely unworthy recompense, perhaps y'all would be diverted to hear an ancient Indian tale of love and loss that attaches to this very place."

On Honeyman Bald

5.

After the ancient tale was told, the ladies' chorus sang one more hymn to ease the departing on their way, and Derwood and DB disappeared into the woods on the south edge of the Bald, doubtless following one of their imperceptible manways and singing "Little Brown Church in the Vale". The last we heard of them was Derwood's *"O-oh, come, come, come, come..."* A half hour after that, we were bedded down again.

We could hear Bethany and Suellen in their tent, giggling about the DB Cather, and about Derwood's Indian legend. Suellen launched a joke that had to do with "manway," but the punch line - evidently a rouser, for Bethany and she cut loose with treble bellows of laughter - was too quiet to hear.

Lee stretched herself across the sleeping bags and whispered at me.

"You wont to think about a little punkin?"

"Sorry," I said, slow on the uptake from Suellen's martinis, however cautiously sipped. "A little ...?"

Lee swore mildly. "Never mind," she said, slowly. "I meant to say a little 'something', but what I really, really meant was a fuck. A good old fuck. I can still say that fine. Well?"

I could see her arms, luminous in the near-perfect gloom of the tent, reaching for me. "What say," I suggested, "It's our turn to enjoy the constellations tonight. If we get right out there, we can probably establish squatters' rights."

"You have the best damn ideas," she whispered. "You always did. That's why I fell in love with you the minute I laid eyes on you, sitting there in that ridiculous pool bar at Wallden." She gave a little snort of reminiscence and gathered up an air mattress and a sleeping bag.

Outside the tent, the sky was so spangled and cosmic that it gave you a scare to look up, as if the crammed heavens could burst, drowning the listless world in starfire. In that world, west of Honeyman Bald, tiny sparks gleamed, one every ten miles of complete blackness, to mark a place where people pushed it back with light bulbs or kerosene. I suppose one of them marked a spot where them unto whom they would minister awaited the advent and comfort of Derwood Barnes Cather and DB. The light of all those stars was more than enough to find a flat place on the granite, a little sheltered by a stunted cedar. We settled on it, gently undressing each other, shivering, slipping into the slick cavern of the down bag, warming each other with belly heat that had waited all day for the chance. We both smelled pleasantly of unwashedness, an ancient human smell that was probably abundant around the Looks Far household. I kissed Lee's ear, and whispered in it.

"Wallden? You can't tell me you gave a damn about me then. Or you sure put on a good act. Not to mention for a whole year in Gabbro."

Her eyes in the starlight locked hungrily on me, and she spoke slowly. "Hap, listen to me, and remember. I have loved you since the day I was conceived, since the day the world was made. I will love you just the same until there is no more world for anyone. Don't you ever forget that."

Well, there was no topping that; not that I didn't try. I

turned my attention to what my son Taylor, shortly after his introductory birds-and-bees lesson, referred to as the "ucky stuff " involved in ... well, in a good old fuck. But don't think that Lee's declaration didn't run through my mind then, and through all that followed; and through what I finally realized was Lee's foresight of the heartbreak that must come; though neither of us could possibly have foreseen what the form of that heartbreak would be.

*   *

We woke to blindness. Day had come, since the starlight had dissolved into something brighter. But except for the top of Lee's head, tucked under my chin, and the corner of the sleeping bag, the rest of the world consisted of shining fog, so dense that my hand dimmed perceptibly as I extended it to arm's length. The shine told you that somewhere, this cloud was lit by sun; but there was no direction brighter than any other.

I gently extracted myself to take a leak and trod carefully into the cloud, splitting my vision between the rock ahead and the sleeping bag behind. I could see the ground out to ten feet or so; beyond that it was a blanket of splendid ignorance, and I didn't care to celebrate our lovemaking by pitching over the edge of Honeyman Bald.

I found another cedar - careful studies of soldiers in desert warfare have shown that men peeing in the outdoors are acutely uncomfortable without a structure to target - and when I got back to the sleeping bag I found Lee, as naked as I, standing on it and marveling, stretching her arms and legs out to admire how the fog faded them away at the tips.

"How's this for a change of weather," I whispered.

On Honeyman Bald

"This is something. My god, let's not even go near the edge until this clears up."

"I wasn't thinking of going anywhere but back into the sack."

"Show me where you were. I need to pee too, and if I go by myself, I'll never find you again."

So I showed her, and after she'd smirked at the wet patch on the trunk of the little cedar, she dismissed me into the discretion of the fog. I walked a distance that reduced her to a crouching egg at the spooky edge of visibility, and waited for her to find me again.

When she did, she had a plan.

"What time is it?"

"No telling. I usually wake up around five thirty. It could be that, maybe six. I don't think it could be any later than that."

"The girls won't be conscious for hours. Let's find a place where we can't see anything but each other."

It wasn't hard; in five steps, we hit a patch of featureless grey lichen. A toe's length beyond our bare feet, it was like walkable fog. Not another structure, not a shadow or shrub or pebble broke the sphere of luminous cotton around us. There was not a sound in the world but our breathing, nothing to see but the woman I loved above everything else in my life, naked as Eve. I have never stood in such an erotic setting, before or since.

Lee turned as if we'd walked onto a dance floor and held me, looking into my eyes with the same hunger she'd shown last night. She was shivering just a little, and we were both growing a slick coating of moisture. It gave last night's smells an oceanic note.

"This is it," Lee said. She was squinting at me, her head

a little tilted to one side. "This is good. Now; do you remember what I said last night?"

"I'll remember it until there is no more world for anyone."

She raised a finger. "Just the same."

"Just the same until there is no more world for anyone."

She raised her face to me. It was covered with dew, and the dew was beaded up on her curly hair and shining like constellations; in our bubble of fog she looked like something out of a very good dream. "Like this. This is what heaven will be like."

"If we forget how to walk..." It was getting hard to say long sentences. "... on the tops of the clouds, and fall through?"

"That's right. If we fell into a cloud. And not even God could see us. What more heaven could anybody wont?"

Only exactly what happened. One of her legs snaked up the back of my thigh, then the other.

When we woke again the fog was still there, pierced now by a yellow flicker and the smell of bacon. Lee and I ghosted back to our tent, glad of the cover of fog, speculating in whispers which of the girls had smuggled bacon into her pack - it was no part of our rations, since we hadn't planned to cook breakfast - and then found the enterprise to get up, find dry wood, and start frying. I was ready to nominate her for sainthood, or at least advanced maturity, until I dressed and found their tent still sodden with girlish slumber. A stab of alarm and annoyance turned me toward the source of the yellow glow.

"A most cordial good morning to you, Harper,"

rumbled Derwood Barnes Cather. He was crouched over a rimless iron skillet, dressed still in his quasi-ecclesiastical flannel shirt, and seeing to the frying-up of what looked like at least a pound of thick-cut bacon. "The little flock we served last night gifted us with more home-smoke than DB an' me could consume in a year. I thought y'all a'd be of a mind to help us out with it this morning. And ain't this one of God's most beautiful morning creations?"

"It certainly is, Rev," I said, not ready to return cordiality fire. "DB here too?"

"One of our parishioner ladies went into premature labor during the service. DB stayed with her to offer what assistance and comfort he could, and to baptize the child in case of mortal peril. I don't know when to expect him back."

"In case... I get it. Good of him."

"He's a good boy. It won't have escaped you folks, DB's a little bit of a lost soul, and a worry to me. I do wish he'd learn to relax and be himself around folks."

Derwood sighed and scraped moodily at the pan to loosen the bacon. "I been taking in stray boys for a long time. Ever one of them, they started out wild and awkward and in trouble with the law, and they all proved to be susceptible to the fathering every boy needs. In five or six years, eight at the most, they'd turn to me one day, and thank me, and say they'd found a job in Knoxville, or met a girl in Rutherfordton, some such thing, and let me to understand they were grown up and ready to cut loose on their own. They're well settled now, and I'm proud of every one of them."

Derwood turned the coarse strips of bacon over, lining them up as neatly as they'd been when they first started frying. "Oh, DB too, of course. Just, it's been quite a time now, and still I don't believe he's come all the way he's got to come, particularly in the way of self-respect. He lived a rough and desperate life before I found him, and paid the price for it. Now it's a struggle for him to present himself ... Well, you heard how he talks, like he learned it in a reform school, in the Depression. I wish to goodness he'd meet a sensible, amiable Christian girl who'd take him just as he is, and help him believe in himself. He knows I love him, but I'm getting on. It kills me to think of passing, and leaving DB to fend for himself."

Derwood looked at me a little expectantly, maybe thinking I'd say, why, Bethany or Suellen was in the market for a nice mountain boy, particularly a bashful ex-thug. I opted for silence. He sighed, and poured excess bacon grease into the fire, where it sizzled and flared demoniacally.

"I don't mean to intrude on you folks," he said. "Folks come here to get away from company, not have it keep popping up like bad pennies. Thing is, I know these here grey-outs. They happen in the Smokes pretty regular, end of the summer, and folks get lost regular, missing their way." He leveled a rueful gaze at me. "Kilt, even, they take a wrong step where they can't see."

He tossed his head southeast. "We don't live all that far from here. I got up restless, couldn't help thinkin of you folks waking up in this, and take a wrong direction out your tents, and bingo. Whyn't I take some a that bacon up there, thinks I, and share it out, make sure them folks are safe?"

The bacon was very tasty, I have to say. It wasn't long before Suellen and Lee joined us, neither of them much more cordial than I'd been. Derwood dove to the rescue just in time to head off stumbling Bethany as she exited the tent and headed for the brink, grabbing her elbow so that she shrieked at his sudden appearance, and then got impossibly flustered at having her life saved by the Greatest Living Ecopoet.

I don't think any of the rest of us was all that thrilled that Derwood was back with us. The girls, after they'd gotten over the change of weather, and after Lee had escorted them to the pee tree, settled on an air mattress and stared grumpily into the fire. Lee was unhappy about them, I could see, and her face showed it. My fog angel morphed back into a stressed-looking matron with a pair of young girls to shepherd through the wilderness, who - we thought then at least - needed just as much protection from each other. We passed around a bottle of Tang and some coffee. I did what I could to get us packed up, so we could start down as early as possible.

When Derwood saw what I was doing, he asked me flat out:

"Harper, are you thinking to take these ladies back down that trail this morning?"

"We need to get back home," I shrugged. "And we've got more than a day's hike back to the car."

"As to that," he said, "I can point you a way that'll save half a day over any trail that's on your map. You can really afford to wait a bit for dryness and visibility. And, I gotta tell you. The upper stretch of that backside trail, where you came up, it's a leg-breaker right now. Those rocks are as slick as frog ribs, and you can't see what you're getting into in the way of snake pits. Where it was rocks and dust yesterday, it's soap and clay now. I think DB and I have taken eight or ten hikers off a there with broken legs, collarbones, often as not made worse by snakebite, in exactly this weather. My earnest advice to you all is to bide a while, and let the sun burn this fog off. It'll be gone no later than midafternoon, and you can tackle the worst of it in dry, sunny conditions."

I turned to Lee. She sighed. "That sounds like sense, Hap."

Derwood nodded. "It is sense, little lady. Set down here and try another cup a this splendid coffee. I believe I read a headache in your eyes, and there's nothing for it like coffee."

And when Lee had settled fidgeting against a fire-warmed boulder with a cup of coffee, Derwood beamed around the unenthusiastic circle of us, and said,

"I expect you ladies are about sung out. Would one of the family be willing to exchange a story for the one about Looks Far and Windshadow?"

A longish silence. "Well," Suellen said then. "I could tell you about a preacher fella my mother and I knew, out in Wisconsin. That be of interest to you?"

Derwood tipped his head and gave her a look, as of What you fixing to pull, little lady? But he could hardly turn it down, since Suellen's was the only story on offer.

Suellen settled herself, and then held up a finger, reminiscent of Lee's. "Hold it a second, though. Nobody's driving today, and everybody looks kind of cold. Anybody mind if I heat up the coffee and put a little vodka in it?"

Nobody objected.

On Honeyman Bald

6. Suellen's Tale

Me and Mom had a pretty good life in Chicago for more than a year, when I was about twelve. Working bars and clubs up toward Evanston, and down the other way, toward the University. Awful lot of country boys show up there at Northwestern, that'll be good tippers once you kind of let 'em know where it's at. We'd be there yet, I don't doubt, but in the fall elections of '98, some holy roller got elected Alderman in the ward we did most of our work, on a platform of cleaning up the night life. They didn't let students vote in those elections, so none of the guys that wanted to keep it free and easy had a voice in it.

Of course, that sort of thing comes and goes all the time, and most of the time, the cops'll see to it you don't go on the street. But then we hit a string of bad luck, a rent raise and dentist bills for a toothache that Mom got, that was so bad she'd toss and turn all day. When times like that came along before, she'd have to turn some tricks to make the rent. Mom was awful good looking, and she knew about all there is to know about sex, so most of the time she could about name her own price.

But when she got this toothache and couldn't sleep, she got kind of run-down looking, and the number of tricks and the price both went south a little, which made her even more upset and run-down. It was a feedback loop, you know, kind of like global warming. Couple of guys she brought home tried to get her to name a price for me, instead of her, and she threw them down the fire escape.

So the next thing was, she couldn't pay off the cop any more, so she didn't get protection from the civic improvement. They actually busted her <u>and</u> me for vagrancy and prostitution, which was ridiculous - we had a perfectly good apartment, and she'd never once let a John at me. But we didn't trust the public defender more than to plead to a lesser charge, and the end of it was a pair of one-way tickets out of the Trailways terminal at five in the morning, Easter Sunday. The tickets were for Des Moines, but Mom said for God's sake nobody owes Society that much. She - I'm so proud of my Mom for this - she took a hard look at herself in her compact, and she said, Suellen, I look like a hooker on the downside of forty.

She held her breath and went into the stinko little toilet on that bus, and she scrubbed herself shiny and started from scratch. Changed clothes to a sober little navy blue dress and a sort of sailor hat she used for tricks sometimes, for a certain kind of customer. She'd spotted a likely looking guy sitting by himself a couple rows back, and when she came out of the toilet she kind of sauntered up the aisle, watching the road ahead. And when the bus hit just the right kind of curve, she let it fling her into this fella's lap.

She kind of shrieked and apologized, and squirmed around like she couldn't wait to get off his lap, which let him cop any amount of feel, if he was so inclined. And I guess the results were encouraging, because she got herself out into the aisle just in time for the next curve, and back she went, and off he went on a tour of the goods again.

When I saw how it was going, I pasted my hair down flat with spit and put on my glasses, so in case I got into the act, he wouldn't get distracted by this cute little thing that looked so much like her momma, but - you know, fresher. Which was

On Honeyman Bald

luck, because the next thing I know, Mom's standing over me telling the guy I'm her baby sister that she's taking to visit our granny in Trempealeau County, and I should shake hands with Reverend Doctor Baxter.

Reverend Baxter looked a little skeptical about the sister act - Mom was twenty years older than me, after all - so I said, well, really, stepsister, but I love her just like she was a real sister. He gave this little coo, like wasn't that the sweetest thing he'd ever heard, and he said, little girl, it is all one to me whether you are her granny or her parole officer. I scour southern Wisconsin for souls in need, from Kenosha to Trempealeau County" (which he pronounced completely differently from the way Mom said it, I don't know why she couldn't have just said Buffalo County, which is the next one north and would have been the same size lie; Mom never was one to take the easy way) "and I stand in need of assistants. Attractive, modest, and virtuous female assistants like yourselves. I cannot pay a princely salary, but it is my conjecture that the two of you right now would see about any salary at all as princely. I promise you that I will not let that cheapen my standard offer by so much as a penny. I can also offer modest, comfortable accommodation. And, by the way, an eternal crown of pure gold awaits you when your service is done."

Well, he talked that way all the time. You never could tell if he was being dead serious or sarcastic, whether it was about eternal salvation or the best road from Madison to Dubuque. Generally, he was pretty serious about salvation. He had one of these real preacher's looks - big round handsome face, and a lot of white hair, big gentle-looking hands, a gold tooth and a gold watch the size of an English muffin. Mom asked him if we could get a loan against the pure gold crown to come, and he just *laughed in a funny way, and said by the time we got it, everybody else would have one too, and it wouldn't be worth a hoot, in money. Mom said she'd figured something of the sort.*

The bus had a layover in Beloit to wait for a connector, and he took us into the coffee shop to buy us some breakfast, which I must say was nice of him and plenty welcome; we'd had a Twinkie each since last night's jail food. It was lighter and steadier in the coffee shop, and he had a chance to size Mom up a little more accurately, and we had a better look at him. I don't think any of us came out the better for it; even me, since I was the age where your nose and chin are growing about as fast as - well, anything else. Anyhow, it was super-obvious that Reverend Doctor Baxter's white hair was a wig, and he was probably ten years older than he talked.

But he could talk, boy. He said he was looking for a pair of attractive ladies to help make real the concept of the Rapture to Come to a population of farmers and feed clerks that had no more poetic imagination than a gas pump. He quoted us a salary that was more than reasonable for what sounded like pretty easy work."

I gazed into the silver fog in the direction of the valley while Suellen told the Reverend Derwood Barnes Cather about the Resurrection Angels and the wet-robe show. It wouldn't have been polite to be too obviously checking his reaction. But I have good peripheral vision. He lifted his coffee mugs to smell the alcoholic steam and bent a narrowed gaze at her. Beside me, Lee seemed to have drifted off to sleep.

Well, for a while, Suellen said, *it went very well. We traveled around in a converted school bus with bunks and curtains, but the whole back end of which had been welded into a gigantic baptismal tank, with a plexiglas window cut into the side, so the folks who came to services could watch sinners get washed clean. Mom and I made good money, which he paid us every Monday afternoon in cash out of a lockbox that he kept in his suitcase.*

If you ask me we earned every penny. Reverend Baxter always made sure the baptism tank was full of fresh, cold water, so we'd show a lot of nipple through the robes. I was starting to get my figure, and even before that, you could see some old boys looking more at me than at Mom. So I was holding up my end. Some weeks, Reverend Baxter had to go to the bank and change the offering money into big bills, and even then sometimes he could hardly stuff it all into that lockbox. But toward the end of the summer of '99 the whole show started to come apart.

See, the thing was, Suellen said, wanting us to understand.

The thing was, old boy really believed in all that stuff about the Rapture. The Robe Show was something that had come to him in a dream, which for him meant practically on direct orders from God. He was given license, he said, to use even the Devil's tools to do the Lord's work. If he could bring ordinary sinners to salvation by catching their attention with us, then there would be more joy in Heaven over that, than worry about the sex end of it.

Derwood Barnes Cather snorted about that. "Classic Devil's logic," he said. "The end justifies the means. I'm ashamed of you, young lady."

On Honeyman Bald

Suellen reminded him that the notions being reported were not necessarily those of the reporter, but were an accurate account of what she had experienced. "I never argue about theology," she said.

He had a different approach for women and old folks, of course. He was the bait for them. We were there for the men. He'd always have us walk over from the tank to pass under his lectern, to pull their eyes along, and just when we'd pass under him, he'd fling a bathrobe over us to cut off the show, and he'd pull out his big gold watch and hang it down where their eyes were, and tell the sinners that the time cometh and now is, and start reading from Revelation and talking about what he called the Raptur' to Come.

But that wasn't all that came in dreams. He dreamed huge books of important, life-and-death information about the Rapture in an ancient language that he had to figure out and master in a hurry, since the time was getting short. He took to shortening the evening services so he could work over his Bible and his dream journal, trying to decipher what the Lord was telling him; and that tended to cut into the offering take.

He got short with us, too, when we asked about working conditions. Come this time of the year in Wisconsin, it can get pretty chilly in the evening, and Mom and I were like to freeze some nights. Mom tried to get him to let us wear some kind of bodysuits, even just on top, and she showed him how if you got the right material you just about couldn't tell it from skin, particularly under a white robe; and how nipples would show just about the same.

"Just about," he said, "is going to be the difference between Raptur' and eternal torment for some soul, when he sees a panty line through that robe, or where the bodysuit ends

on your necks. You look at these outfits figure skaters wear; sure, it looks like skin when they're spinning around, but it don't fool a baby when they're standing still. A farmer sees we're trying to fool him, his heart will turn to stone, he won't hear the message of salvation, and we've lost him. You want to show up before the Throne of everlasting judgment with the weight of a dozen Wisconsin farmers' souls around your neck, why you go ahead, little lady, and I'll find another set of Resurrection Angels."

Mom said, well, when people see us coming up there with pneumonia, some of them'll figure out how we got it, and then where's their Raptur'? So the compromise was, he'd draw the baptism water as soon as we got set up, and let it warm up a little in the sun before we had to get into it; and then things were a little better.

Course, he'd been sleeping with Mom; he said lying with a woman seemed to clear not only his sinuses but the channel for the Lord's message. Plus she was supposed to wake up after he'd had one of his prophetic dreams and take dictation right then, in the middle of the night, before he forgot everything he'd seen. I could hear it; you could hear everything in that dumb bus. Some of it was pretty crazy stuff.

When I started to grow, he started giving me looks, and patting my butt a little extra when he'd pass me in the aisle. He started trying to get Mom to switch off with me, to see if that helped clarify the dreams. Mom had always protected me from Johns and from other guys that wanted into my pants. But she got a cold from that damn water tank along toward the end of August, first of September, which turned into bronchitis and flu, and she didn't have the strength to fight him any more. She sat me down and told me what to do, and what to say, and what not to put up with, and...

On Honeyman Bald

Suellen sighed, and looked off into the fog for a moment. But her voice stayed as steady as the gneiss under her.

and we did it.

It wasn't too bad, I guess, all in all. Reverend Baxter woke me up about four in the morning, and said he'd never had such a vivid and curious dream, just full of significance. The Lord had led him into a kind of control room, like you see at NASA, and there were angels with crew cuts and pocket protectors sitting at computers and calling out this significant stuff to each other. He realized that he was meant to hear it and remember. And then he started dictating all this stuff, half of it was in foreign languages, and full of numbers and equations and signs.

Derwood Barnes Cather shook his head. "Delusional. You shoulda had the silly bastard committed."

Suellen shrugged and took a little sip of her coffee.

Not long after that, we're taking a pit stop at this little city park outside Boscobel, Wisconsin, and Reverend Baxter looked up at us from where he was sitting under a tree with his Bible and his calculations, and he's white as a sheet. "What day is today?" he yells at us. "Damn it, what day is today?"

"It's Wednesday, damn it yourself," Mom answers him. "And we haven't been paid yet."

"I mean the day of the month, you stupid slut," he yells.

So Mom tells him it's the fucking eighth of September, and don't dare talk to her that way. Reverend Baxter starts running for the truck, and says get in, quick, we got less than a day to get ready.

On Honeyman Bald

So we did. What else could we? We're way out in the middle of nowhere. While we're tearing down the highway, Reverend Baxter keeps pounding on the steering wheel, and saying it's so simple, it's so simple, why didn't I see it before? And thanking God for letting him at me at last, so he could have this big dream that had the answer wrapped up in it.

"Answer to what," Mom asks him. "The Raptur', the Raptur'," he says. "It's coming tomorrow at 4:39 in the afternoon, and we got to be up north of Winona, Minnesota to be there."

"Well," Mom says, "If you don't slow down, you'll get a trooper on your butt, and that'll cost you a couple hours, not to mention whether this wreck is licensed and inspected properly. And anyhow, how come only up there? I thought it was supposed to be the end of the whole world. Why don't we just wait here for it?"

"I'll try to keep it simple," says the Reverend. "Look here. Where do we know about the Raptur', and the Last Things?"

"The Bible." says I, trying to show I give a rat's ass.

He gives me this patient look. "Fine, little lady. Happen to know where? Never mind, of course not. In the mighty Book of Revelation, which is the work of Saint John the Divine, him that is also known by the symbol of the mightiest of raptors, the eagle." 'Course the difference between the Evangelist John, John the Baptist, and John of Patmos went right over our heads, whatever he thought of it. I know for Mom, one John was pretty much like the next.

He starts to hunch over the wheel, which makes his foot crunch down on the gas, and that raggedy old school bus starts flying down the road again, heading for the Mississippi crossing at Prairie du Chien. And over the rattle and bang of pots and shoes flying around the bunks, and the booming of the dunking tank, he lays it out:

The key to understanding Revelation, he says, is the number seven: the seven churches, the seven seals, the seven visions, the seven-headed harlot (where he gives Mom and me a look). But the figuring the last day, the last hour and moment when the Raptur' is gonna hit, that's what's been stumping him. The Revelation is crammed with multitudes and numbers, and he figures it's got to have to do with math, which is also the message of this NASA dream he got by screwing me. But he's a man of the Bible, what does he know about math?

He says he finally became as a little child, and gave up on anything higher than just simple counting. The last day, the last hour, he figures, is gonna be the last number, the number 9. And here we are in 1999; that's a start, right there. And if Revelation's any guide, there's got to be a seven in it somewhere.

He's doodling around with numbers, like 97, or 7 plus 9 (which is 16, the digits of which add up to 7; that false trail cost him days, looking for a 16 somewhere) or 7 times 9, another false lead. And then, sitting in that crappy little rest area, dumpster full of stinking diapers under his nose, he sees it: seven seals, seven churches, <u>seven nines!</u> Meaning, not 63, but a simple string of 9's, seven of them, laid out side by side like the seven candlesticks. He's getting hot now, he says. He thinks of 9/9/99 almost right away, but he's not sure of it until he sees where the other three 9's come from: the 999th minute of that day, which is to say, 4:39 pm. Figure it out.

He wrote it down on a piece of paper, and he says it felt like an angel was guiding his pencil. And when he'd finished writing it, he heard a trumpet blow, like he'd broken through to the next level.

He kind of closed his eyes then and leaned back in the

On Honeyman Bald

driver seat, and it came out of his mouth in this voice I'd never heard from him before in my life, a voice like there was a whole men's chorus inside him, in nine-part harmony: "Thursday, September 9, 1999, at 4:39 in the afternoon." Every hair on my body stood up. Mom grabbed the wheel to keep us out of the ditch, and she's laughing at him like he's the seventh stooge. But I could see her hand shaking, just the same.

I won't drag this out. Where he was headed in such a tearing hurry was Eagle Point, Minnesota, which is a bluff over the Mississippi where there's always a lot of eagles. We'd passed by there more than once, on the Wisconsin side, and you could always see three or four of 'em circling around. Reverend Baxter figured an eagle had to come into it, because of John the Evangelist. So he wanted to get to somewhere high up, where there would be eagles.

We did sure enough get busted for speeding the minute we crossed over into Iowa and started up the river. They wouldn't take a check for the fine, which meant he had to break out the cashbox, and you show a cop a box full of cash, he's gonna have a lot of questions, the first nine of which are gonna be, how much of that can I get my hands on. Time we're loose, it's almost midnight, and Reverend Baxter was fit to be tied, particularly when he found out Mom took the distributor cap out of the bus engine, and won't give it back.

Listen, she says, it's a four hour drive max up there, and you're in no shape to keep driving. I'll wake you up tomorrow, I promise, first thing, and you can make Winona easy by late morning. Give you five, six hours to say your prayers. You don't want to go into the Last Day all ragged out like you are right now. Come here, now, I got something special I saved up for the Last Beddy-Bye. Well, he raved and swore, but when Mom made up her mind on something like that, she wasn't going to move.

On Honeyman Bald

She'd tucked the distributor cap into a Tampax box, which she knew he won't look into.

He kept us up so late crying and begging, and getting pacified between us, we didn't wake up till like 8 or 9 on the Morning of the Last Day. Plenty of time, still, Mom says. But the next thing, it's come up with a fog as thick as we got here today, you can't see squat. Reverend Baxter's big gold watch had stopped, because he got so busy being mad and pacified, he'd forgot to wind it. He called the time and temperature number and set it again, courtesy of La Crosse Provident Mortgages, and he had another fit, seeing how late it was. We got out on the highway, and after Reverend Baxter ran us off the road, going faster than he could see ahead, Mom kicked him out of the seat and told me to take him back in the bunks and quiet him down.

We made Eagle Point at 4:25, fourteen minutes to spare, and we were the only thing moving on the road. The fog was heavy as sin, and there was sure as hell not one eagle in the air that day. What were they gonna do up there, but bump into each other?

Reverend Baxter never wavered a hair. He gets out of bed and puts on one of our white robes, and he walks out barefoot to where there's a kind of scenic overlook, and he climbs up on the wall the Park Service has put there to keep tourists from falling off the cliff. Mom and I tagged along, I guess, figuring if there wasn't anything to it, he'd need some kind of comfort and calming down; and if there was, maybe we'd get sucked up in the undertow with the gum wrappers.

When we got there, he's wavering around up on top of a stone pillar at the end of the wall, and looking at his watch, and up at the sky, which is exactly the same blank grey crap we got here. It's 4:36, he says, and he showed us the watch. You best get down on your knees.

Mom never budged but to ask him where he kept the key to the money box.. But I tell you, I was scared good. I mean, he was a fool and a lecherous old fart who had as much knowledge of Divine secrets as a doorknob. I'd figured his whole ministry as a scam and a way to get laid regularly, all along. But where did that voice come from?

Four thirty seven, *says Reverend Baxter. And a little bit after that, Mom gets down next to me, whispering to me this is the lamest crock she ever saw, but let's humor the old dope.*

An eternity later, Reverend Baxter looks down at us. **Four thirty eight,** *he says, in that big, scary voice.*

I started counting seconds, and then I got mixed up and lost count, and tried to remember the last number I'd got to, which was up in the twenties somewhere, so I put down a few seconds to the confusion and started over at thirty. Mom put her hand on my shoulder and said, Don't worry, honey, eagles don't fly in the fog. She didn't sound too relaxed about it. I passed forty seconds.

Mom yelled up at Reverend Baxter, Hey, what happens to the rest of us? What happens to them that don't get Raptur'd?

Reverend Baxter looked down, and it seemed to me his face had changed into a giant clock, you could see the gears and springs whizzing around inside his head, and the second hand was just passing his eye on its way up to the top. Fifty seconds.

THEY GO DI-RECTLY TO HELL, *he said, and it sounded like a brass band. Fifty five.*

And when I got to 57 seconds, we heard the hugest, most horrible sound of feathers and wings, and we looked up at this shape coming down through the fog, you couldn't see what it was except it was pretty big.

And then an eagle, I swear it had wings ten feet long,

On Honeyman Bald

comes out of the fog, and its talons are stretched out in front of it, and it's headed straight for Reverend Baxter. Mom and I screamed and dove for the ground, and the eagle screamed back louder. Just before I covered my eyes, I saw it snatch that silvery wig right off the top of Reverend Baxter's head, and zoom back into the fog.

I looked up again, and there's Reverend Baxter standing on top of that stone pillar, bald as an eagle, and he's got a hard on that puts a big point on the front of that choir robe. I started to laugh, and I bent down and pulled Mom's arms off from over her head, and said Mom, Mom, it's OK, look. And slowly, Mom straightened up and we looked up at Reverend Baxter.

And he's gone.

Just plain gone. The next second, the fog lifts like magic, it's a clear, sunny day. There's a bunch of other tourists there, looking up at the eagles with binoculars. All of 'em were regular size eagles.

We jumped up and ran to the wall, and it's nothing but a straight drop, maybe a couple hundred feet down to the railroad tracks that run along the Mississippi.

7.

"Right", Derwood said, after a little silence. "The addlepated old lecher fell or jumped to his death. You were well rid of him, child."

Suellen looked at him over her cold coffee.

"That," she said, *"or that <u>was</u> the Rapture, and this is Hell."*

8.

Suellen acknowledged applause and went to root around in the girls' tent. She left her rump sticking out of the tent flap, straight at Derwood. I think she got it from Mozart doing pretty much that to the Archbishop in Amadeus; when she crawled out backwards with a roll of toilet paper and her Hoffmann, wiggling under Derwood's nose, I was sure of it.

When her head cleared the tent, she stood up more or less the way a cobra stands up when the fakir plays. She stretched elaborately, and winked at stunned Derwood.

"Where's the latrine?" she asked.

Well, we hadn't established one. That was one of the universe of little logistical matters we'd gone into this with no plan for. And it turned out that we couldn't be as carefree about it as most forest mammals.

"Folks," said Derwoood. "DB and I would take it as a kindness if you'd be circumspect about that. We do live downhill from here, and this kind of rock substrate, there's not much natural filtration to the hydrology. We do of course have our own facilities, built to specifications of the US Department of the Interior, Forest Service inspected, that I'd be more than pleased to share. It would be more pleasant for you, and it would ease our minds somewhat on the score of sanitation after you're gone back to Gabbro."

I could see some mixed feelings on our side of the fire. Woodland sanitation is rarely pleasant, either for the user or for those who follow behind. On the other hand, I think every

On Honeyman Bald

one of us but Bethany had spent all the time they cared to in the company of this generous, charismatic, possibly even holy man. Suellen had her face fixed to say No thanks, when Lee came back to life.

"That'd be just fine," she said, and she roused a little shakily from her doze. She gave Derwood a speculative look that might have given a sharper observer - one who hadn't been screwed comatose twice in the last eight hours - pause. "I think I got poison ivy from one of my stops yesterday, and you can't hardly believe how itchy that is."

I couldn't, because I knew perfectly well it wasn't true. But Lee's elbow was hard into my ribs - God, but she always was an old-fashioned woman - so I said what she wanted me to say.

"Very kind of you," I said. "Don't want to put you to any trouble."

"Not a bit," Derwood beamed. "Put it down to enlightened self-interest."

Derwood led us across the rock in a southeasterly direction, stepping confidently over the cracks and potholes that appeared out of the fog as we got away from the naked dome of rock, and into the meek and mossy fringes of vegetation.

"All this'll be forest, another six, eight thousand years," he opined placidly. "You can see how the lichens start it, and them little dwarf weeds colonize where dust and dirt have caught in the lichen to make soil, maybe a crack or a hollow catches moisture, even out of the fog. Course, you know this fog sometimes is loaded with acid, which is killing trees on the hilltops all through the Smokes. Seems a little tangy today, even, though it tends to be cleaner on a weekend."

On Honeyman Bald

Bethany piped up from beside him. "Maybe it won't be the same kind of forest."

Derwood chuckled at the thought. "Good, Beffie. Maybe get the same kinda trash grows in cities. Nice stand a mulberry and locust, that's the ticket." Bethany looked a little crushed at that, but chuckled dutifully.

Getting there took a good fifteen or twenty minutes of near-bushwhacking along a "manway", which turned out to mean a line through the underbrush mostly devoid of opportunities to break your leg. In the dripping forest, the fog didn't seem quite as thick as it had on the open rock. I had a moment of wondering if we were getting clear weather at last, and decided not, that being surrounded by trees prevented a sightline long enough to get swaddled to death.

At one point, I would have sworn we doubled back, but there was nothing to navigate by. One tangle of trees and laurel after another loomed out of the fog and disappeared into it again. We were now utterly dependent on Derwood to get us where we were going and back again. We came about again, and walked a log over a rocky gully and into a cemetery.

A small one, certainly. A dozen tombstones, heeling from side to side like buoys in a choppy harbor, most of them smothered in brambles and brown oak leaves. " - 1923" said one of them. Another spoke of "Beloved Consort." Away from the trail, a ragged row of wooden crosses bore no legend at all. Bethany knelt immediately at a tiny stone, with the dates 1919 - 1921 carved into moss-drowned marble.

"Aw," she said.

"All too common in them times," Derwood said. "This here ain't virgin forest. You could believe it, they was a farm up here once upon a time. Crazy folks tryna make a go of it with pigs, goat's milk fudge, tobacca. Tobacca, up here! Figured since they could claim the land for next to nothing, it'd all be gravy, whatever they could make on it. Some went crazy first and then broke, and some went broke right away. They reckoned without the costs of just breathing from day to day."

"The Second Law," Suellen said, and I glanced involuntarily at her left breast. "Ask me about it. Geez, will you look at this. It sounds like your newspaper friend, Beffie."

"*Stranger, pause as you pass by,*" she recited slowly, tracing with a finger the words held lightly in shallow marble grooves.

As you stand now, so once stood I
As I am now, so you must be.
So think on Death, and follow me.
Sacred to the Memory of
William Barnes Derwood
Nov 30, 1861 - Aug 10, 1932

"Great-uncle of mine," Derwood said. "Always was a gloomy old coot. Plus pause, pass together in the first line is weak diction."

The Cather residence was a place you were well into before you realized it was there. We were in deep woods, slipping ever downward through wet undergrowth and trusting to Derwood's assurance that there was firm walking underfoot, when I smelled kerosene. Lee, ahead of me, stopped abruptly because Derwood, ahead of her, had.

We bunched up as a consequence, and found ourselves in a hollow space made by gigantic slabs of rock. They were leaning on a cliff of gneiss and on each other like a house of cards - though more sturdily, I hoped. The forest kept a distance, so the overhead was clear; it looked like what might be a sunny, intriguingly shadowed courtyard in good weather. At one end, weathered grey planks took over from the rocks, increasingly enclosing the space until it amounted to a screened porch; and within that, shadowily, I could see a doorway leading to interior space. A spring trickled down the face of the cliff, occasioning ferns.

"Welcome to Apostle House," Derwood said; and sure enough, a rustic wooden sign over the doorway bore that carved and blackened label. "I see DB's back from his service. How'd it go, son?"

"Healthy baby boy," DB reported as he emerged from the fog. "Didn't look all that premature to me. I think she lost count, is all."

Bethany was lost in admiration of the way Apostle House blended into the forest and rocks that cradled it. "This place," she said. "It looks like something out of a storybook. It's just so... I don't know. At <u>one</u> with its setting."

"DB and me have lived happily here for - how long's it been, DB?"

"If you mean the two of us, over ten years," DB said. He turned to us with a broad half-smile. "Papa lived here for many years before I joined him. I believe his tenure is about coextensive with that of the hills themselves."

We chuckled appreciatively, and started looking for the bathroom. "A lovely spot," I nodded. "Obviously a pleasant, cozy spot in any kind of weather. We're obliged for your kind hospitality - "

Derwood grunted. "But some of you stand in need, I believe. Will you allow me to show you the way, little lady?" He took Suellen's arm and led her down a path - an easily visible path, by gum - into the all-concealing wall of fog. Before anybody had time to worry, he was back.

"Took the liberty of checking the facilities for supplies, and for the Brown Recluse," he said.

Lee raised an eyebrow. "Lower down, I always thought."

DB pooched out his lips. "For many years, they were largely confined to a band between the Piedmont and the high mountains. In the last few, they have spread upward, probably as a remote consequence of the great increase in tourist traffic in these parts. Much more commerce, more garbage and waste, thus more rats, more fleas and ticks, more of everything living. A lady was bitten in her privy near Smokemont last year. That bite festered and got infected, like to kilt her. Got her to the clinic barely in time."

"Great," Suellen said. "A new kind of snake."

DB shook his head. "A spider," he said. If you were to see it, you could scarcely credit its fearsome reputation. It is just a little brown spider. But their venom can be very troublesome, to the susceptible."

Derwood broke the ensuing pause by opening the door to Apostle House. "You all look wet and uncomfortable," he claimed. "Come in the house while you're waiting your turn, and we'll acquaint you with a tea that grows in these parts, and was certainly served by Ms. Windshadow to Mr. Looks Far."

It sounded good. We went in.

Apostle House was deeply back-country. The smell was of woodsmoke and kerosene, with an undertone of something richer. Cooking, maybe, and men living together. When Derwood lit a couple of lamps, we could see that it wasn't a big space, but as neatly kept as a destroyer, if destroyers plied the sylvan depths. One wall was of naked stone, the others of wood, draped here and there with animal hides and, on one of them, anomalously, a parachute and a telephone. A single, sturdy-looking door led off to what I guessed would be sleeping quarters. On either side of the single window, bookshelves groaned with a collection of religious books on the right, and a more eclectic library on the left: poetry, the works of John McPhee, and a batch of Dick Francis stories. (Or, to be fair, the same story told over and over in different settings.)

The same could have been said for the other bookcase. It proved to hold maybe a hundred Bibles, in a rainbow of bindings, sizes, and languages, many of them titled in exotic alphabets impenetrable to me.

"Not a one, but that's plain King James," DB said sturdily. "We hold with no other. Of course, we're not so dense as to think it's the literal words of Jesus, being that English wasn't invented yet back then. But we do think it was good enough for our forefathers, and it's good enough for us. All the translations come from friends who do nothing but that - translating the Good News into every one of the forty thousand languages that sprang from the Tower of Babel."

Over the fireplace, a passable amateur portrait of Derwood beamed at the thought.

Derwood had busied himself in a utilitarian-looking corner by the fireplace, shaking a wood stove into fiercer life, dipping water from a barrel, and pulling crockery from a cabinet. By the time Suellen rejoined us, he was handing around mugs whose steam sent messages of - I don't know, something like taking a nap in a forest clearing, attended by Bambi and Thumper.

"This is really, really good," Bethany said, after she'd

managed a scalding sip. "What in the world is it?"

Derwood smiled broadly. "Not something you would ever find in a Starbucks. Grows in the tops of trees, down in the deep timber. The old loggers knew about it, because they felled the trees. When logging died out in the high hills, acquaintance with pussyflower tea died away with it. It only blossoms for a week or so in the spring. Folks on the Appalachian Trail pass back and forth under it all summer long, and never see it."

Lee sniffed the steam cautiously, and touched a lip to her tea. "You're giving us something very precious, then, evidently."

"No more precious than the privilege of your company, Ma'am," Derwood rumbled. "DB and me - aw, I don't want to make too much of it, but we get a mite bored with just each other's company, up here. Your singing, and that, that remarkable and provocative story that Miss Suellen - "

"Pussyflower?" I asked, thinking Georgia O'Keeffe.

DB confirmed it by blushing. "There are some," he allowed, "who claim that the blossom somewhat resembles, ah ... well, a lady's private - "

Suellen snorted. "I get it. What they serve on TWA."

Lee put down her tea. "I'll enjoy this better when it's a little cooler, and when I have room for it," she said. "Suellen, would you show me the way?"

When they'd gone, DB looked after them. "That young lady has a most lively apprehension," he said, a little stiffly. "She will be nearly irresistible when she learns to govern it with an equal measure of discretion." He picked up the teapot and offered topping-ups.

Bethany bristled at that, and opened her mouth to rebut, but Suellen came back in looking a little chastened, and I speculated that she'd received a quick earful from Lee. I offered a diversion.

"I take it you men don't make many trips to the grocery store. How do you put it together, make a living up here year-round?"

"We hunt and fish and gather," Derwood said, waving an open hand at the woods. "We believe and preach that the body and blood referred to in the Communion are those of Earth itself, and those who seek perfect communion live as directly as possible from them."

DB nodded. "Of course, from time to time, we trade our services for flour and salt, or for luxuries like that bacon. The woods are full of game year round, in one season and another. Squirrel, deer, wild pig, long pig; sassafras, all manner of greens, roots and berries; hickory, walnuts, and other types of mast. Acorns, of course, which have to be treated carefully to remove the bitterness."

"Uh huh." I felt a little sleepy, and I was content to let DB's Robinson Crusoe catalog slip in one ear and out the other. I may even have dozed off. Lee came back from the privy and pointed me the way.

The privy was, like the cabin, neatly kept. It featured a calendar painting of Custer's Last Stand, underwritten by the Anheuser-Busch Brewing Company of St. Louis, Missouri. Custer stood handsome and erect in a sea of corpses and scalpage, firing a six-shooter into a wall of Indians. Them Injuns looked savage as hell. I nodded off, and caught myself toppling from the throne.

Reconstructed, I exited and gathered some condensed mist off a tuliptree leaf and rubbed my face. It restored enough mental activity to find the path, but I was getting more and more uneasy and oppressed by the fog. What started as romantic, sexy and transcendent had become a prison. It seemed impossible that there had been a time when I led a little party of singers under a shining sun.

When I got back to Apostle House, Derwood was passing around some biscuits while DB stood next to the wall with the parachute.

"Thereby," DB was saying, "hangs a tale".

9. DB's Tale Begun

All this, you must realize, he said, dates from the time before Derwood and the Lord found me and started me on the One Way. There is nothing in it of which I am proud.

Derwood grinned at his adopted son. "More joy in heaven," he quoted. Suellen looked up at that, but then yawned and settled across from Bethany on the floor in front of the fireplace.

No, DB said,

I was a no-good, smart-alec kind of fellow, the sort who'd drink and carouse and flirt with women for no other reason than to lie with them for a night, or an hour, and then go find another one. I was a petty thief, a coward, a tinhorn, a cheat, a louse, a jackass jerk, and a betrayer who was headed on a straight, if at that time remote, course for the Eternal Fires. I drank and cheated and lied, and I avoided fighting only because it was too much trouble, and because I couldn't stand pain of any sort. I worked when I had to, to get the money to pay off creditors and start another round of sinfulness. I had a friend, if you could call him that, a man even more corrupt than myself, who happened at that time to be holding a job with a video rental firm in the town of Gatlinburg, Tennessee. His name was Douglas, and I called him Doug.

This firm owned four or five outlet stores between there and Alcoa, and since Doug was a big, rough, cruel sort that no one would want to meddle with, they hired him to pick up the weekly cash proceeds from these stores, and deposit them in a bank in Knoxville. He wore a trumped-up kind of uniform that said "Special Security Detail" on the shoulder. No real police force or security service in the world would have had him.

On Honeyman Bald

Doug - and I am not going even to mention his last name, since he is still alive and nurses a grievance against me - had a woman friend, Clara Banks, who flew a helicopter for a rides concession out of Pigeon Forge. Clara was tough as leather, a great sport who took no shit from anyone. So she was a good match for Doug. When she felt like it, she could usually come up with a girl for me so we could go on double dates, some of which would consist of going up in her helicopter and parachuting for sport. I gloried in the cheap accomplishment of jumping before easily impressed country girls, and in their fear and reluctance to jump with me. I would tease them into putting on a parachute, and then horse around inside the helicopter and rassle with them, pretending to pretend to push them out the open door; and then really pushing them out. I gloried in their screams of terror and, as an experienced jumper, could maneuver myself next to them in free fall, purloin a kiss and a feel while they pummeled on my back, and yank their ripcords for them, getting myself clear before it was too late. Usually.

Later, I found that the experience had made them pliable and grateful to be alive to yield to me. I apologized for nothing, of course. Finding a date for me involved scouting out girls who hadn't yet heard of me, since none of them who had, would have anything further to do with me. One or two of course, because they were dead.

Usually, what Clara found to hook me up with were lame, underage or ugly. But one night, Clara came up with a real prize. Alice Avery was her name, and she was red-haired and green-eyed, as tall as I and with a figure that you would expect to see only in Hollywood. It is true, she had a slight harelip, and this it was that had left her available for Clara, and thus for me. The helicopter was in the shop for service, and we were on our own to generate such amusement as we could from the resources of Sevier County, Tennessee.

Clara and Doug came by for me one Friday afternoon shortly after I rose for the day, and we drove out to a squalid trailer park to pick up Alice Avery. From there, we left Gatlinburg, heading for the bars and nightclubs of Pigeon Forge. Doug and Clara sat in the front of Clara's pickup truck, and Alice Avery and I settled in the truck bed with a ratty corn-shuck mattress and a quart jar of moonshine. I ignored Alice until we'd gone through a Burger King to line my stomach against what lay before it.

The harelip was of course unsightly, but after I'd bolted a Whopper with enough moonshine to slide it down, I was drunk enough to overlook it. When we had visited a half-dozen low establishments, drinking and dancing and getting into fights with local toughs foolish enough either to hit on Alice or to joke about her, Clara suggested that we drive into the country and, as she put it, park. Doug acquiesced readily enough, and we set off for the wooded country along the French Broad River.

When we found a suitable glade, moonlit and secluded, he and Clara stumbled a short distance away with an air mattress. Alice and I remained in the truck bed, and before morning I had prevailed against whatever virtue she may have possessed, not once but several times.

Suellen opened her eyes, rolled one of them at Bethany, and winked the other. "Are you sure this is the kind of story you'd want to tell in front of a young girl?"

"Excuse me," Bethany said, sleepily. "I think it must be that tea." And she slipped out the door, evidently heading for the privy.

"Forbear," Derwood begged. "It will soon take a more

On Honeyman Bald

uplifting course."

Literally. Toward dawn, Alice, who seemed to be perfectly indefatigable, expressed admiration at my broad-mindedness in overlooking her disfigurement.

" 'Fn I had a fella like you, steady," she said, "there isn't hardly nothing I wouldn't do for that fella, and as many times as he could stand it."

I expressed willingness to consider the job. Alice let on to be skeptical.

"Thing is," she said, "I like, you know, nice things. I can't stand tacky. Place I'm livin now, you couldn't un-tacky it with a steam hose. You're nice and all, but I need a fella with the money, I could slam the door on that double-wide and never look back."

I protested that I could have all the money I wanted, any time I felt like working regularly; she laughed and stuck her tongue in my ear. "Liar," she whispered. "Big talker."

I was ensnared. I spent what was left of that night, and the weekend - during which Alice twice rebuffed my appeals for a second date, having decided, she said, that she wasn't the kind of girl to spend her life in the back of a pickup - cudgeling my wits about where I could come by some really big money. And on Sunday afternoon, help came as the rain falleth from Heaven. The phone rang.

It was Doug. Big job coming up, he said, and he wasn't confident he could handle it by himself. And though he made it perfectly clear that he had no respect for me as a man or as a friend, he didn't really have much choice. He was frank about that, and his frankness made it easy to do what I then resolved to do.

It seemed that the next cash run was to be an especially

big one, and would include certain transactions that the video company carried out without leaving a paper or electronic record. Possibly money laundering, possibly proceeds from salacious movies, in which they were implicated. Why they confided this information to Doug I have no idea; unless he was more deeply involved in the business than he let on.

In any case, there would be something over one million, three hundred thousand dollars in cash, not to mention the usual cash pickup from the rental outlets, which generally ran to a few tens of thousands. Enough, I felt, to set me and Alice Avery up somewhere in the Caribbean, fornicating for life; or at least until one or the other of us lost interest. I called Alice and hinted at what I had afoot; when I said I needed a favor from Clara, she said Clara was right there with her, and put her on the line. I explained my needs and my plan, not mentioning Doug's part in it; and what her share in it could be. Clara agreed readily, and promised to call back when everything should be ready.

I dressed in a black sweatshirt and jeans so dirty as to be essentially black; a black watch cap and black basketball sneakers. Doug called and told me to meet him at the video warehouse at ten that night, for the run to Knoxville. Thing is, he said, we have got to make the pickup run from these little flick shops, so it looks like an ordinary night. You got a gun? I told him I had, not bothering to add that I'd gotten it out that morning and cleaned and loaded it.

The evening passed slowly. I sat by the phone, not daring even to call out for pizza, so as not to miss Clara's call. I must have gone to the toilet a dozen times, and emptied and checked and reloaded my pistol at least that often. At last, minutes before ten, as I was about to call Doug to fob him off with some kind of stall, Clara called. All, she said, was in readiness.

On Honeyman Bald

Doug demanded to see my gun as soon as I jumped into the "Vacation Videos" pickup van. When I handed it to him, I couldn't keep my hands from shaking. He looked up at me with suspicion writ upon his face.

"What're you so jumpy about?" he wanted to know.

I managed to convey - and no great ruse was involved - that I was simply a coward who was wringing his hands over the possibility of danger and violence. I asked him where the money was to be picked up, and he said it was already aboard, in two big sacks in the back of the pickup van. I could see them back there, a pair of US Mail bags fastened shut with heavy canvas webbing and steel clips.

I started back to look at them - to heft them, really, to see how heavy they were going to be; but Doug grabbed me by the hair and slammed me back into the passenger's seat. "Siddown, punk," he snarled at me. "Don't think you're getting your slimy hands on it."

Well, of course, that was what I needed to clear my head. I sat quietly next to Doug, going over my plan one detailed stage at a time.

The first cash pickup was in Gatlinburg itself, a litle mom-and-pop operation that was either a negligible source of revenue for Vacation Videos, or a front for something more lucrative. After that, and after two in Pigeon Forge, we had a long, quiet stretch before the fourth pickup in Maryville. And it was in that stretch, where US 321 passes under the Foothills Parkway, that I planned to make my move.

As we approached the underpass, some time after midnight, I could see - because I knew to look for it - that Clara had done what she promised. I told Doug to stop under the underpass, that I needed to take a leak -- that was the way I talked in those days. He, of course, refused, claiming I could

On Honeyman Bald

hold it until Maryville. So I had to insist, and finally - just as we came up to the Parkway - I said, all right, then and I knelt on the seat and rolled down my window, prepared to urinate into the night wind that came through it. As I anticipated, that was enough to convince him to stop. As soon as the van was at a standstill, I pulled out my gun and shot my friend through the head.

DB looked around the shocked bunch of us. "As you see, I am being perfectly frank. That is not the last of the crimes I will relate, and I tell you about them in a spirit of penance and humility."

Derwood grunted. "Also, it would be fair to add that I have long thought, and have enforced this with all of my boys, that restitution toward the victim does more good in the world than punishment of the criminal. DB anonymously double-tithes toward that end."

As it turns out, the shot did not kill Doug; though it appeared to, and he has never been fully functional since that night.

As quick as I could manage it, I took the ring of keys from the ignition, and ran around to the back of the truck. It was a fumbling eternity's work to find the right key, but I eventually had the back doors open, and the two sacks of cash out onto the shoulder of the road. I dragged the first of them to the far side of the overpass. As I dragged it, I could hear the engine of Clara's helicopter wheezing and bursting to life by the side of the road just ahead.

She was in the pilot's seat, fiddling with controls and yelling at me to hurry; and believe me, I did. On the trip back for the second bag, I glanced up at the cab of the van, and saw

On Honeyman Bald

Doug's face flattened against the window. It was smeared with blood. He appeared both furiously angry and dead, and his lower jaw was displaced at an angle that allowed me a glimpse far into the smashed workings of his skull. That sight has remained with me ever since.

I glanced at Lee. She appeared to be half-asleep, and she had no reaction to the gory tale. Suellen was staring at DB in fascination. Her hands were half-open on the floor beside her, utterly relaxed. I tried to fidget, to let DB know that there were things I wasn't willing to hear, just for the good of his soul; and found it too much trouble.

I got all the cash into the helicopter. Clara hauled me into the passenger seat, and strapped a parachute onto me, and clipped another, small one onto the sacks of cash. The idea was that they should fall as straight down as possible, gently enough not to break them open, and to give me something to mark the spot where they fell.

Clara yanked the helicopter into the air, and we headed straight up to ten thousand feet. From the air, I could see a glow under the bridge, and I realized that I'd left the van headlights on. I cursed myself for a fool, and then relaxed; they would not show during the day, and it would certainly be day before anyone started looking for us.

We flew straight toward the Smokies, gaining altitude slowly. I told Clara to shut off all lights in the cabin, to give me a better view out the window; location, as the realtors will tell you, is everything. It was a dark night, with a waning moon just rising in the east. I'd checked that detail, but I could see that we were a little ahead of time; I wanted it to be well up before I committed to the next step. Which was to dump out the

On Honeyman Bald

sacks of cash, to follow them down myself by parachute, to a place called Tuckerman Overlook, off the Blue Ridge Parkway. There, Alice Avery was going to meet me in a rented van, which would carry us and our million three all the way to Panama. After that, I figured to improvise, aided by such cash payments as seemed unavoidable. I tried to get Clara to take a circuitous route, to give the moon a little more elevation, but she told me it wasn't on, that the helicopter would run out of gas before the moon was enough higher to make a difference.

"You're just going to have to do your best, sport," she said. "And don't forget to put my share on the front seat before you ditch."

I was pissed ... quite angry at that, and I screamed at her that she was nothing but a faithless, er, pussy. But she just smiled at me, and pretended she couldn't hear. She made the helicopter tilt and swoop down so that I almost fell out the door, just to show me that she could. I was furious, and so keyed up I almost shot her; but reason took over in the nick of time.

I opened the money bags, and almost fainted. I'd never seen so much cash in my life, even if you count all of it that passed through my hands from the age of three. I counted out her share - fifty thousand - on the seat; I did up the bags and got them ready. The moon was high enough now that I could see the faint gleam of Fontana Lake, down to the south. I guided Clara toward Tuckerman, and when I was pretty confident of where I was, and I could see there wasn't any traffic on the Blue Ridge, Clara took us up high enough to make it safe, and I pushed the bags out, and jumped out myself. As I fell away from the helicopter, I thought I heard Clara yelling something about "Tuckerman" after me. I yelled, "What?" but of course, there was no answer. The helicopter sloped away

On Honeyman Bald

toward the Overlook, and I turned my attention to my own situation.

I don't know if you all have done any sport parachuting. You really ought to. The free fall part is what it's all about, particularly in a group jump. There's no sense of falling, once you reach terminal velocity; indeed, who can say who is falling, and who is rising, when all are in free fall? Particularly at night, you could easily think you were experiencing the Rapture, or I suppose something like what the Indian couple experienced in Papa's story.

Of course my first concern was for the money, down below me. The idea was, I would steer myself through free fall until I caught up with it, and then open my own chute, hoping the money and I would come out close enough to Tuckerman to make hauling it up to the Overlook parking lot not too exhausting. I spotted it, and I could see I had some altitude to lose yet, and a little lateral correction. These were no challenge at all to an experienced parachutist like myself. I soon overtook the money. I could hear it fluttering in the wind, like a crowd of voices saying, A million three. Saying, As many times as you can stand it. I felt like the happiest, smartest, royalest king that ever was. I just gave over to the beauty of flying through the night sky, watching the moon, watching that lovely money just ahead of me. When I saw it was time I pulled my ripcord. I heard the chute pack open, and the sound of the shroudlines running out behind and above me, and I braced myself for the jolt of the chute. And it never came. The parachute flat failed.

The moonlit forest rushed up at me. The smartest man in Tennessee, floating on a cloud with his fortune, changed back to a two-bit punk with twenty seconds to live.

Lee stirred next to me. "Where's Bethany?" she asked,

On Honeyman Bald

so faintly that I could hardly hear.

    "Went to the loo," I said.

    She frowned. "Tha's long time ago. Whyn't she back?"

10.

I held a time-out finger in the air toward the plummeting punk, roused Suellen from her sprawl, and sent her to the privy. She returned, yawning, to report Bethany not there. She seemed unworried about it; and I wasn't sure there was something to worry about. That's how far gone I was. Lee dragged herself upright and looked me hard in the eye. She spoke as if drowning in molasses.

"Hap, something is wrong. Every one of us is about asleep on our feet, and Bethany's missing."

I gaped for oxygen like a beached trout, and turned to Derwood. "Wha's going on, Cather?"

He smiled gently. "We see this a lot. Y'all have a little headache, right over your eyes?"

I examined that. "Huh."

"Altitude. Seems to me Gabbro's in a part of the state that's by and large about ten feet above sea level. You're more than a mile up, here. And a course, it's aggravated by high humidity, which takes another part of the oxygen out of the air. I've known sea-level folks like yourselves to take a hot shower and plumb pass out, up here. I expect your little girl's settled down somewheres to sleep it off. Le's go see can we find her. Little exercise'll work wonders for y'all."

He and DB led us out into the leaning-rock courtyard. Derwood leaned his head back and bellowed, "Beth - anee! Ah - hooooeee!" The last part sounded a little like hog calling. It sliced through the fog like an auditory laser, echoing eerily from the rocks and trees. When it died away, there was nothing but the drip of water from the forest.

Derwood scowled. "Now look, folks. There's about no ways she could come to serious harm, hereabouts, but I'd hate like Time to think she could have wandered back up onto the Bald, if she's in the kind of state y'all are. I sure don't want the rest of you wandering off looking, get scattered and lost, yourselves. Promise me, promise me, you'll stay together here, and stay in sight of the House. DB'n me will track her down quick enough."

I promised him, promised him, with a mental reservation that as Bethany's father, I was entitled to say the same to Lee and Suellen, and do a little poking around on my own.

Derwood walked down the path toward the privy, which we already knew was empty. DB vaulted up one of the leaning rocks to the top of the cliff that formed one wall of their dooryard and started scanning futilely into the impenetrable fog. The direction they left unchecked was the path along which we'd come to Apostle House, so as soon as the pair of them were out of sight, yodeling, "Bethaneee, Beffeeee," that's the direction I took.

And found her almost right away. She was crumpled on top of the child's grave in the little cemetery. Her shorts and panties were down around her knees, and there was an oozing scrape on her forehead. Behind her, the gravestone noted: *As I am now, so you must be.*

I knelt by Bethany in a fog of shock, trying to see how badly she was hurt, checking her thighs for obvious injuries or the leavings of rape. There was nothing. I was peeling off my shirt to cover her when she opened her eyes.

"Daddy, what in the world are you doing?"

"Bethany! Did you see him?"

"Who?" She started pulling up her pants. "Do you think you could give me a little privacy, here? I mean, OK, you're my father, but - "

"Honey, never mind that. And maybe you should just leave your pants down until we see if there's evidence that shouldn't be wiped away." I was shaking with outrage, trying to keep my voice soothing. "Just lie still for a minute, honey, and - "

"Evidence of what, for heaven's sake? I came out to pee. Is that some kind of Federal crime?"

I cradled her head, smelling her Ginseng Mist shampoo, resisting her efforts to wiggle out of my arms. "Beffie, honey, somebody jumped you, and knocked you on the head. Don't you remember anything after that?"

She started to shake, and I thought, well, now it's coming back to her. "There, Beffie, it's all right now. You're going to be just fine. Did you get a look at him before he hit you?"

Turned out she was giggling. "Daddy, relax. I'm sorry I scared you, but nobody raped me. I got on the wrong path, and I wound up here, instead of the privy. I really, really had to go, so instead of floundering around in the fog, I just hunkered down behind that big gravestone. Thing is, though, I was so sleepy, I think I must have passed out when I stood up to pull my pants up. I expect I hit my head on it."

She rose to a kneel and got her panties back in place, yawning unconcernedly. "So unless Speedy Gonzalez or somebody came by while I was conked, I'm still a virgin."

What flooded through me then was that strange amalgam of relief and fury, a parent's reaction to a child unhurt after a risky escapade. But it was heightened beyond control by the stresses and blows of these months: Lee's illness and "cure" and symptoms of relapse; Bethany's sexual dalliance with Suellen; the oppressive, apparently never-ending fog, and our entrapment in it with a maybe reformed thug. I stood abruptly and looked down at Bethany, gritting my teeth. "Well, I suppose that may be technically so, unless you and Suellen brought special equipment."

"Special what? What's that supposed to mean?"

The fact that I didn't know what I wanted to mean, only made me more furious. "Got me, Bethany. But I expect it's made out of leather and rubber. You little idiot, you damn near broke your mother's heart."

Her jaw dropped in exaggerated disbelief, and then she looked away into the mist. "We were checking each other for ticks." She must have heard how that sounded, so she stood and yanked her belt buckle closed. "Not that it's anyone's business but ours. Who asked her to police my sex life?"

"Sex? With ticks? She wasn't policing anything but the smell of pot, following it upwind. Apparently, she almost tripped over the ...." I waved an arm. "The scene. She's completely wrecked about it."

"Yeah? How kind of her to share that with my stepfather." She sighed then, and put a hand on my arm. "I'm sorry, Daddy. The pot wasn't us. We smelled it too, but it wasn't, wasn't, us. Maybe somebody else was camped upwind. Maybe somebody was burning leaves. Well, that's pretty dumb. Maybe there was a forest fire somewhere far away. Don't let's fight, Daddy. I didn't even like it all that much."

The fury drained, leaving relief tinged with depression. "I'm sure your mother will be glad to learn that, if you should wish to share it. Right now, there's so much else going wrong, I guess it seems like small potatoes to me. Let me look at that bump on your head."

She tipped her head back and looked up at me. A tear stood in the corner of one eye, and she looked just the same as she had for twenty years, wanting me to fix a bruise.

I kissed the abraded spot. "It doesn't look serious. Do you have a headache?"

"Who doesn't? I'm real worried about Mom. You know she's coming down with those, those symptoms again. Can we get out of here, Daddy?"

"You bet we can," I darkwhistled.

*   *

When we got back to Apostle House, Derwood and DB were still out looking for Bethany. That wasn't too hard to take, and nobody pined about missing the end of DB's tale when I suggested that we see if we could get back to our camp again. After all, it was on the peak of this mountain; I figured we could find it again by retracing what steps we could, and going uphill when in doubt. I left them a note, saying Bethany had been found, and thanking them for the tea, the use of the privy, and their many other kindnesses. We hadn't been on the trail more than five minutes when the fog took on a golden tone, and in another five, a spot of actual sunlight crossed the forest ahead of us. It wasn't all that different from a choir of angels beckoning us to the Rapture.

Not that everything went fine from then on. The fog came back and we lost the trail, which was of course completely unmarked. Going uphill when in doubt led us to a forested peak that was probably within easy sight of the true peak, but nothing that was farther than ten feet away had a chance against the cloak of invisibility. It took two more such false leads before the vegetation thinned to bushes, to shrubs, and to the lichen at the bare top of Honeyman Bald. A faint cheer went up from the girls; Lee sat down immediately on the rock, shivering and soaked. She looked incapable of further effort.

I turned to Bethany and Suellen. "As I recall, back when we could see anything, this rock is really big. We're not out of the woods yet. You guys run ahead - well, don't run, for God's sake, walk carefully - and find the tents and such. Then one of you stay there and stoke up the fire, and the other one come back and get us, so Lee doesn't have to wander around looking. Bring her extra sweater, so we can get her into something warm and dry."

They headed uphill, and I had a second thought. "If it's real far from here, which I don't think, work out some kind of whistle or signal, so we don't lose the place again. And for Pete's sake, stay away from the edge."

When they were gone, I sat and looked into Lee's eyes. She looked back and tried for a reassuring smile; but she was just very clearly in distress. I began to think about how much food we had left, in case we had to stay another night to give her a chance to regain the strength to hike back to the car; and about how I'd decided against bringing a cell phone, because this was supposed to be vacation.

But while we waited for Bethany or Suellen to reappear and guide us back to the camp, an amazing thing happened. The fog brightened up again, and I saw that it was draining away from here like water from a bathtub. We could look up and see swirls and blotches of blue, where the clear sky overhead penetrated. I stood up, and found my head so nearly out of the fog that I could see the neighboring peaks, basking in sun above a level deck of whiteness, into which I sank when I sat again to report this to Lee.

And as I was telling her about it, we both heard a penetrating whistle from ahead of us, probably Suellen serving as beacon while Bethany came back to find us. I heard Bethany yodel in reply. I stood again and waved my arms. "Over here, Beffie."

Bethany waved back at me from perhaps a hundred yards away, and then disappeared again into the cloud. I turned to Lee and got her upright, making encouraging noises, speaking of hot chocolate around the rekindled campfire, thinking about reconnaissance of the rocky gorge that would lead us back to a walkable trail, and the day and a half of hiking that lay between there and our car. We would be lucky, I thought, to negotiate all that without further deterioration in Lee's ... God, she would have killed me if I had referred to it as a "condition."

It took Bethany longer to reach us than seemed reasonable. But then, I didn't want her to run, trip, and hurt herself, either. I was at the stage of wondering whether to worry when I heard boots scuffing on the rock, and a shape approached through the remains of the fog. "Over here," I said.

"Thanks, Doc," DB answered. He had Bethany's wrists clamped in one hand, and a knife against the angle of her jaw in the other. Her eyes were wide, and she strained against his grip like a spooked horse.

"I'm sorry, Daddy," she croaked. "Mom, I'm sorry. This is my fault, this whole thing."

DB's nose was bleeding sluggishly, and there was a swollen knot at the corner of one eye. The legacy, evidently, of subduing Suellen and Bethany. "Don't take it on yourself, little lady," he soothed. "They're not sorry at all. Now they get to hear the rest of my story."

On Honeyman Bald

11.

DB's Tale Concluded

I was reduced at once to a screaming primitive, hurtling through the night sky. I remember a warm rush of urine, and an abject attempt to bargain salvation. God, I cried, Great Lord of all creation, spare me, and I will serve you untiringly for as long as you can stand it. And so sooner had those words left my mouth than I plunged at killing speed into the forested mountainside.

DB walked into my field of view as he recited. The knot by his eye was turning into a shiner. Fine, but that was the extent of it.

He had us arrayed at the top of the bald. Lee and I were closest to the edge, bound back to back against a gnarled and stunted cedar that was crooked enough that there was no way to work our arms over the top; but he'd made the mistake of leaving Lee's knots within reach of my hands. I found that I could get my fingertips onto one of the knots that held her. I tapped her wrist to warn her to silence, and began to pick at it.

I remember a rush of wind and a blurred sensation of plunging through pine boughs, and then an almost unbearable force on the harness of my parachute. My feet brushed the

On Honeyman Bald

earth. The next second, it was not the forest below me but the rising moon; I rose again above the forest, and again descended into it. This transformation repeated itself no less than five times, if you can credit it, before I hung safe, dizzy, and disoriented, thirty feet above the earth, swinging back and forth with ever-decreasing amplitude.

Bethany was ten feet away, her wrists tied to one of the pitons that were jammed into the rock; Suellen was still farther away, out of sight except for a bare foot that emerged from behind a boulder. "God, this is exciting," she said. Her voice was strained, as if she were bound tightly to the rock.

"Suellen, shut up," Bethany snapped. "Don't give him an excuse."

DB turned from Suellen and smiled lazily at Bethany. "You think I need a excuse, honey? You're gonna see otherwise over the next little while. Take your pants off like Suellen, here."

"That'll be tough tied up like that, won't it, Einstein?" Suellen grunted. "Why'ncha let her loose so she can undo her buttons?"

DB strode behind the boulder, and I heard a smack and a short cry from Suellen.

"That all you got to say, Blondie?" DB was shrieking with fury. "Cause if you got anything else to suggest, try it now, and see how hard I hit you when I really try. I'm tellin this story, God damn it."

He hitched himself up onto the boulder behind which Suellen lay, and began idly to tink the blade of his knife on it as he told her the rest of his story.

You can call it a lucky natural accident if you like, or you

On Honeyman Bald

can call it God's generous response to an offer of perpetual service. Just as I plunged into the forest, my useless parachute had caught over a limb, high on the biggest pine tree in that part of the forest. It stopped my fall not all at once, which might have cut me in half, but by looping me over and around that branch, again and again, dissipating the force of my fall into a harmless circular motion that eventually died away into that gentle rocking.

When I stopped screaming and blubbering long enough to realize what had happened, I just hung there in the harness of that parachute and I said, Well, OK, God, thanks a lot. You watch how I carry out my end of the deal. But the first thing I did for the greater glory of God, was to pass out, from the fright, exhaustion, and relief at what I'd been through.

When I came to, the waning moon was far to the west. Nearly dawn, then. Of course, as soon as I saw I was going to live for a while, I thought about the parachute with the money. That was a lot of money, and the Devil's money at that, and it seemed clear to me that it was mine to do God's work with. But of course, my first job was going to be getting myself down from that pine tree.

I made a start toward releasing the chute harness, and stopped myself just in time. I was high enough in that tree, that I could still kill myself just falling the rest of the way from where I was. I started pulling myself up the shrouds, hand over hand, to the safety of the limb. And before I'd gotten there, I made a very significant discovery. The harness had been cut cleanly on one side, just below where the shroudlines fastened. My parachute had been sabotaged.

But, I thought, that's not possible. Clara packed that chute herself. I paid her full asking price, fifty thousand dollars, with hardly any haggling. I racked my brain to reconstruct

On Honeyman Bald

what it was she'd yelled after me, about "Tuckerman". All I could really remember were the two syllables, "...ucker..." I must say, I didn't like anything I could make out of that, if it wasn't about Tuckerman Overlook.

"Is he still facing Suellen?" I asked Lee, at the edge of audibility.

"Yes."

"Your wrist is almost loose. When it comes loose, see if you can get my hands loose. Then head for the woods, and let me handle DB."

But just the bare possibility that I'd been set up and double-crossed gave me a kind of blazing caution that was utterly unlike anything I had felt before that night. I believe that shrewd fury came into my heart directly from the hand of God.

I crept to the highest part of that tree, and scanned the moonlit forest. And there, not fifty yards from where I had fallen, I saw the money parachute. I descended my pine tree with the feline caution of a mountain lion, and I crept toward the money, every sense quivering, probing the dark forest, alert to the scent of treachery.

And it was the scent that gave them away. I had smelled it, after all, for hours on end: a cheap toilet water that Alice Avery used to cover the stench of her ravenous body. My nose led me toward her like radar, like a heat-seeking missile. Rather, toward them. In the time I had hung unconscious and in imminent danger still of dying, Clara had landed the helicopter at the Overlook, and she and Alice had clambered down to collect the money. And there they lay in a pool of moonlight, naked in each other's unnatural embrace.

On Honeyman Bald

Lee barely moved when her ropes came away at last, and she started to work on the knots that held me. But it was hopeless; DB had yanked my wrists so tightly against the cedar that the knots were half-sunken into the skin.

"Forget it," I whispered. "Watch your chance and undo Bethany if you can, and both of you head for the woods. If you can't get her loose either, just run, quick, before he finishes."

I hardly need tell this company how deeply repugnant I found this sight. But as my fury mounted, so did my caution. There may be some bizarre but innocent explanation yet, I thought. There is no rush to condemn them. Wait.

And I was right to wait, for bye and bye dawn came, and they awoke. I will not defile my lips with the endearments, the gloating, the self-incrimination that poured from them. It seemed my amateurish plot had come as a godsend; Clara, thoroughly sick of Doug, had formed an abominable relationship with Alice. She had been scheming to get rid of Doug, and I had provided not only the means, but a literal fall guy and a handsome cash bonus.

The only decision left to me was which of them to kill immediately, and which to kill slowly, in as protracted and satisfying a way as I could devise. I decided finally to grant Alice the quick death; she had been amiable, for as long as I'd known her. I nourished Clara, when she became hungry enough, with Alice's flesh.

DB walked to the edge of the cliff and stood looking out over the mildly tossing sea of cloud at his feet.

"There is a moral to this story, people," he said. "If

anyone can articulate it, I would be very much inclined to listen sympathetically to any pleas for mercy."

"The Lord works in extremely mysterious ways," I hazarded.

"Wrong," DB said. "There was nothing mysterious about any of it. But you are for the jump anyhow, Daddy."

Bethany spoke from behind me. "Don't fuck with Hoppy?" I think she was trying to get DB's attention away from Suellen; which I guess I would have to count as a pretty significant token of affection for her.

"Not bad, little lady," DB said. "It's a sight how a saying like that, which must be a total mystery to a youngster of your age, survives yet. All right, Beffie, we'll consider that a serious contender if you can answer one simple question: Who's Hoppy? No help allowed from the older generation."

"Give me a minute to think about it," Bethany said.

"Easy," Suellen said. "Hopalong Cassidy. That old show where the guys with the tiniest dicks had the biggest knives."

DB's face distorted. "Bad answer, sister," he snarled. "The moral is this: lesbian sex is a waste of two perfectly good pussies. You two young ladies could have learned something from the handsome and imaginative coupling of your elders here, some of the prettiest I ever watched. Surely it must have come very near what Adam and Eve practiced before the Fall. Instead of that, you fumble and fool with each other, makes me sick to see it."

He shucked his jacket off and tossed it on the ground at the edge of the cliff, and stalked toward Suellen, unfastening his belt. "Lemme show you how it's supposed to go, you smart-mouth little bitch."

Before the end the end of what followed that, Lee was crouched behind Bethany. I could see the end of a rope flying from side to side as she undid the knots. DB's head appeared from behind the boulder, his face distorted in what could have been ecstasy or despair. He lifted it and howled to the sky, and then dropped out of sight. I could hear Suellen breathing hard, like someone who has just vomited and is still nauseated.

Bethany sprang to her feet and shook off Lee's urgent arm. She ran to where she could see DB and Suellen, scooped up a handful of rocks, and started pelting them at DB as fast and hard as she could, grunting like a tennis queen. The first one shattered against the boulder above DB, but the second thumped into something that sounded like a watermelon. DB yelled and stood up from behind the boulder. I heard his knife clang on the rock as another rock caught him hard on the elbow. He staggered back and grabbed Lee, and held her in front of himself as a shield while he ran to where his jacket lay near the cliff edge. Bethany got in one more shot that took him in the side of the head while he bent over the jacket. He roared with pain and rolled on the ground, dragging Lee with him away from the tormenting barrage. I felt an instant of hope.

"Great, Beffie," I yelled. "Do it again!"

Bethany didn't need coaching, but she was out of rocks. While she scrambled frantically for more, DB staggered to his feet with blood streaming from a lump on his temple. He clamped an arm around Lee's neck and began shaking his jacket frantically with the other hand. As Bethany started pumping rocks at him again, he shook a pistol clear of the jacket and jammed it against Lee's head.

"Drop the rocks, you little bitch, before I blow your mother's head off."

Bethany stared at him and dropped her rocks on the

ground. She burst into tears of frustration and knelt beside them.

DB relaxed and smiled on us. "My stars," he said. "That was exciting. I gotta tell you, though, there's gonna be shit to pay. You think what we done up to now was - "

"DB Cather!" Derwood's voice boomed out of the middle distance. "Just exactly what the hell is going on here?" He walked toward us from behind Suellen, looking from her to DB in astonishment.

I sagged against my cedar. "Your lonesome fella got tired of waiting for that amiable Christian girl and learned to be himself, Derwood. He just raped Suellen."

Derwood was stunned, no mistaking it. "You _what_? God damn you, you shameless, lawless boy, what the hell has gotten into you? Give me that gun."

DB wiped the blood away from his eyes with the hand that held the pistol. "Cut it out, Poppa. She was asking for it. She is nothing but a dyke, and it done her good to get it the right way for a change. You - "

"Silence!" Derwood swelled like a thundercloud. "Not another word from you." He turned to us, his face and body a study in devastation. Tears shone on his cheeks. "My God, this is unbelievable. Suellen, Jesus, we can never make this right. But I promise you, this boy is going to face justice for this. I will see to it." He walked toward DB with his hand out. "DB, put down that gun. Give it to me."

"As you wish, Papa." DB leveled the pistol at Derwood. It made a slamming noise, and Derwood clutched his chest in disbelief. As Derwood sagged onto the rock, DB swiveled toward me.

"No witnesses," I think is what he said. The gun blammed again, I saw a brief flame at the muzzle, and a twig jumped from the cedar beside my head. I ducked, trying pathetically to hide behind the stunted cedar.

Lee began to twist and struggle in his grip, and the pistol fired twice more, the bullets humming and whining off the granite of Honeyman Bald. "Damn, little lady," DB panted. "F'shit sake, hold still."

Lee fastened her eyes on me while she continued to buck and struggle in DB's grip to keep him from drawing a bead.

"Remember what I told you. I'll explore later. Damn, *explain.*"

It occurred to DB too late, simply to shoot Lee. He was putting the pistol to her head when she jammed a boot against the rocks and heaved backwards with all her strength. I saw what she was doing, and screamed in fear.

"Hey," DB said.

It was the perfect last word for him. Propelled by Lee, he stumbled with her off the edge of the cliff. His mouth opened in a scream a foot wide. Lee winked and smiled at me as she fell, but not a sound came from her. I screamed for her as they tumbled together into the heaving sea of fog. For an instant there was a small indentation in its surface, and then that filled in forever. From far below, I heard a despairing scream. And seconds later - some handful of shocked and stop-heart seconds later - a shot.

12.

Lee stood before me, and her hair was straight and black again. It was spread around her head in a wind-whipped cloud, as if she were riding in a convertible, but it was not moving. In the enveloping fog, with the mist sparkling on it, it looked like the night sky on Honeyman Bald. She was naked, and so was I.

"Lee," I said. "Why?"

She smiled and shook her head.

You know why. Plus, I told you, if that business came back, you'd have to take me out and shoot me.

I nodded. "Did he shoot you on the way down?" Not knowing which way I wanted it.

She snorted. Not him. He shot himself.

"Then you fell all the way ..."

She shrugged, making the skin of her belly rub against mine.

I'm still falling. Seems like it's fixing to take forever. But I'll tell you one true thing that boy said. After a little, you forget that you're falling. It's like you're flying instead. It's pretty lovely, really.

"Lee," I mourned, filled with horror and sadness. "Jesus, what am I going to do without you?"

Not one thing, cause you won't be without me. They don't tell you the rules, but that's the one thing I've figured out so far on this deal. You wont to see it again? The family that cries together, ...

On Honeyman Bald

She didn't finish the rhyme. Her leg snaked up the back of my thigh, and her mouth opened against mine. And she flowed into me, like water flowing into dry ground.

*   *

For the next year or more I was clinically, certifiably insane. It was my only armor against killing myself. Part of the insanity, its chief sign and symptom, was the calm maturity with which I worked at recovering from Lee's death.

I almost wrote "the loss of Lee," but night after night she came to me. Often, she would comment in her sensible way on things that had happened that day. Sometimes she would tell me how deeply she had loved our life together, or laugh with me about some passing drama from years before. But just as a church service, whatever its occasion in the calendar, must always include the basic message of the Gospel, so Lee closed her visits always with the same message.

And that message, coded in the melding of her self into mine, was that she had been glad to discard her doomed body in exchange for the lives of Bethany and Suellen and me. That the quick, airy death it found on Honeyman Bald was infinitely preferable to what awaited her at Duke, if she had gone down that mountain with us. And that, as she had been a part of me of all those years, she was part of me now, and always would be; that she would be present in my life, not as a memory but coded in the very flow and grain of my thoughts. Some of the code was contained in "I will love you just the same until there is no more world for anyone;" and some of it in the cryptic riddle about "The family that cries together ..."

On Honeyman Bald

So he who accepted the awkward sympathy of students and the consolations of friends who - truthfully - had loved Lee better than they'd loved me, was not just Hap Maryland but was also in some part and in some way Lee Morgan Maryland herself.

And in the end, the justice that I would bring to a murderer would come from the hand of his victim as much as from her avenger.

13.

Wetmore Parsonage slumped onto the CCC bench where Lee once sang Amazing Grace, and threw a wad of chewing gum into the forest below.

"Don't skip that part. I gotta hear it."

I lifted a hand. "As you wish. I didn't see much of it; they had me tied on the edge of the cliff with my back to her. But anyhow, DB raped her."

He nodded and drew breath through his teeth. "He hit her?"

"You know he did, Wet. You saw her when we got back."

Wet ignored that. "How many times?"

"I wasn't counting. Once before he started .... " I sighed. "Before he started in on her. A few times during. It sounded more like slaps than punches."

He grunted. "But some thump to it."

I nodded. Wet didn't need a sound track, and he didn't need my description of the blows. He'd seen Suellen, seen the abrasions on the back of her head where the force of DB's pummeling had scraped it across the rock.

Wet pounded his fist on the bench, and broke one of the 70-year-old slats. "Slimy piece of shit scum. Makes me want ta dig him up and stomp his bones. The only thing keeps me sane is the way Lee took him out. Christ, that was a woman."

"Look, you want a piece of advice, don't try. I'm not."

On Honeyman Bald

"Keepin sane?" Wet shook his head. He was starting to get his breath, after our long climb. "I could miss something. You want to stay sharp, you don't take aspirin."

"I'm not talking about loony bin stuff. I'm talking about monomania. Kind of a..." I shrugged. Wet didn't have to know where it came from. "A shrewd fury."

Wet chuckled without smiling. "I always admired how you could talk about stuff without actually gettin your hands all that bloody. You'd rather find a new name for shit than flush the toilet."

"Watch me on this one, buddy boy. There's something very weird going on out here."

He rose from the bench, reluctantly. The next thing was to get him up the steep and snake-infested trail of boulders to the top of Honeyman Bald. I will leave it to you to picture that, but I will say that Wet's hiking outfit was the same rumpled raincoat, fedora, and wingtips that he wore day in and day out back in Cumberland County to gumshoe deadbeats and shoplifters. No amount of joshing or hard-headed reasoning had gotten him to even think of wearing proper hiking clothes. He did carry his share of the gear, which amounted to a small tent, meager food for two days, a couple of self-inflating mattresses, and sleeping bags that I hoped would be adequate for this fall weather, up there at six thousand feet.

It had been Wet's idea to drive out here and see the place where we'd fallen afoul of DB and Derwood Cather. For once, I was glad to fall in with one of his sleuthing schemes, which mostly struck me as a lot of histrionic overkill. In the days following our return to Gabbro after Lee's death, some eerie features of our encounter had begun to emerge from the chaos of grief and horror, mostly during sleepless predawn hours, and had finally convinced me that we'd been very badly deceived; at least about Derwood Barnes Cather, DSc (Hon).

Half-way up the rock scramble, I showed Wet where I'd found the bone - a dead match for the first ring-finger joint, right hand, of Gabbro College's teaching skeleton.

"What kinda bone?"

I gave him a look at it, and he turned it over in his hand. It didn't take long for him to find the match, either.

He wiggled the relevant finger speculatively. "Figure them guys might of made a habit of doin hikers?"

"Yes. That's what they were going to do with us. I even think it was going completely according to script, until Lee ... did what she did. They couldn't have figured on that. Raping Suellen was just the start of it. "

"That's start enough for me. We gonna camp on this rockpile, or you wanta get on up top?"

It was hard as hell to see that place again. The only merciful part was the difference in the season and the weather, which were now autumnal. The view over the Smokies was as vast as before, but chilled under a slaty sky. Wet stood at the brink, looking out over it, rocking on his ridiculous city shoes for a minute or two, and then turned to me.

"OK, Hap." It was maybe the second time in our acquaintance he'd called me that. I guess he was feeling compassionate. "Where were you?"

I showed him the cedar, a yard back from the brink. I sat on the edge and put my arms behind me to demonstrate. He nudged me to one side and sat where I'd been, turning his head as far as he could over his shoulder.

"Couldn't see squat, could you?"

"Not hardly. Lee kept me informed."

Wet stood, and I guess had a little dizzy spell from it, or from the neck-twisting. He gave me a funny look, and started to walk sideways toward the edge. I clamped onto his wrist just as his foot rattled off the rim of forever.

He gasped, "Ah, shit," and grabbed my wrist too, and for maybe four seconds it was an even thing whether I would pull him back and rescue him, or he would pull me over. I had a split second of relaxation when I realized that I didn't care all that much, but the thought of sharing terminal velocity with Wetmore Parsonage gave me a jolt of strength. I yanked him back from the edge.

"Holy crap," he said. "I suppose I owe you again."

"Forget it. I didn't fancy going over myself, is all."

He nodded. "OK, then. Show me where Suellen was, and the others."

I did my best, caveating freely that, after all, I hadn't been in a good position to see anything, and that Suellen had been out of direct sight most of the time. When I showed him the pitons DB tied her to, he gritted his teeth and laid himself over them. I don't think he was being prurient or morbid; that was just Wet's approach to detection, sharing the viewpoint of the victim and the perp to make it real to himself. Still, it was making things too real for me. I looked away.

When he stood, brushing the rock dust from his raincoat, the look on his face was one I'd never seen on Wet, or anyone else. If DB had been there, I'd have given him a life expectancy of less than a second.

"An' the others?"

I walked him through what had happened, including -

he insisted on this - reciting as much as I could remember of DB's squalid tale, and exactly what I had seen and heard during Suellen's rape.

"But after Lee went over the edge with DB, I just collapsed. Bethany eventually remembered to go and get DB's knife where he'd dropped it to pull out his pistol, and cut Suellen loose, and the three of us pretty much fell in a heap on each other."

I looked out over the miles of forest. On a sunny day, seen by someone whose life had not fallen apart, they would have been beautiful, a hilly spectrum of autumn colors. It looked like a graveyard to me.

"It was a while before any of us could think of anything but Lee, and then it was Suellen, trying to comfort her. She kept insisting she was OK, it wasn't the first time it had happened to her, and it was no big deal compared to Lee, but you could see otherwise. When we'd helped her put herself together a little, we started down the mountain. I guess we were fifty yards down the trail when somebody finally remembered to go back and look at Derwood. And by God, he was gone."

"Gone? The guy's plugged in the chest by his own son, and he gets up a zillion miles into the wilderness and hikes off?"

"Yeah, maybe. Or maybe they faked it, like in 'The Sting'."

"Fucking movies. You heard shots pinging off the rocks."

"Not too tough to put a blank in the first chamber and live rounds in all the rest."

"Why'd they do that?"

"Got me, Wet. Part of some elaborate fakeout maybe,

that would have ended up with us scattered, unable to defend ourselves, dead. All I know for sure is, Derwood was gone, and he didn't leave a blood trail. And I think he was hand in hand with DB the whole way."

"Why?"

"I can't exactly say. A guy's adopted son goes bad, and shoots the guy. Must happen all the time. But there were enough little funny hints, that I just can't buy it."

"Intuition, God's gift to the moron. Where was he after the kid shot him?"

I waved vaguely at an area of rock with a faulted crack in the granite. "Best I can remember, it was about here. But remember, the next thing after he went down, DB started shooting at me, and then Lee ... did what she had to."

Wet gave me a look that somehow combined sympathy with impatience at a bathetic plea for sympathy, then got down and looked at the rock, and wound up sniffing all along the base of an eight-inch step close to where Derwood had fallen.

"Might be a little blood smell there. Been a lotta rain out here, I expect."

"Sure. But it wasn't raining that day, and there was no blood, and no blood trail."

Wet heaved himself upright and looked around like a pissed-off bear. Looking for the spoor, I guess, of a wounded eco-poet with white whiskers.

"I don't see no trapdoors, anything like that. Or any sign of him."

"You realize," I said, "there've probably been dozens of people up here since then."

"Suellen said you didn't see nobody but them two."

"Well, sure, but - "

On Honeyman Bald

"Well, that was a hot weekend in the middle of August. High season. I don't expect people come up here much."

I thought about that. "Seems kind of odd. You'd think this would be a big hikers' mecca. It's a great view and all."

He scratched the back of his neck. "Next time you see one, ask him about goin up Honeyman Bald. I bet you'd get some kinda funny reaction."

"Well, there was the owner of that bone. Former owner."

"Yeah, and a few others over the years. Not so many, would you think? That trail up here looked like nobody'd been on it in a year."

Yeah, I thought. And I had another visual memory that gave me a shock in the solar plexus. "You ready for the next part?"

"No. I'm ready for whatever supper is, and a drink. I'm completely wiped."

On Honeyman Bald

14.

It rained a little that night, and the rattle of it on the tent woke me, and then put me back to sleep. Lee visited, and expressed admiration for Wet Parsonage's skill and dedication.

"You could never stand him."

He thinks well of you, and he's been a good father to Suellen, such as he could. You see people more whole; that's another piece of this deal.

This deal. That was the only way she ever referred to her death.

"Uh-oh," I said, unsure to what extent one joshes the dead. Lee smiled, and ran a hand through her blowing hair.

You got nothing to worry about, hotshot.

She began to shimmer somehow, and flow. *The family that cries together ...*

*   *

In the morning, we had fog. Not as thick or as shining as what we'd had before. That had been a summertime, high-pressure, no-wind fog; this was just a continuation of rain by other means. Wet's clothing, of course, was no match for the temperature and humidity, but I knew better than to tell him I told him so. After a cold breakfast of granola bars and Tang, I led him toward the forest, looking for Apostle House.

On Honeyman Bald

At first, I was pretty confident of where I was going. Derwood's voice in my ear called out the landmarks: the lichens colonized by dwarf weeds at the edge of the open part of the Bald, the first part of the "manway" that led through the heavy brush. I tried to reproduce, as closely as I could remember them, the pattern of bends and doublings we'd followed. After ten minutes, Wet's raincoat and city shoes were drenched and useless.

"You sure you know where you're goin? I'm goddamn soaked."

"Nope. Didn't I talk to you about the right kind of clothing to wear in the woods?"

"Yeah, Eddie Bauer stuff. Catch me in that yuppie crap. How'd I look in teal spandex?"

"You'd look darling. I just meant proper boots, wool socks and such. You'll be lucky those pimp shoes don't fall apart."

"They been wet plenty of times. I paid eighty bucks for these shoes."

"Eighty bucks," I whistled.

After another twenty minutes, I stopped and tried to get some kind of bead on where we were. Nothing looked right; but then, nothing looked wrong, either. We'd been surrounded by fog and wet laurel then, and that's where we were now. We'd have been out there to this day, if Wet hadn't tripped over one of the headstones of the little graveyard. Don't ask me how we hit it without crossing the log bridge; obviously, we were lost and lucky.

I had a theory about that graveyard, but it would take some uninterrupted time to check it out. In particular, time not interrupted by Derwood Barnes Cather emerging from Apostle House, guns blazing. I squatted on the ground next to Wet and got him quieted down about his bruised shin.

"The place is no more than a hundred yards from here," I whispered. "It's reasonable odds that Cather is there, if he thinks nobody's looking for him. We're going to have to split up, and come up on it from two sides. Keep hidden, and keep quiet. As far as I know, there's only one door, and it's well hidden under a rockfall. If he surprises you, you're a lost hiker." I looked at Wet's wing-tips and shrugged. "Way lost. Or make up something better than that."

I showed Wet the path that led to Apostle House and sent him on a line parallel to it, twenty yards to the right; I did the same on the left.

Walking through the forest was tougher even than the manway. Mountain laurel was thick, and in places impenetrable. I detoured twice, hoping Wet could do the same without getting lost. I have to say, though, he kept it quiet. At last the jumbled and leaning rocks of Apostle House's dooryard showed ahead on my right. I could hear the water of the little spring trickling down the bluff that made its back wall.

I eased out the Glock I'd picked up at Gabbro Pawn and Electronics, and checked it for load and safety. After that, there wasn't much point in pussyfooting; I rushed the place as quietly as I could. When I was under the shelter of the leaning rocks, and well back toward the screened-porch area, it came to me that the place was deserted.

Wet appeared at my elbow. "Nobody home," he grunted. "Not a single fucking apostle."

"You so sure of that, you're ready to chat about it, out here in the open?"

"Yeah. There's a window broke on my side, and a curtain half out of it. Curtain's all stained, like it went through a few weeks outdoors. And anyhow, you can pretty well tell."

I remembered that curtain, but not whether it might have been stained already. But I wasn't going to split hairs. "Let's go in, then. Where's your gun?"

"I never carry."

"That's funny. I remember pretty clearly you drawing a bead on Lee one time."

"That deal cured me. You can do fine in almost any situation, you're willing to use other means. Look what good guns done Derwood and DB."

"OK, fine. You'll excuse me if I leave mine handy."

"Just don't plug me. Let's go."

The instant we walked through the front door, we heard a rattle and bang from the little kitchen area, and something fell on the hearth and shattered. Wet and I hit the floor and each other, and I let fly a shot toward the source of the noise. It plucked the fedora from Wet's head, ricocheted off the stones of the fireplace, and put a good scare into a raccoon, who gave us a burglar's glare and waddled at speed toward the broken window.

"Holy shit," Wet said.

"Telling me. My pulse has got to be 200."

"I meant the stray bullet, not the badger, whatever that thing was. Put the heat away before you shoot your dick off. Or mine, more likely."

I stashed the Glock unhastily.

Apostle House was wrecked. I couldn't tell who'd authored it, whether human vandals or wild animals, but every cupboard in the kitchen was open, with empty bins and containers scattered over the floor; the books were pulled out of the bookcase, and lay about the floor like broken birds.

On Honeyman Bald

Rain had come in the broken window, and stained and warped everything in reach. The animal skins were gone from the walls, as was DB's parachute. The portrait of Derwood hung at a drunken angle over the fireplace.

"This place has been completely ransacked," I whispered. "It was cozy and neat when we were here."

"Wait a second. You were here? Nobody told me that."

"How'd you think I knew where it was? I told you, he fed us some tea that about knocked us out, which I expect is how they do it."

I realized for the first time that Bethany's disappearance in the cemetery was all that had saved us from death; DB and Derwood had been unwilling to make their move with a possible witness lost and unaccounted for. And another thing ...

"Those ratshit devils had been spying on us for hours. Days, maybe, before they showed themselves."

"Yeah, Suellen told me how DB said he peeped at you and Lee. Pervert."

"It was earlier than that, even. When Bethany wandered off and sacked out in that graveyard, they called her "Beffie" when they went off yelling for her. I don't think any of us called her that the whole time they were around. They had to've picked that up on the trail. Oh, shit, of course, and the singing, that they said was so fucking angelic. There was no singing going on anywhere near the top of the Bald; we were separated and out of breath the whole last hour of that climb. They shadowed us all the way up that trail, and told us so. I'm a stupid, careless, no-mind - "

"Nobody told me nothing about Bethany wandering off, neither."

"Well, she did. We can re-enact that when we go back

to the graveyard, Sherlock. Let's shake this place down."

"Fine. Lemme just say, you could of sat on your thumb down in Gabbro for another six months and never thought of any of that. You gotta go where the thing was coming down, and relive it. That's what makes stuff come to your mind."

"Such as it is."

There was nothing in Apostle House that looked as if it had been touched by a living hand - not counting wildlife - since the day we were there. The mugs we'd had our pussyflower tea out of were still sitting in the sink. I took one that had a crust of flakes in the bottom, hoping to get forensic confirmation of what I already knew. The one surprise came when we pried open the heavy door at the back of the living area.

A corridor led away into darkness. We had no flashlight, but there was a switch on the wall. When I flipped it, a hanging bulb sprang to yellowish light, and after a fading second or two, we heard the noise of a gasoline engine cranking, coughing, and thrumming to life somewhere down the hall. The bulb perked up some, and the shadows receded.

"So much for the Man of Nature," I said. "Wonder what kind of berry juice that thing runs on."

The walls of the corridor were solid rock; we were under the low cliff against which Apostle House stood. Three doors led off the corridor. The first was a severe bedroom, with a pine dresser - completely empty - a straight chair, a desk, and a bed. The bed bore a naked mattress, with the usual constellation of stains. There was a small, smeared window high in the back wall, that appeared to give onto a light well from above. A spider - a brown recluse, I hoped - had covered it in web. The desk had no drawers, and nothing stuck to its underside but a collection of boogers. The depositor appeared to be left-handed.

When I pointed that out to Wet, he patted me on the head. "For that purpose, anyways. You know anything about handedness in them guys? They write anything down, throw a rock?"

"DB had his gun in his right hand." I said, eventually. "I can't think of anything else that would tell us that."

When we felt we had sucked the room dry, I insisted that we either post one of us as a lookout, or at least check our rear before going farther. It was just the kind of situation where you know damn well the rightful occupant is going to ambush you while you exclaim over incriminating finds.

"In the movies," Wet said. He shivered, and stuck his nose into the corridor. It, and the house and the dooryard, were innocent of enemies.

I was prepared for the second room to be another sleeping chamber, and so it proved. But a Honda electric generator was in there, thrumming busily. It certainly would have ruined my sleep.

There was no window; and no other furniture than the bed. The stains on the mattress were altogether darker and more abundant than those in the first bedroom. Wet scowled at them and looked around the little room, his nose wrinkling. He lay down on the bed, which alarmed me; and when he sat up, he lifted the mattress at the foot of the bed. Lying flat against the spring were two broad leather belts, or straps, bolted to the corners of the bedframe, and ending in buckles. A single strap lay under the top of the mattress.

"OK," I nodded. "Tell me DB could have had something like this in here, and Derwood didn't know about it."

"Uh huh," Wet said, and he shivered again. "Hard to keep your girlfriend tied up in a place like this, and not have

Daddy notice."

"Papa. You knew those things would be under there?"

He cocked his head vaguely east, toward the flatland. "See this kinda thing all the time."

It was my turn to shiver. All the time, in hideaways like this all around me, this kind of thing going on all the time.

The third door opened on a staircase that smelled of dampness and welcome fresh air. Stone steps led to a kind of mud room or utility room, in which were clabbered together a congeries of buckets and mops and rusting tools. A pick and shovel, a posthole digger, a wheelbarrow, and a collection of those cement blocks, two-by-fours, tarps, and minor machinery that the most lawful household will collect. What we had seen made every scrap of it suspect.

The utility room in turn opened on a tangle of laurel and boulders that would have made it impossible to spot from more than ten feet away, or from the air. I pushed through it and emerged on Eternity. Another step, and I'd have pitched into the thousand-foot fall that Lee and DB had shared.

"Holy - " I said, cartoonishly.

"Goddlmighty," Wet agreed. "Where the hell are we?"

I scooted myself carefully to the lip of the drop, and looked up. "We're on a ledge about twenty feet below the top of Honeyman Bald," I said. "I think we're about twenty feet from where we started out this morning."

Wet saw the point of it right away. "So when that guy evaporated on you, he was taking the short way home."

"I expect so. They've got some kind of god-knows-what figured out. A bolt-hole. I don't know, I suppose a hidden stairway or a thing you shinny up and down. That's how they got up there ahead of us, to ambush us when we found our way back to the tents."

I tossed a pebble over the ledge, and then remembered to pray nobody was camping down on Fall Creek. Where Lee had landed, after getting shivers from the voices in the water.

"Getting back down might have been tough though, with a gunshot wound," I mused. If it was real, maybe Derwood couldn't do it, maybe he fell, the scum bastard, serve him right. More likely, he was healthy as a ... He told us early on, there was a kind of ledge just under the top of the Bald, with an overhang that keeps you from seeing it from on top. This probably connects with that, somehow, if he wasn't lying about that too. Honestly, as long as he's not sitting on that ledge, laughing at us, I don't give much of a crap one way or the other."

At one point, the ledge we stood on pinched out against a rocky prominence. Just there a slender, tough-looking tree had lodged roots in a crack and improbably flourished. At shoulder height, its bark was worn smooth.

"Swing yourself around that, I expect," Wet shuddered. He looked very un-inclined to try it.

I was, too, but the thought of Derwood standing on the other side of that rock wall, or crouched with a pistol, was unbearable. "Lend me your hat," I whispered.

"Already plugged once," he said. "Why the hell not?"

I put Wet's fedora on the end of the posthole digger and cautiously eased it around the prominence. No shot. I tried another ploy, shaking the little tree and popping the hatted tool into the space where a person would appear, swinging over thin air on the tree. Nothing.

"OK, fine," I whispered. Either he was there, unfooled, or he wasn't there at all. I led Wet back into Derwood Barnes Cather's mud room. "Bring the pick and shovel," I said.

On Honeyman Bald

"We've got one more place to look."

*   *

Wet Parsonage tossed the shovel out onto the ground, and it clanged against the baby's gravestone like a muffled bell. He lifted a hand toward me.

I stood above him, hands on my knees. "You want me to pull you out of that hole? I don't know if I've got the strength left."

We were both filthy, mud-smeared and sweat-soaked. We'd dug two deep trenches in the little graveyard, one on each side of the row of unpainted and unmarked wooden crosses, without finding any trace of a coffin, a vault, or remains. I was getting a little discouraged.

Wet got his butt up on the lip of the trench, started to stand up, and fell back into it. He slumped against the muddy wall and looked up at me.

"I was sure you was onto something here," he said. "Still am. But damn'f I can see what the deal is. A bunch of grave markers, an' no graves." He heaved himself back onto the lip of the hole and fished a rumpled cigarette out of his suitcoat.

When he had it lit, he said, "First time I been warm this whole damn trip. So why would a couple criminals put up grave markers for nothing? And what's the case that they put these here anyhow?"

"Who else? DB said Derwood had been living here for a very long time. I don't see much evidence of a lot of traffic up here with hearses and stuff, people bringing flowers on Memorial Day. This is deep wilderness."

Wet shook his head, like I didn't need to tell him that.

"Plus, them markers don't look all that ancient to me. Couple of 'em look like treated lumber. Maybe they chopped their victims up and tossed the bones over the cliff. Put the markers here because it's consecrated ground."

"Maybe so," I said.

I was going to have to come out with it. "Maybe they not only robbed, raped, and killed people. Maybe they fed off the bodies."

Wet snorted and looked at me slantwise. "Yeah? What's your evidence for that?"

"Same as for all the rest. They told us. I think they must have figured we'd never survive to spread the word, and anyhow, we were all sitting around in a stupor after they fed us that drugged tea. Derwood and DB were telling me in this smug, this men-of-nature way of theirs, how they lived off what they could hunt and gather in the forest. DB actually included 'long pig' in the list. Which is what sailors used to call human meat, when they were talking about cannibals or I guess getting hungry when they were marooned. I was too dopey at the time to notice it, but it came back to me one night. Another thing I should have noticed and didn't."

"So every one of these little crosses is for pot roasts? Holy Mother of Mary."

"Why do it at all?"

"Remorse." He shrugged. "Indigestion. Maybe they were hoping if they go through the motions, put the remains in consecrated ground, God won't get 'em for murder, rape, cannibalism, what not."

"Huh. Maybe they wanted to get caught."

Wet razzberried smoke in the direction of Apostle House. "More movie shit. They weren't takin that big of a chance. Nobody hardly comes up here, and them that do, chances are, they don't go back down."

"All those Bibles. All that religion, going through the motions. Maybe there's not a whole body under each of these. Maybe just a little token. What if we looked directly under a cross?"

"Run gimme that posthole digger."

When I came back with it, Wet had pulled one of the crosses out of the ground and was examining it. He showed me the top of it, weathered but smooth and rounded.

"No sign they had to pound this thing inta the ground. I think maybe they stuck it in a hole and filled in around it."

He took the posthole digger and addressed the leaf-cluttered spot where the cross had been. A foot down, the blades clanked on something hard.

"Bingo," Wet puffed. We knelt around the shallow hole, and Wet dug at the muck in the bottom with his fingers. "Feels like concrete."

It was. We had to shift our digging six inches to the side, and dig parallel to uncover the side of a foot-long plug of cement. And below that, a rotted rag wrapped around a pathetic bundle of small bones. Fingers, ribs, a collarbone. Wet pulled it gently out of its niche, and put it to his nose.

"Not hardly no smell to 'em at all," he said. "I expect it was already bones when it went in the ground."

"Aw, Jesus." I sat on the ground, sick and dizzy. "Consecrated ground, sure. This isn't a cemetery. It's a garbage dump."

I gave Wet a hand to stand up. His hand was as hot as a mug of pussyflower tea. "That's where we were supposed to end up. Suellen, and Bethany, and Lee and me. After they ate the good parts. Spare ribs and roasts, and ... aw, no. Aw, shit. Shit, shit, shit." I turned and stumbled blindly into the underbrush, my stomach heaving.

"An', what?" Wet sighed, after a silence. He sounded like a man at the end of his endurance.

"Bacon," I gasped.

15.

It is a flat-out miracle that I got Wet back down from there alive. For starts, he'd caught a cold from the constant chill of being ill-clad and sweaty; and after we left the grisly horrors of Apostle House, he began to express passionate hatred of the silence and isolation of the woods.

"I mean, for shit's sake, Maryland, there's nothin going on out here."

"Murder, rape, and cannibalism, that's nothing?"

"We got that back in Fayetteville. I mean, where's the people? Where's the - I dunno. The movies. The traffic."

"Some people like it quiet."

"Perverts."

So he got even with the wilderness and with the way it failed to forgive his failure to dress for it. He refused to respect the difficulties of descending a rocky path, which are ten times those of climbing it, particularly when one is tired. He fell three times, bruising much but breaking nothing, and twisted his ankle by treating a slope of cobbles as if it were as level and firm as a sidewalk. By the time we got back to the car, he was so foul of temper and mouth that I was reduced to hand signals to communicate with him.

Still, we had to do something about what we'd found at Apostle House. The ranger I'd talked to in August had told me that all that territory was National Park, so it was to the ranger station in Smokemont that we went first.

The folks there were polite, sympathetic, and

completely dedicated to keeping hikers from starting forest fires. They came up with a file, labeled with Lee's and DB's names, that they'd created when they went in to retrieve the bodies.

Because of my status as bereaved, they stretched a point and let me look in it, under the close scrutiny of one of those paper-management ladies that dead archives always have. The top sheet in the file was dated August 31st, a little over two weeks after Bethany, Suellen and I stumbled into the Ranger station with our grief and our tale of fog and rape and death. The entry reported failure to turn up Derwood in any of his usual haunts, including Apostle House. There was nothing newer in the file.

"What, you folks have given up on it? Is that it?"

"You'd have to talk to the Super about that," the paper lady said. "My job's keep the records."

"Well, can we?" I very dimly recalled the station Supervisor, a tall, mild-looking guy who apparently spent a lot of his time filling out requisitions and reports about lost hikers.

"Today?" She sounded as if I hadn't heard about World War III. "Super's over't Mount Sterling. Raft swamped on the Pigeon River, drownt three ladies from Charlotte." Her tone was that of a farmer whose incompetent neighbor had gone bust again. What can you expect from Charlotte ladies, but trouble, death, and paperwork? Or Gabbro ones, I expect.

"Look," I said, prepared to be sane and undemanding. "My wife was killed, and my friend here's daughter was raped back in August, and I haven't heard a thing from here about any progress in catching a guy who could tell us a lot about it. I don't want to be a lot of trouble to you, but - "

"What I recall, that fella got kilt the same time your

wife done."

"One of them, yes. The other one, who I think was just as guilty, disappeared. Derwood Cather."

Her face closed down, and she shook her head. "Hope you don't think ill of him," she said. "Hard to believe it."

I felt my blood pressure snap into fury mode. "You can believe it, Ma'am," I gritted. "I was there."

"And your deposition is right here in the file, sir. Any time - "

I felt Wet tugging on my arm, and I shrugged him off. "Listen," I roared. "You just listen to me for once. That goddamn file - "

I felt serious pain in my left elbow. "Scuse me," Wet said. "Ma'am, thank you for your time. We'll be moving on. Thanks again."

With every sentence, Wet walked me a step toward the door, keeping a death grip on my funnybone. When we were outside, he relaxed.

"That what you mean by fuckin 'shrewd fury?' Where's the shrewd? That was about the un-shrewdest interrogation I ever seen. That dame wouldn't tell you the weather now."

"What's with her, Wet? Just because I came in from the flatlands, I'm some kind of enemy?"

"Probly," Wet shrugged. "More to the point, she knows something about Cather, and she won't let it out."

"You think so? Jesus Christ, I'll subpoena her so hard, she'll get whiplash."

"You're not gettin squat outa her you didn't already get, hotshot. Subpoena away, you want to waste more time and money."

"Waste of time, you got that right."

Wet grinned. "Not completely. We learned a big thing

in there, you stop and think about it. Cather's still around, and he's in touch with folks. How else is she gonna know to shut up on us?"

I sighed. "OK. And the Park Service isn't going to do anything about it."

"I'd guess not, though that may not be exactly policy. Couldn't hardly be. But you can make a lot of stuff happen or not, just knowing how the wheels turn. I'd guess the Super won't even hear they was a couple flatlanders in there today, wouldn't you?"

"I guess. How much else do you think might not have made it into that file?"

Wet nodded approvingly. "Very shrewd, hotshot. Hard to prove a negative, in't it?"

We didn't bother visiting the Swain County sheriff. I'd already talked to him, or to his anti-client firewall, several times since August, and learned only that he considered it either a closed case - Lee dead, DB dead, and lucky for us DB had no relatives or witnesses coming forward to charge Lee with his death - or a Park Service matter. Depending on who picked up the phone. Besides, I got more than all I could stand of Swain County when I went unwillingly to the morgue to identify Lee and reclaim her body.

"They was both pretty smashed up," the morgue attendant said. "Not much in the way of facial features on the fella, though the lady come through it remarkable. I know this is tough, sir, but we do need a positive identification 'fore we can release her."

I had planned to ask if I could identify Lee by a small, curled scar on her left knee - a scar I had thousands of times kissed and tickled and asked her about - at any price not to see her face. But I gritted my teeth and nodded, promising myself that I would consider this an episode of controlled insanity, and nothing to do with reality.

Her face was unmarked, though her head lay against the slab in an ominously asymmetric way; and it was far from clear that it was still completely attached to the rest of her. She looked serene. Her expression was pretty much what she would allow herself, when I would swear to her that there had never been a more beautiful, virtuous, and clever woman in the history of love, and that I would worship her eternally, and so forth. Back in that part of my life.

I looked away, nodding, and the attendant whipped the sheet over her.

"Wonder if you'd care to do the same for the fella," he said. "Being as nobody else has come forward."

"I wouldn't look at the ratshit bastard if it would save me from the fires of hell," I smiled.

He nodded, palms spread toward the floor. "OK, sir."

In the end, Wet and I drove back to the flatland. By the time I left Wet off at his dubious Fayetteville hotel he was flushed and sweating, and coughing constantly.

"Get a doctor to look at you, you dumb flatfoot," I said.

He shook his head while he bent double on the sidewalk by the door. "Suckers are bad luck," he gasped. "I'm OK."

*　　　　　*

I'm sorry, no one can take your call right now. Please leave a message at the tone.

The voice was masculine, but I wasn't fooled. "Hi,

On Honeyman Bald

Beffie, it's Dad. I'll be a little later than I thought, so don't expect me for lunch. I've got an errand to do on the way up, don't think it will take long, but don't hold lunch. I'll see you this afternoon, honey. Bye."

I am not a Catholic, even lapsed. I had a brief fit as a Presbyterian elder, but Presbyterians do not feature the sacrament of Confession. Episcopalians do, and it is available to anyone; but Gabbro has no Episcopal Church. Thus I found myself seated before the rector of Saint Joseph And The Incarnation in Bozlee, North Carolina, a week or two after Wet and I returned from our trip to Honeyman Bald.

"You look very troubled," she said.

"I've hardly eaten or slept for a week. And what I was doing before that - well, it wasn't all that restful."

"Can you tell me what is troubling you?"

I explained about the bacon, and how I'd told myself that eating human flesh could hardly be a sin - I hoped - if one were tricked into eating it, but that its taste had poisoned my mouth, and soul, since the horrible suspicion had dawned that Derwood had undertaken to fatten us on the flesh of prior victims, up there in the fog. The Rector was a very cool customer, who probably heard a lot of rough stuff - Bozlee is a rough town - but nothing like this.

"But if what you say is true, these men are deeply, horribly depraved. Have they been apprehended?"

"One of them is dead. It appears the authorities have no interest in pursuing the other."

"I see. And do you?"

"I think 'interest' is not a good description. I feel I have a duty."

She fingered the cross at her throat. "To what end?"

I opened my mouth, and closed it. And, hell, opened it

again; I was confessing. "I may need to kill him."

She paled, and sat quietly for an interval; and then looked up at me. "The intent to murder is not different from its achievement, as far as your soul is concerned. Could it be that 'duty' that is poisoning you, and not the innocent, and apparently unproven, cannibalism?"

I thought about that. "I can't tell them apart. The whole business tastes of rancid, ... nasty ...."

I began to shake. "I loved Lee. I wanted nothing more than just to be an ordinary man, growing old with her, watching our son and daughter marry, have children." I tossed a hand. "You know. The American dream."

"The dream of human love. I know about Lee. Tell me about the son and daughter."

She asked for it. I told her about my own daughter, who'd died in a fire when I was too drunken and self-absorbed to keep her from danger; about my son, grown and distant, married to an African-Italian but so far childless; and about Bethany, committed but, in those days, unmarriageable and childproof.

"How do you perceive her homosexual union with this person?"

"As just that. Homosexual. Barren. Plus, Suellen is a - Well, she's had a hard life, God knows, but she's not a pillar of strength and sanity for Bethany."

"Do you resent her presence in Bethany's life?"

"I do. Darn right I do."

In the end, she absolved me of the possibility of cannibalism, and set as a penance that I reach out to Suellen, as a way of reaching out to Bethany, and not losing her from my life.

I said I would; but I doubted even then that I would do

On Honeyman Bald

it.

Suellen broke the hearts of the Gabbro College chemistry department by dropping out of college indefinitely while she undertook to heal herself, and to help Bethany heal, from what they had suffered. They moved to Carrboro, which is a kind of suburb of Chapel Hill, a month after we came back from Honeyman Bald, setting up housekeeping over "The Little Shop of Horace," a florist in a gritty strip mall next to a bar, a mailbox franchise, and a laundromat. When I walked up, Bethany was hanging wet underwear over a clothesline in the hall.

"Hi, Daddy." She gave me the small formal hug that was as intimate as things got between us these days. "I got your message. Thanks for calling."

"Hi, Beffie. How's it going?"

Bethany shrugged. "Suellen got a techie job with some genetics outfit over at Research Triangle," she said. "It helps. She's still got the bladder infection. How's Wet?"

"Still on antibiotics." Wet's shivers on Honeyman Bald had deepened into bronchitis, pneumonia, and a stay at Fayetteville General. The last I'd seen him he looked terrible; but it didn't seem useful to say that. "Listen, about that infection, has Suellen had a... you know, does she know her status? For HIV?"

"She'll be home in a while, you can ask her yourself. But it's negative. How's the College?"

I tried not to look relieved. "We installed Tim Summerton as president last week. I sent you an invitation."

"Uh huh."

"He spoke very movingly about your mother."

Bethany went to stand in the door of her apartment. "I

bet. You wont a drink of something? Juice, or tea?"

She seemed so like Lee that it gave me a scare. I opted for tea, just to see if she made it as sugar-heavy as Lee had.

"So," she said, opening a cupboard in the kitchen-pantry-dining room. "What'll you do now?"

"I don't know. Go back out there, see if I can find Derwood. See if he'll tell me what he and DB were up to in that little house."

She cocked a hip against the fridge. "They weren't 'up to' anything, anyways not Derwood. You heard him, he did his best about DB, and got shot for it."

"Doesn't it strike you as a little funny, how he disappeared like that?"

"Strikes me as luck and God's grace, he wasn't killed. You think he'd hang around up there waiting to see if we'd come back, when the boy he put so much of his life into had just shot him, and then got killed? I expect his heart was about broken."

"Poor guy. Of course, what killed DB was your mother, taking him with her before he could finish us off. Insensitive of her."

She put her hands over her ears. "You think I don't have nightmares about that all the time? And I just get back to sleep when Suellen tunes up? We get to where we've woke each other up three or four times, we don't bother going back to bed."

I didn't want to hear about bed arrangements; but in any case, I was still a long way from clear on Derwood myself. I couldn't see how the things we'd found at Apostle House could be seen as anything but damning. On the other hand, what did that business on the cliff top mean? I couldn't dream up a scenario that didn't fail the imaginary test of trying to sell it to Wet Parsonage. Movie shit, he would have said about almost any explanation I could think of, other than an innocent Derwood being shot by his miscreant stepson.

Well, not innocent. Not by a long pig. But I wasn't willing to trump Bethany's defense of Derwood Cather by telling her he was the kind of guy who had fed her human bacon just for fun.

"Beffie," I said. "Let's not fight over it when we're both grieving. Just, don't build up Derwood as some kind of martyr over this. Wet and I found things up there that I can't begin to tell you about."

"Oh, well, of course. Nobody can discuss with somebody who hints about secret facts they aren't at liberty to share. What I know for myself is, it was DB that raped Suellen, and Momma took care of him. Derwood was nowhere around."

She softened, and put a hand on my arm. "And while she was at it, she took care of herself. It's taken me a while to see this, Daddy, but it wasn't such a terrible thing that she did it that way. You heard her, you saw her. What'd she have to look forward to but more sickness, headaches, getting her words tangled up, more operations and chemo, and then dying anyhow?" She thrust the tea at me. "Is that what you wonted for her?"

I tasted the tea. Unsweetened and green. "Of course not, Bethany. So we just shrug off what happened to us up there, just let it go?"

"Good for you. That's exactly it. If I can manage to never, ever think about Honeyman Bald for the rest of my life, that'll be a real achievement, seems like. I can't imagine why you want to spend the rest of yours obsessing about it. I think we got a lemon somewheres."

The new assertive Beffie. She squatted and rummaged through the bins in the bottom of the refrigerator while I surveyed the poky little place. The walls were smudged and dented from other people's furniture. A lime green dining table was shimmed level with books under the outboard legs; I thought I recognized works of Derwood Cather and Roald Hoffmann. A cheap exhaust fan that braced open the window had clogged the screen with dust and lint. The refrigerator bore hip feminist cartoons and hundreds of little magnets, each bearing one word, arranged into wisecracks and poetry.

you and me heal in life river, one of them said. *chickies dig sticky figs*, sang another.

Bethany, whom I had pulled into this life from her mother's womb, was grown and gone, like her brother before her. Launched on adulthood in a ratty lesbian love nest.

"And you're happy here?"

Her face closed. "Happy enough. What's happy?"

"If you have to ask, then you're not, is what I think. And your mother..." I started. I shook my head and walked toward the door. Some things, oh yes, how true. Better by far left unsaid. Chickies hate sticky dads. Though sometimes not saying them is no improvement. Bethany flared at me over the top of the fridge door.

"Don't you dare represent my mother to me, Mister Maryland. Don't you goddamn dare. I loved her as hard as I could for as long as she was alive, and I don't need to be beat over the head with her corpse, just because who I sleep with makes *you* uncomfortable."

I tossed my hands, nailed by a mind-reader. "Far be it, then," I barked. "I just wish you'd had the decency to show up down there last week, the pair of you. You could have done that in memory of her."

"Listen. I got all I could take of fucking Tim Summerton at the Memorial Service." She slammed the refrigerator, and dislodged part of a poem. "'This ideal of Southern womanhood, this mother, sage, and loving teacher.' Hey, he ought to know. He had a thing going with Mom for years after you married her."

I would not have been more shocked if she had morphed into a gorilla. "Bethany! For God's sake, how can you say that about your mother?"

"Not that I was looking for a chance to."

"Well, I want you to apologize."

"To her?"

"To her memory, sure. To me. Even to Tim Summerton, who I admit was never one of my very favorite people."

"Shit, mine either, Daddy. But I will not, sorry, I will not apologize, for telling you something you probably already knew. Or you should have."

"Should have known it? I don't believe it even now, and what I absolutely can't figure out is why you're dirtying yourself by peddling a tale like that. Is it to take my mind off you and Suellen? Is that what's going on here?" I don't know why I bothered to ask. I was sure of it.

Bethany didn't answer, but turned on her heel and stormed out of the kitchen toward the back of the apartment. I stood for a few moments uncertain whether to call out a goodbye and go off to let her cool down, or to go after her and try to mend what was hideously broken. I was never fast on my feet in these situations, and had slowed some from that lately. I was drawing in a breath when she reappeared. She slapped a creased 3 by 5 card on the kitchen table.

On Honeyman Bald

"Here you go, Daddy," she said, no longer storming but tearfully firm. "I hate to do this to you, but you asked for it. I've saved this since I found it in the pocket of her jeans one time. She should have checked stuff like that before she lent me clothes."

She picked up a green book bag. "Stay as long as you like. I have to go to Chapel Hill, to the library."

"Wait up," I said; and I looked at the card she'd given me.

I don't remember the door closing behind Bethany, but when I looked up again, some later, she was gone. She couldn't bear to be there while I read what she'd given me to read.

Lee, my darling -
My God, you are still magic. Your taste is on my tongue. I can't possibly wait more days to kiss you everywhere. Call me tonight.

Your Tim.

16.

The good part of that was, it got my mind off of riding
west to bring Derwood Barnes Cather to justice. Compared to
the news that I'd been regularly betrayed by the woman I
worshipped, his crimes, if any, were a backstreet squabble in
Uzbekistan.

I do not remember going back down the steps to the
street. I may have stood unseeing and unmoving in the dirty
little entranceway for some time; it was getting dim outside
when Suellen found me there on her way in from work. She
greeted me, as they say, effusively, and told me that I was not
to leave until I'd given her a rundown on Wet, whom she had
taken to calling "Daddy."

"He's doing OK, Suellen. I wish I could spend longer,
but I really have to ... uh, to..."

She drew back and stared at me. "Holy shit, Hap,
what's eating you?"

I tried a little laugh; it came out as one of the strangest
noises I'd ever made. "Nothing you want to get into, Suellen.
Thanks, though. How's the new job?"

"Boring. You look like hell. Come up and have some
tea or a snort. I got some of that one-ninety lab stuff."

"I just had tea; I don't need sympathy. I could take a
leak, but not up there."

She glanced up the steps, then grabbed my arm and
spun me out the door and past the florist to some fake-tudor

frontage that turned out to conceal a bar. I had no interest in a cozy drink with Suellen Ransom, but no will to resist.

When we were in a booth, she said, "Go, leak, and get back here. I got something to tell you."

Washing up, I tried to collect myself. What I saw in the mirror wasn't encouraging. By the time I got back to the table, it held a pair of Pilsner Urquells, and Suellen had a foam mustache.

I tossed small talk over a wall of pain. "How'd you know this was my favorite?"

"I could say you look like an Urquell guy, but it was Mom."

It was like a dying man being told the phone was ringing. Flattering, in a way. "Get out."

"No shit. I never sort of passed this on, but she told me a ton about you. Lee, too, and Wet and the whole scene here, before I came. What kind of mother would she be, put me on a bus to Fayetteville and not brief me on what I was going to find?"

I opened my mouth and closed it in time not to say that I'd thought her mother about the worst of the species I would ever know. Not an ideal of Southern womanhood. I gave a little gasp and changed the subject. "What was it you had to tell me?"

Suellen squinted at me with tilted head. "I'll get to that. The reason Mom described you so good was, she wanted to tell me not to fuck with you. You look to me like somebody has."

I twiddled the beer coaster, tempted, and shook my head. "Sort of. It's a long story that I don't think I'm ready to talk about. I just got badly disabused."

"Something about Beffie?"

"No." She had no right to call Beffie that.

A corner of her mouth twisted. "Well, I been abused and I been disabused, and believe me, they both suck. But OK." She looked past me toward the entrance, and leaned forward.

"Here's what I wanted to tell you. I'd call Daddy, but I think he's going to be out of it for a while yet. I'm pretty sure I saw Derwood last night."

I lowered my glass slowly to the table. As far as I knew, Suellen was in the dark about Derwood's crimes, but she sure didn't look happy about sharing a town with him. "You saw him here?"

"Not right here. In Chapel Hill."

"Does Bethany know about this?"

"I left her a note. We haven't both been awake at the same time since I saw him."

"Did he see you?"

"I'd guess not, but I don't think it matters. I don't think he'd remember me out of a crowd of other blonde lesbians."

"Shit." I couldn't think how to go on from there.

Suellen shrugged. "The guy's a saint, right? So what if he's here?"

"I think you know better than that. I'm not sure how, though."

She grabbed my arm. "Doesn't matter. There he is, over by the bar. Don't turn around."

"Why not?" I turned. Against the wall with the dart board, a knot of student-looking kids surrounded a massive guy with white whiskers and a ponytail. His back was toward us; immediately in front of him, a short, intense girl with vaguely French-Canadian features gazed up at him. She looked entranced but worried, which was enough to convince me that it was Derwood. Probably talking about the granite boulders in his dooryard and the aeons-distant heirs of this fleeting millennium. It couldn't fleet fast enough for me.

I rose unwillingly; if it was Derwood, Bethany and Suellen were coming back to Gabbro with me tonight. Or anyhow, Bethany. When I got close enough, I could hear the rumble of his voice, and the short girl's alto response.

"OK, sure, but a Diels-Alder cycloaddition, that's going to give you the 8,9 *cis* isomer, isn't it?"

The white-haired one clapped her on the shoulder, and let his paw dribble down her arm a little. "See," he nodded. "But in the first step, that's what you want. It'll invert to *trans* in the next reaction."

That sure didn't sound right; I shouldered into the circle and put a hand on his shoulder to make him face me. It wasn't Derwood.

"Excuse me," I said. "Thought you were somebody else. Familiar touching of students violates an Orange County ordinance. I can let it go once, but don't let it be a habit, OK?"

The paw jumped as from a hot stove. Fear and pissed-offedness competed in his face.

"Fuck off," he said finally; but it was the sort of thing not even a chemist could be sure was total bullshit. I fucked off and rejoined Suellen.

"False alarm," I said. "You sure that was the guy?"

"Ya, well," she said. "Pretty sure. Same shirt and all." She slumped in the booth. "God, that's a relief."

"You don't buy the innocent-Derwood picture."

"I wouldn't trust that fucker any farther than I could piss."

I hated to smile at that, but I had to. "Me either. Not

even as far. But why not? DB shot him."

"What's that prove?"

"Well... nothing, of course." I turned over the beer coaster and drew a circle on it. "Let's break it down either way. One, it was a faked shot, like a blank. The other, it was real, but maybe not for the reason it seemed to be, which is that DB was a rotten thug who couldn't be civilized even by an ecopoetical saint."

"Or it was a real shot, and that <u>was</u> the reason. Beffie thinks Derwood walks on air, but DB was definitely a rotten thug. Whatever, you can forget the first one. It was no fake; I saw the bullet hit him. He kind of twitched back, and he was plenty surprised."

"So DB really shot him. Did it look - I don't know, fatal?"

"How would I know? Guy gets shot, grabs himself like in the movies, and falls down."

"Did you look at him while he was lying there?"

"Huh uh. There's these other shots going off, and then you and Bethany started screaming about Lee. I was trying to see what was going on."

"Yeah. Let's not talk about that. Can you think of any reason DB would shoot Derwood, that would lead you to think Derwood's guilty of ..." I censored myself; I didn't see any reason to tell Suellen about the bacon if I didn't have to. "Of anything?"

"Sure." She put a hand on the table, and looked me in the eye. "He's a horny old bastard that's used to getting his piece of ass regular, and I know what I'm talking about on that one. Maybe he's pissed at DB because the deal is, Derwood's supposed to get first crack at the girls, and here DB went ahead and did me out of turn."

On Honeyman Bald

When she said "did me", it was like a cop talking about street crime. I sat back in the booth. "Boy, does that sound possible."

I told Suellen then what Wet and I had found in the back reaches of Apostle House, and in the graveyard.

"Holy shit. That whole scene with the pussyflower tea and the goddamn Bibles and the parachute story, that was all just setting us up. I gotta tell you, I had the creeps the whole time. Something in that place, it just put my hair on end."

I glanced at the blonde frizz. "You hair's always on end."

"Not that hair."

I snorted, minimally. "OK, now I've got the creeps. Go take a close look at that guy, and make sure it's the one you saw."

She did, and came back. "I can't be sure, but I think so. You wont another beer?

"Yep. I'm buying, though. You learn to say 'want' like that from Bethany?"

"Prob'ly. Sure not at my mother's knee."

I waved the empty Urquell at the bar, and got a nod. I could feel the first one starting to work, numbing the pain, and the replacements were just as sweaty and crisp.

"Your mother's knee. You know, I didn't have a lot of use for your mother, by the time she headed west with you. Truth is, I hated her for shooting Lee. Still, I'm sorry she had to die like..." I shrugged.

Suellen swigged her new beer. "In a bloody mess on the floor of a cheesy bar in a cheesy town out in the Ozarks, with a circle of rednecks watching her go? Suellen looked away, and her eyes filled. "Hey, they had a use for her. I bet that scene's on a dozen home videos."

What do you say to that? "You're a lot like her. And I mean it as a compliment," I lied.

She patted my arm, and headed for the Ladies'. By the time she was back, I was through the second Urquell, and starting to think I might try drinking myself to death. She caught up with me in about two gulps, and we switched to rum sours. At some point, the false Derwood left with his devotee, who flipped me a bird as they passed.

Suellen smirked when I told her why. "Def'ly the guy I saw before. Sorry I scared you."

"F'get it. Took my mind off things for a while."

*   *

Things.

"The way I see it," I said, "either Bethany has some very compelling reason for lying to me about that, and forging evidence to support it. And of course, that in itself would crush me."

Or?

"Or, you had something going with Tim Summerton for years after we were married. Oh, well, quite all right. Bygones - "

She swung her head from side to side.

Either, Or, Either, Or, Either. That's such a ... a <u>life</u> way to see it.

"Excuse me. That's my status for now. I'm ready for a change, though."

The family that cries together.....

"Dies together. Too bad we didn't."

Don't say that. Not that I wouldn't like the company. This deal isn't all floating in space, it turns out. Plus, it might give you a chance to see things from a little ... more general perspective.

I said nothing. She sighed and reached toward me, but it only pushed her backwards.

"Why don't you just tell me, then, so I know, one way or the other?"

Why do you wont to?

"That's easy, I'd think. It would help generalize my perspective. And not knowing is hell."

It's one kind. Knowing is one.

That infuriated me. "Be so kind as not to pull that I'm-dead-so-I-know-stuff-you-don't business," I snapped. "I'm not Ebenezer Scrooge."

She smiled as if I'd mentioned the pranks of a school chum.

I wear the chains I forged in life. (She sang it to the tune of "I Dreamed I Saw Joe Hill Last Night".) He got that right. Remember how Beffie loved to watch that at Christmas?

"I don't see any chains."

Not all chains are made of iron. All my life, I felt like if I wasn't careful, I would fall. Down, somewhere, maybe somewhere bad, maybe just fall. Now here I am, falling. Forever, seems like.

I saw then that Lee - or her image - was fading a little. The star-points in her hair were not as bright, and the hair not as firmament-black as when I first saw her. And though she was still naked, I couldn't feel the skin of her belly against mine; it felt as though a layer of flannel had slipped between us.

"I remember," I said. "Do you remember what I just asked you?"

I do, and I don't. Something about Beffie, though, I

know that. I have to go.

"Lee - "

Her leg crept up my thigh, she flowed into me. But when I looked down at myself, I saw that she had left a gritty residue on my skin. It tasted like soot and tears.

17.

I woke, and thought I really had gone mad at last. None of the windows were where they should have been, and the impostors on the wrong walls admitted urban glare that Gabbro never knew. A massive and unmoving bed partner the size of a davenport had me shoved against the dropoff edge of the mattress. I had a vague understanding that it was Lee's nurse, in her afterlife. I shoved back, and pushed myself backwards to the floor.

I remembered then that I was bedded on the ratty couch in Bethany and Suellen's living room in Carrboro. I hadn't got quite drunk enough to risk driving back to Gabbro, as drunk as I was; though it was the possible loss of innocent life, and not my own, that deterred me.

Not a great place to wind up, when you thought you were drinking to forget. But it certainly was better than spending that night in the Gabbro bedroom, Lee's and mine, that I'd occupied for twenty years. That was the extent of the upside.

The downsides were massive. They began with a dry mouth, a sore throat, and the knowledge that I'd been snoring thunderously. Lee was dead. The hangover had started early, my bladder was full, and the only bathroom opened off Bethany and Suellen's room; I would piss out the window first. Derwood Cather was, or maybe wasn't, around, and Wet Parsonage, my only ally, was seriously sick. Long before the catalog reached the matter of Lee's infidelity, I was angry, afraid, and depressed. When it got there, I became suicidal.

How could she? How the hell could she turn her back on what we had, for that all-too-perfect example of Southern manhood, that pretty boy whose manly good-naturedness about Lee's choosing to marry me over him turned out to be not so terribly admirable, since it involved no real loss of access, did it?

How could I have been so wrong about Lee? How could she lyingly live with me through thick and thin, better and worse, for all these years? How detonate from no-nonsense, self-contained scholar to the lithe and lovesoaked queen of the sheets who always, always left me dazed and limp, and then do it again with someone else? How so perfectly feign the one-man woman, the settled matron of Gabbro, the severely coiffed president of Gabbro College, when all along - or at least, on Bethany's testimony "for years," - she had a thing going on the side with Tim Summerton.

A thing, going! With Tim Summerton! Would I have done that to her? Could I have sunk so low as to gut and cuckold someone I loved for the dubious thrill of motel sex? Could I have betrayed Lee for... oh, Suellen Ransom's mother Trudi, say, who was - after Lee, of course - the sexiest, most compelling woman I had ever known?

Well, to be honest, I only got the chance once, and took her up on it. Before Lee and I were married. But after we were promised, vowed, and bedded, married in all but fact. Irrelevant that we'd had a falling-out, that at the time I doubted we'd ever marry and hadn't fathomed the depths of Trudi's rottenness, that I was then younger, stupider, and more headstrong than .... well, than I became, later. So perhaps, perhaps. I do not set myself up to be more moral than average, and we all know where that average sprawls.

But does one tearstained coupling weigh as heavily as a having a "thing going"? A going thing is betrayal that happens more than once, that worms its way through months and years of spousal deceit, denial, weekend trips, late work, lunches stolen at the Bozlee Diner, registration at the Holiday Inn under fake names. Phone calls, close calls, click-offs. Lee did that. Lee did that, and now she was dead, oh, Jesus. I would never know, could not bear to know, how many of her education-bigwig trips were legitimate, how many not. There could be educators in North Carolina who thought Tim Summerton was me.

OK, I did it too, once, without all the machinery, and it was over in 15 minutes. Is betrayal nobler for being rare and brief? Never telling Lee made my perfidy equal hers in longstandingness, if nothing else. So, yes, I did it, and I was not dead, but I longed to be. If this was seeing whole, if this was the more general perspective she touted - man, I couldn't wait for more.

I found myself on the sidewalk outside The Little Shop of Horace. Beyond the bar - locked and dark at this hour - an alley opened to the street. I went into it, sought the deepest shadow, and pissed against the wall. Probably good for a fifty-dollar fine, if there'd been a cop there, a death sentence if the alley'd held its quota of cutpurse muggers. Neither were on duty just then. I moved a few feet and slumped against the wall.

OK, no more bladder issues on the list. Anything else we can tick off? Well, I wasn't snoring on my lesbian daughter's fleabag couch any more. After that, I couldn't think of one goddamn thing to celebrate, and I gave it a try. I gave it the rest of the night, walking the streets of Carrboro and Chapel Hill, stopping once in a while to fold myself into a doorway and weep or just to breathe, with my face clenched hard enough to start a dull headache. A rainstorm swept through and soaked me, then headed for Durham to soak the Blue Devils. Maybe I slept. In a freight yard on the south side of Chapel Hill, I pulled out the little card and read it by the glare of sodium lamps off puddles and polished rails. *My God you are still magic.* He had that right. Even dead, she was still magic. The kind that makes your life disappear, pulls dead rabbits from your hat, and saws your heart in two right before your eyes.

At dawn, I was back in Carrboro, stumbling down the main drag reeking of vomit and fatigue, hoping not to see a cop before I was back at the florist. It took a long time to find it, and when I did I crept up the stairs, hoping to pick up my wallet and keys and get out of there without further dialogue. But Suellen was standing at the sink in shorts and a sweatshirt, a cup of coffee cooling beside her. She looked ten years older than she had last night.

"Hi," I grunted.

She said nothing I could distinguish over the running water.

"I'll be headed home now," I said. "Thanks for the hospitality"

"Forget it. You guys get anything settled?"

"What's to settle? She's dead."

She turned from the sink and looked past me. "Where's Beffie?"

"Beffie?" It was Bethany's baby pet name, and anyone who used it was a parent or other dominating.... Oh, stop it. I looked at my watch. Eight thirty.

"In bed, I'd think. Give her my - "

"No, she's not. She went out to meet you."

That made so little sense that I just shrugged. Even that minimal effort made me dizzy.

Suellen grunted and slapped a sticky-note down in front of me.

D called and wants to talk. I'll be back around 10 or so.

"The phone rang about six. Beffie got it, and talked to you for a while, and then went out. Are you saying that wasn't you?"

"Not. I didn't even have a quarter in my pocket. Why would I call, when I could just come here and talk to her?"

"How the fuck would I know? Even sober, you do a lot of things that don't make sense to me."

I looked at Suellen then, and saw the shock hit her an instant after it hit me. "Derwood."

She inhaled coffee and choked. "He's got her."

I knew it was so. My hangover evaporated. "Get some things together, fast. If we go right now, maybe we can get out there before anything really bad - "

"What things? Let's go."

I suppose it says something that neither of us bothered to suggest waiting until after ten, calling the cops, wasting hours giving descriptions of Bethany and Derwood, answering stupid pedestrian questions, listening to calm advice about how missing people generally turn up on their own. Hours that Derwood Cather would use on I-40, heading back to Apostle House with Bethany.

On Honeyman Bald

"Open the glove compartment, and see if the tope sheets for Honeyman Bald are still in there."

Suellen rummaged briefly, and came up with a handful of dirt-smeared paper. "Uh huh. What if he's taking her someplace else? What if it isn't even him?"

"What if she's sitting in your apartment right now, calling the cops because we're missing? What do you think the chances are of that?"

"None. Anyways, I left a note where she'll see it. No, he's got her. That's what I thought first thing, and that's what I still think."

"Me too. And I don't see him going somewhere else. His house is all set up for taking care of abducted women. How close can we get to it by road?"

Suellen opened the tope sheet and squinted over it. "There's a secondary road, comes out of Smokemont. Least, where it goes off the edge, it says 'Smokemont, 11.4.' Any luck, we might find that."

"What's it say, going the other way?"

"At the other edge? Bryson City 7.6. Wait a second, there's actually a town on it, Hahnemann, not that far from Honeyman Bald. Bet that's the original name. Cluster of shacks, more likely." She rattled maps for a moment longer. "There's no Hahnemann on the highway map."

"Does it show a road between Smokemont and Bryson City?"

"Nope. We'll have to go into Bryson City and ask."

"Isn't Smokemont closer?"

"Closer to Honeyman Bald, but it's quicker to Bryson City on paved roads. Also, Bryson City is smaller, it'll be easier to spot the road to Smokemont from it, and they don't know us there."

"You have a most lively apprehension."

Suellen glared out the windshield. "Beffie told me about that," she snapped. "Not funny."

"Sorry. I wasn't trying to be."

Suellen hunched herself into a corner of the seat and said nothing for five miles; then she reached over and touched my shoulder. "I'm sorry, too, Hap. We need all the shit we can muster here, and it's stupid to waste it on each other."

I drew a breath. "Tell you what, Suellen. I'm as close to being out of shit, whatever that means, as I've ever been."

"As in, get your shit together. Beffie told me what she told you about Lee. I'm not surprised you looked fucked over when I found you on the steps. How long were you there?"

"I don't know. I don't think there's much use in dissecting it, Suellen. Thanks, though."

"Bullshit. You go up against Derwood in this shape, you're gonna be no good to anybody. Anyways, I flat don't believe that about Lee."

"You'd rather believe Bethany would lie to me about something like that?"

"I bet there's more to it, that's all. She could be mistaken."

"What there is, is plenty."

"In this case, more is less. What do you really know, just Lee's supposed to have had a thing going - "

"Her very words. Consistent."

" - with this guy. If that's all there is to it, that's the worst it could be. I bet you'd find out, I don't know. He made her, guys do that all the time. He was blackmailing her about something. He's dying of cancer. Something like that. "

"Not fast enough for me. I don't want to discuss it,

Suellen. Would you just please drop it?"

"Ya, OK."

She sounded so much like her mother then, that I almost stopped the car and kicked her onto the shoulder of I-40. I drove on, seeing Bethany hauled up to Apostle House over Derwood's shoulder. Bound and gagged in the second bedroom while the Honda generator chugged and Derwood got things ready.

At 11:30, when we'd been on the road for four hours and had another three to go, Suellen stirred, scratched her thigh, and announced that she was hungry.

"I've had a beer and five peanuts since yesterday lunch," she said. "We get off here, go to a McDonald's, we can be back on the road in ten minutes."

"Every minute is another minute he has alone with her."

"We won't neither one of us be worth a damn if we don't eat. You want to bust in on him and fall down from hunger? Plus, we'll have all that woods hike to do when we're there."

"All right." I lurched the car into the exit. The McDonald's was backed up ten deep at the drive-through, but there was a Burger King another mile down the road. I laid a trail of rubber out the McDonald's exit ramp.

So, well, it was more like twenty minutes than ten, but we were back on the road, Suellen now slumped slit-eyed with anger behind the wheel, a foot on the dash, a whopper in her hand and country music blaring on the radio. I mistrusted the setup, but the hood ornament never wavered a hair from the center of the lane. I sluiced my own burger and fries over the hemorrhage of dread at the base of my throat and let my eyes rest on the passing farms and junkyards.

*   *

I'm so sorry she told you that.

"I bet."

She said nothing, but turned her eyes to the road and flipped on the radio. She scanned past the country stations, looking for something. Her hair was beginning to fall into a messy tangle and her fingers fumbled with the radio as if she had forgotten how to work it. She passed a woman's soft voice reading some kind of script; scanned back, passed it again in a storm of white noise, and then found it.

Here it is, she said. It's a long story.

On Honeyman Bald

18. Lee's Tale Begun.

He grew up next door to my folks on Church Street in Gabbro, North Carolina. Our mothers shared babysitting and a nanny, colored of course in those days. Carrie was a big, motherly woman who smelled of chamomile, and called us "young mister Timothy" and "young missy." I don't remember much more than that about her, or much of anything at all about those days, except that it was always hot and sunny, and we were always together. And I do remember one other thing.

She slammed the wheel, and her hair sprang back to its accumstomed halo. *Jesus Christ,* she yelled. *We barely got started.*

On Honeyman Bald

19.

Suellen slammed on the brakes and yanked the wheel over, and we began a smoking, slithering waltz down the shoulder of I-40. What I could see out the windshield - when the windshield was pointing down the road - made no sense. Clouds of dust, cars leaping into the air. A truck backing down the lane ahead of us, another flopping from jackknife to humpback like a dying fish. The next time we came around, the truck that had been facing us was lying on its side, still progressing our way, an extravaganza of sparks mushrooming from under it. I had time to gasp into a fetal curl while the fountain of sparks loomed against us. We crunched sideways into it. The door next to me moved inward an inch or two, and we were stopped and it was our turn to act as stone wall.

A big SUV came rolling toward us - that is, the whole thing, rolling ass over teakettle like a giant silver football. Through the spinning, arcing windows, I could see blood and a deployed airbag. It hit Suellen's side of the car with a bang, rebounded, and pivoted on its roof to give us another smart rap with its rear panel. A second later, something hit it from the other side and nudged it firmly against us. And our part of a twenty-car pileup was done with.

"Holy shit," Suellen said. "You all right?"

"No," I said, "but I'm no worse off." Even I could hear how stupidly self-pitying that sounded. "What happened?"

She looked at me and burst into tears. "It started too

far ahead to see, but some asshole passed us going about one-fifty. I expect he hit somebody up there, or scared 'em into somebody else. Or just lost it himself, the stupid fucker. This is the last goddamn thing we needed."

"Easy does it. First of all, are you sure you're OK?"

"I'm OK, I'm OK. Jesus Christ, though. It's gonna be hours getting out of this."

Four and a half hours, in fact. And damn lucky at that. By the time they got ambulances and a medevac helicopter to take away the worst of the human wreckage - and I hope I never see anything again like what was jammed up-side down, dangling from its seat belt in the SUV against Suellen's window - and then wreckers and cranes to pick apart the metal, and fire trucks to hose away the gasoline and blood, the sun was slipping toward the rampart of Smokies ahead of us, and we were still two hours from Bryson City. Suellen was inconsolable.

"Shit, we lost four-five hours, plus it'll be dark before we're there, so might as well add on overnight. He's already had her almost a day already." She floored it, and we began shimmying again, as we had at any speed over fifty since the accident.

She shook her head angrily and slowed down. "All right, all right. Just don't say 'Easy does it' again. You sound like a goddamn bumper sticker."

We limped into Bryson City at dusk. The road toward Smokemont - the road to Hahnemann, maybe - was marked by a skinny white sign with black diagonals that directed us up a paved, but leaf-littered woodland road that looked like it hadn't been traveled for weeks. Suellen spotted it and yelled, and I swerved us onto it. She reached over and punched the trip odometer, this lively-apprehensioned girl.

"Good thinking."

"Thanks."

The pavement played out in less than a mile, when we passed the last of a string of prosperous and xenophobic-looking spreads, the kind of quasifarm that North Carolinians favor when they acquire a little money from urban enterprise but don't want to leave the country. Big mailboxes, white rail fences, eagles on the chimneys, massive security lights that were flickering on now.

With the gravel road came hills, smaller houses, dimmer lights, flags more faded. Dogs that rushed the road and barked. Then came woods that were broken occasionally, and then rarely, by clearings, battered log-hauling trucks, mobile homes, trailers, shacks. Darkness deepening, ears popping, engine straining, temperature gauge edging redwards. We'd lost a headlight in the accident, and the one that was left was a little wall-eyed. I slowed and downshifted.

"We'll sleep in the car," Suellen said. "Take off soon as it's light enough to walk through the woods. Looks to me like where their so-called goddamn Apostle House was, it can't be more than a mile from Hahnemann. There's a crick we can follow for a while, drains away from the top of the mountain."

"We'll have to be damn lucky."

"Ya, we got all kinds of luck, don't we? No, but Jesus, look here! Derwood Cemetery! Bet that's that little cemetery we saw, had his uncle in it. Aw right, damn it, we got him."

"We got him located. His house. That's a long ways from - "

"Oh, all right, then. What's the deal, Hap? You wanta keep telling me how we'll never make it, and all this time he's got Beffie, and he's fucking her, he's making up new ways while he rests up to do it again. We just going to give up, or are we going in there and grab that bastard and pound him into dogshit?"

As rotten as I felt, as depressed and hopeless, I had to smile. "Dogshit. Thanks, Suellen."

"Fuckin' A."

She pulled a foot onto the seat and swiveled to look at me. "How old are you, Hap?"

"56."

"Huh. Beffie told me you were sixty, she thought. Still, I don't think you're going to be able to take Derwood. Mom told me you were a pretty good fighter."

"I don't know where she'd have learned that. There was a time when I was pretty tough. I had a daughter that got killed, and I gave up everything but working out, getting strong to kill my ... the people who killed her. That was a long time ago."

"Did you?"

"Lee came along, and went into labor with Bethany, right under my nose. I had the choice of killing somebody or delivering Bethany."

Suellen tilted her head. "Beffie told me about that. Not the killing part, though. Thanks, I guess."

"For saving Beffie for you?" I lifted a hand from the wheel. "Any time."

She turned back to watch the road. "Does it bother you so much?"

I didn't say anything for a while, and when I did, it was, "That's 7.6 miles from where we turned off. We ought to be on the tope sheet now." In spite of everything, I felt a twinge of anticipation in my belly.

Suellen sighed, and opened the map. "OK, yeah. We're going down, cross a railroad track, and then left and back up."

We did. The road was down to a single lane now, with wildflowers growing in the center.

Suellen nodded. "OK, got us. You got a right, up a long straight, a left, two rights, a long left. That ought to be Hahnemann."

"Maybe we should stop before we get right into town, and find a place to hole up."

She mulled that, and said, "No, drive straight through, give us a chance to scope the place, then we can turn around and kind of drift back with the lights off."

"That'll fool the cops."

She snorted. "Cops? Hahnemann, North Carolina, amounts to four, eight, nine, ten little black squares and a name in the tiniest print they got. They'd run out of able-bodied citizens before they could staff a squad car."

"So there's no real reason to stop there anyhow. What's the nearest point on this road that looks possible to hike back in from, to find Derwood?"

She nodded. "Maybe... wait a second... six hundred feet, little over a tenth of a mile past the last shack, a little creek crosses the road. We could hike up it, and not get lost."

"How do we know which shack's the last one?"

She stretched back and turned off the domelight. "It's a church. Shut up and drive."

The church was easy to spot. It looked like nothing more than a quonset, but it had a big illuminated sign, Hahnemann Charismatic Testimony Chapel. The Reverend Cloyd Hunnimon, Pastor. A tenth of a mile down the road, with the woods closing in again, Suellen pointed to a dumpster by a culvert. A small tin sign said Flat Creek.

"There," she said. "Behind the dumpster. Perfect."

As soon as we parked, she raked her seat back, turned away from me, and said, "We're going to be up before first light to kill Derwood Barnes Cather and rescue Beffie. Don't dare think anything but that, don't snore, and don't whine at me, you couldn't sleep. Good night."

On Honeyman Bald

20.

It was cold as hell in the car. A sorrowing cusp of moon hung over the road. Suellen was snoring lightly but solidly. Lee appeared as soon as I opened my eyes.

The second my back's turned, you're sleeping with that girl.

"Jesus, Lee, is this the time to be making jokes?"

I'm not making jokes.

"Lee, listen to me. Derwood's got Bethany. He'll rape her till he's tired of her, and then he'll kill her." I reflected on the classical notion that the dead, far from having special knowledge and powers, are in fact slow-witted, out of touch, and jealous of the living.

Bethany. I need to talk to you about what she said, about.... Tim Summerton.

"Lee, I can't be distracted by anything, even that. I hope to hell you enjoyed your little flings, I wish you all the joy of them. But I can't mess around with it now."

*   *

Lee's Tale (Continued).

One summer day, when I suppose we were three or four - old enough to understand some things, such as that white babies didn't have to pay too much attention to what colored nannies said - Tim and I followed that principle into a world of trouble.

"Aw, Lee, for God's sake, I told you - "

On Honeyman Bald

In Tim's back yard, there was a big old tree, with a swing on it. We had only that summer grown big enough to climb into it and to pump ourselves, and we spent afternoon after morning at it, laughing and relishing the crazy breathless feeling you get when you let go of the ropes at just the right time and fly through the air. Young as we were, we were lucky we didn't break our necks.

There was an old kitchen table under the tree, where Carrie could park the laundry while she was hanging it out, or set pies to cool. One Saturday, I had the idea - a rare case of leadership on my part - that if we could climb onto that table and launch ourselves from there, it would be the best kind of swinging yet. Tim was impressed that I'd had the idea, and after he finished scoffing at it, he told me that it was up to me to try it first. "It was your idea. You have to go first."

But it wasn't easy. Instead of my usual jeans and a tee shirt, I was all dressed up in a frilly dress; Tim was dressed up too, because Carrie was supposed to take us to a fancy birthday party that afternoon. But it never entered our heads to wait until later to try my idea.

There were a dozen jars of new-made apple butter cooling on the table, and we pushed those aside. Tim made a cup of his hands to boost me onto the table, and I managed to get a knee onto the top. I was almost up there when some twist of my foot pinched his hands, and he snatched them away. I started to slide off the table, squealing, and Tim put his hand on my butt and tried to stop me. I remember that moment very clearly.

Well, of course, the table tipped over. Tim and I fell to the ground, followed by a dozen jars of hot apple butter. Not so hot as to burn us badly - there have been guardian angels all my life that delay my having stupid ideas until the apple butter has cooled a little - but hot enough to be uncomfortable. We squalled like wet cats.

Carrie found us in a tangle, our party clothes and ourselves covered with apple butter and broken glass. Her anger was monumental. It looked to her like we'd brought the table down, trying to get into her apple butter, and she scolded us accordingly. Trying - haughtily - to tell her that we didn't give a dang for her old apple butter, that we'd been on the track of something better, only made her madder. She swatted both of us on the fanny and hauled us into Tim's house to get cleaned up.

Carrie had been charged with seeing to it that we got to that birthday on time, and presentable. The time was short by now, and there was nothing for it but a joint bath. She stripped us down and started the bathwater, and put some mercurochrome where one of the broken jars had cut my knee.

The next thing I remember is sitting in a sudsy ocean of warm water, face to face with Tim, glorying in my bright-red knee. Carrie was out of the room, probably trying to clean the apple butter off my fancy dress. And up through the scum of soap came the tip of his penis, supported by a precocious little erection. I was appalled and fascinated, and - sure - some part jealous, red knee and all. Mostly, I was worried, as anybody would be that found a tumor growing on a friend's body.

I don't think Tim had any more idea than I did what it was good for. Or what had caused it, which I expect was the mix of deviltry, disaster, nakedness, and punishment. I reached out to touch the little thing, and Tim giggled at the way it felt. So, of course, what happens next? My mother, who's curious why we aren't on our way to the birthday party, walks into the bathroom just at that moment.

There was a good deal of tight-lipped rinsing and drying

On Honeyman Bald

- I remember that the towel hurt and made my knee bleed again, she dried me so hard - and that was the end of the birthday expedition. And of Carrie's job with our families, which of course meant nothing to us. Tim and I were kept apart for a few weeks after that, kind of to let us cool off, I guess was the theory. But before the summer was out, we were together again, and looking for chances to compare equipment.

I never took it as a bad deal, or something to envy, that I had this clean little arrangement at the bottom of my tummy, much neater looking than his strange, vulnerable stuff. But I sure knew the subject was forbidden. The one question I put to my mother about it, I got a lecture how nice little girls don't ask about that kind of thing.

"All right, fine, I get it. So goddamn dewy and innocent I could about cry. So naturally, there was always this special soapy thing about Timmy Summerton, that just got right under your guard, and you just don't know what got into you."

Lee shook her head, and when she tried to say something, what came out was a wordless gobble that embarrassed her. She averted her face and I saw that the back of her head was horribly misshapen. She had to try two or three times before she could lift her foot along the back of my thigh, and when she flowed into me she left a scummy film, like soap in hard water.

On Honeyman Bald

21.

The car was still dark, but with a faint pearliness to the condensed breath on the windows that showed Suellen, inert as a bag of feed on the passenger seat. In the rearview mirror, a dark shape moved and was gone.

I rolled down the window beside me. Air like a cold washcloth moved slowly through it. I heard a single footstep behind the car, then nothing. I started to open the door, and realized that it would turn on the domelight, illuminating us, revealing the presence of a woman. On the other hand, reclining where I was, having lowered the window and thus informed whoever was back there that I was awake and moving, was a strategy with no good ending to it. I opened the door and spilled myself out low, hoping to roll over and come up fighting. My leg caught under the steering wheel, and I felt my knee pop as I sprawled headfirst onto the muddy shoulder.

A murky shape the size of an easy chair ghosted down the road and into the woods as Suellen's door opened. There was a tense silence, and then a whisper.

"What was it?"

I listened a little longer, and relaxed. "A bear, I think, working the dumpster."

I was sleepy, nauseated, and hungry, and my knee hurt like hell. I had to go kill a man, right now, with no time to psych myself for it. I thought of Bethany on the victim's bed at Apostle House, dreading this dawn, and I needed nothing else.

"Ready?"

"Yup. What's in the car for weapons?"

"I don't know. A jack handle, maybe."

"Get it."

"Yeah, that'll put the fear of God into him." I started toward the trunk to retrieve it, and anything else heavy or sharp I could find. "Why didn't we think of that?"

Suellen pulled aside her sock and showed me a short, scabbarded knife. "I did."

"You slept with that on all night? When did you have time to pick that up?"

"You don't recognize it? DB left it lying next to me, and I've worn it since then. Next guy that fucks with me, it'll be his last."

I locked the car and we started into the woods, following the little creek that drained Honeyman Bald. For a while, we both tried to keep our feet dry, but it meant a lot of detouring and jumping from one slick rock to another. Walking with a sore knee was bad enough without that. I started sloshing through the water, just trying not to slip and break my butt. Before long, Suellen was doing the same.

When she got well ahead of me, she turned and waited. "What's the problem?"

"I wrenched my knee, trying to be cute about going to see who was prowling around the car. I could have saved the trouble."

"From now on, you tell me when you think there's some danger. What if the first I knew of it was a shotgun blowing your head off?"

"Sure would have been tough on you."

She was silent for a while.

On Honeyman Bald

"You sure you want to go through with this, Hap? You're not at an age where... well, where you can tackle the bad guys with your bare hands."

"Yeah, that's what Beffie said. Let me ask you something, Suellen. If I get killed trying to rescue her, what have I lost, exactly?"

Suellen's mouth opened, and then closed. She reached over and put a hand on my shoulder, and we pushed on up Flat Creek.

By the time we reached a place where there was no more creek, just a shallow draw running up the mountain, the woods were loud with bird song. It was light enough to read the map, and Suellen sat on a log to spread it on her knee.

"If we can trust this thing, we're right here, where the creek starts. The cemetery is on the other side of that ridge, that makes the right bank of this little draw."

"Probably where the creek starts is pretty variable, depending on the season. It's been wet, so you'd see water on the surface higher up than average. We could be level with the cemetery now."

Suellen looked from the map to the territory and back, trying I guess to fix herself on the topography. "OK, the cemetery's on a kind of ridge, that's the next one over from this one in front of us. If we climb over here, we should be down in the hollow below the cemetery. That might not be a bad place to be."

She folded the map and put it in her pocket. "Here we go. You're not a bad guy, Hap. I wish we'd had time to help you see how we love each other."

"That'd be a treat. Love Secrets of the Lesbians."

She grinned and kicked my leg.

On Honeyman Bald

"Get going, smart shit." I did. For almost the first time since I learned about her liaison with Bethany, I could imagine liking her a little.

We got up the side of the draw in good order. The wetness of the woods made silence easy. From the top, we could look across the intervening hollow to the next ridge. Aromatic mist rose from Suellen's sweaty tee shirt. She poked me and pointed to a log bridge that spanned the hollow.

"That's where we went across, I bet. The cemetery should be right at the end of it. I think I see a gravestone. See?"

I did. "We're there. Jesus, I thought this place was miles from anywhere."

"Ya, and here it is, a short stroll from downtown Hahnemann."

"Well, at least the road from Hahnemann connects to the outside world. I could have saved Wet a lot of grief, bringing him up this way."

"You look at the tope sheet, you could miss that road easy, it's so secondary. It just about looks like a trail. Don't worry, we know now. Come on."

We stayed away from the log bridge, taking the hard way down into the draw and up the other side until we were just below the top. The little cemetery above us was drenched in birdsong. Wet and I hadn't bothered to fill in the pits we dug, looking for kitchen refuse from Apostle House. If Derwood was there, he knew his secret was out. Maybe he didn't care. Maybe he was sitting behind the first big gravestone with a rifle, ready to defend.

I pulled Suellen close and whispered. "Here, and every time we go around a corner from now on, I'm going first, and you're staying back until we know it's not an ambush. If he shoots me, Bethany still has a chance with you at large. The other way around, she doesn't. Whatever happens, whatever you see up there, don't let yourself get emotional about me or Bethany. She's the prize, and he's the guy we have to beat to get it."

Suellen scowled, and then nodded and patted my butt, and I raised my head above the level of the ridge. Birdsong continued unabated, as did my life. I stood and waited for death, and it did not come. I signaled Suellen up to join me.

"Daddy told me about the crosses," she whispered. "That's where we were supposed to end up."

I didn't reply, because I didn't want her to follow the line of thought that ends in bacon. I started for the path to Apostle House, motioning Suellen to wait until I had cleared the first bend in it. I maintained the distance between us until I stood in the courtyard behind one of the tilted rocks.

Suddenly I knew that Apostle House was as empty as on my visit with Wet. And that Derwood and Bethany were elsewhere, anywhere else on the face of the Carolinas. That Derwood had checked them into some soundproof motel at Raleigh-Durham Airport, timing the horrors to the thunder of departing planes, raping and butchering to his heart's delight while we struggled up here on this fool's errand. The need for action had camouflaged the pit of dread that lay at the base of my throat all day yesterday. Now it was back in full force. I leaned on the slab of rock, and there was no strength in my legs. As I slid down it to crouch in despair, I smelled wood smoke.

I turned and gestured fiercely to Suellen to stop where she was. Keeping the rock between me and the doorway, I crept back to her.

"He's here, by God," I whispered. I felt a surge of joy.

On Honeyman Bald

"We found the son of a bitch. All we have to do is figure out how to take him."

"Let me get in there by the front door. You call him out, like you want to ransom Bethany, and I jump him from behind and slit his throat."

"Mm. He shoots me from in there, comes out to pick up the money, and goes after you. Then what?"

She punched my arm. "I thought that was OK with you. You care whether you live or die, all of a sudden?"

"Until Beffie's safe, yes. Think of another plan."

"Is there a back door?"

"Yes, but I don't think you can reach it from here. The house is built into this hump of rock, and the back door opens onto the cliff. Maybe you could climb up that rock, where DB did, and go across the top. Think you could do that?"

"Get where you can jump Derwood if he comes out, and watch me."

I crept through the courtyard, keeping the leaning rocks for cover as long as I could, praying that Derwood was either sleeping or harmlessly engaged with Bethany, until I stood beside the front door, gripping the tire iron. Suellen loped across the open space and up the slanted rock, making no more noise than a fox might have. I waved her toward the back of the house and went through the door, crouched low.

Derwood had restored order to Apostle House. The mess was cleaned up, the portrait straightened, the window was repaired, and there was a fire in the fireplace,. But its mutter and snap were the only sounds. I tried to assess the emptiness, whether it was of abandonment, or of crouched menace. That had seemed so easy with Wet Parsonage at my back.

On Honeyman Bald

Now I had to go through that door at the back of the room, and into both of the rooms off the little corridor. I was sure that I would not survive it, that only the sound of the shot that killed me would warn Suellen and give Bethany any hope of rescue. Well, so be it. I walked to the back of the room and opened the door.

Nothing, no one. The generator chugged in the torture chamber, and I used its sound to mask my footsteps. I kicked in the door, and saw Bethany's shorts on the bed; but no Bethany. Nor in the other bedroom, nor in the utility room, where Suellen stood, panting lightly.

"Shit," she whispered. "You didn't tell me the damn thing ends in a drop-off. I like to bought it right there."

"I did, you didn't listen. Bethany's here," I said. "Or she was. Her shorts are in one of the rooms. There's a fire in the fireplace. But nobody's there."

"Now what?"

"The fire looked almost fresh, like he built it this morning. He's got her somewhere hidden, which says to me, he saw us coming. What's to keep him from slitting her throat, and disappearing again, like he did before?"

"I don't know. Wanna go back to Carrboro?"

"Nope. I know where he is... I think. The question is, what's going to beat him?"

"We'll think of something. Where?"

"Come on."

I led Suellen to the ledge, and to the pinched-off end where the little tree grew out of the rocks. "I'm pretty sure," I whispered, "he's on the other side of this. He and Bethany, I hope. See where the bark on that tree is worn? I think you must have to swing yourself around on it, onto another ledge. Ready?"

On Honeyman Bald

She looked from me to the sapling, and the hideous drop below it. She nodded dumbly, and stood. As I reached for the sapling, she pulled me back.

"You're not going first on this one, pal. If you're wrong about how to do it, you'll fall. If I am, I can catch myself."

I reached out again. "Forget it."

She stooped and straightened, and the next thing I knew, her knife was under my chin.

"Don't make me argue, will you, Hap? Stand back."

I stood back. Suellen sheathed the knife and pulled her sock over it, and crept to the rocky corner. She made a few rehearsal moves, like a diver practicing body flips on the edge of the pool, then grabbed the tree and launched herself off the cliff. The instant she disappeared, I heard a mutter, and a scream that wailed away into the depths below us.

I grabbed the sapling as Suellen had, and jumped as much like she had as I could. There was a horrible moment when I saw that the ledge on which Derwood and Suellen stood was too far away, that I would never make it. My crippled knee banged against the rocks, and I leaned backward over the void. Suellen reached out and grabbed me, and I limboed onto the ledge.

"Man," Derwood Barnes Cather said. "That was the ugliest anybody come around that corner since a fella from Greensboro tried it and fell to his demise. Me'n DB had to climb all the way down to pick the road kill off Fall Creek and give it a Christian burial."

On Honeyman Bald

22.

The continuation of the ledge was perhaps another fifty feet long and ten feet deep. Derwood stood at the far end of it with a half-inch polypropylene rope wrapped around his gloved hand, his feet braced against the strain where it disappeared over the edge of the drop. The other end lay in a coil halfway along the ledge from where Suellen and I stood.

"Now, here's the situation, Mister Hap Maryland," Derwood said. "I got something on the end of this rope that you want. I'm willing to sell it to you. Or, I guess to be perfectly honest, what I'm selling is a grip on the rope, like you can see I have. Would you like to have a peek over the edge there, and see what it is?"

I knew what it was, but I couldn't stop myself looking. Probably a hundred feet of rope hung straight as a plumb line toward the gravel bar a thousand feet below. At the end of it Bethany dangled by her bound wrists, swinging from side to side. It looked to me as if she was unconscious. I devoutly hoped so.

"My God in Heaven, Cather," I snarled. "You're just one of these Marvel bad guys, aren't you? Let me make a counter offer. Haul her up here right now - go ahead, start hauling while I'm talking to you - and I'll take her and Suellen, and that'll be the end of it, pending what damage you've done to Bethany. If she's injured, or raped, you'll - "

"Oh, she's all of that, Harper. She's damaged goods for

sure. You listen while I talk. I take no dictation from a guy whose slut wife killed my son. Precious Beffie's past providing satisfaction, and I'm tired of her. I want Suellen, you want Bethany back. If you were honest, you'd admit you want Suellen out of Bethany's life, which I can guarantee. Deal?"

"No."

"Yes," said Suellen.

"No," I said. "Shut up, Suellen. Don't be stupid."

Derwood beamed at us. "Call her a stupid dyke, why don't you, Harper? That'll calm her down." He tipped his head at me in a friendly way. "Honestly, don't you want the lesbian gone? Don't you want to take Beffie back to - where was it? Bozlee? Laurinburg? Nurse her back to health, fix her up with some fella that'll teach her how to screw like you and the lovely Lee used to, get grandchildren from her?"

"Derwood," I sighed. "You are of course, a deeply evil man. But you're also as dumb as a rock. If you kill Bethany, you ought to know I won't waste time going to the cops. I will hound you to the end of your days, and I will see to it that your death is as public and humiliating as I can possibly arrange. I won't pretend I was thrilled when Bethany and Suellen got together. But next to you and me, they're like - " I shrugged. "Like children playing in a bathtub. Give me the rope, you fraudulent asshole, and use the trouble Suellen and I will have pulling her back up, to get gone. That's my last word on it."

He shrugged in his turn. "OK, then. Let's get her swinging good, and let's let her fly, shall we? After that, you and I can fight over Suellen. I think I'll win, though, because you're going to waste time and energy watching Beffie fall, and then grieving. Plus, I still doubt you have much use for

Suellen, so you won't fight that hard for her. After I win, I'll pitch you over to join Bethany."

He walked to the edge of the drop, and began walking Bethany back and forth, patiently, taking the time it would need to get a hundred-foot pendulum swinging, while Suellen and I watched, helplessly wondering what we could do to attack him without endangering Bethany. Her weight seemed to put no great strain on him, gunshot or no.

"Stop," Suellen said. She turned to me. "If Lee can kill herself to save us, I can put up with a little discomfort. Give him the rope, Derwood." And she walked toward Derwood with her arms stretched before her, as if handing herself over to the cops.

"Thanks, honey," Derwood said. "I won't bother to say you won't regret it." He grabbed Suellen's wrists, and in the same motion stooped and heaved the coil of rope toward me, and let Bethany fall.

Bethany screamed, and so did Suellen. The rope began to rip and sizzle off the ledge. As I picked up the rope, I saw in an instant that when Bethany's plummeting weight came onto it again, it would pull me off the ledge with her. And I'm sure that was Derwood's idea. I grabbed the end of it and turned my back on them to jam the dwindling mass of rope around the sapling, took a turn around my waist with the last of it, and planted my feet on the dusty granite of the ledge.

The rope was stretchy polypropylene. When it went taut again, the sapling snapped downward like a fishing rod, but it didn't break. I was jammed up against the sapling with the rope cutting into my waist and my hands jammed into the space between the sapling and the rock from which it grew. All of that provided the gradual braking that kept Bethany's arms from being torn off.

On Honeyman Bald

But it didn't protect her from the terror, nor did the unconsciousness I'd hoped for. From far below me, I could hear her screaming, crazed shrieks that went on and on. From where I was wedged against the sapling, I could see her swinging and banging against the cliff, hundreds of feet down in the massive shadow of Honeyman Bald. She was so far down that it made me sick to see it. Much higher than she was, hawks circled in the morning sun.

The first thing was to pull myself off the sapling and get my feet under me again. Then I had to find a way to free the rope from the sapling, because as soon as I started pulling on it, it wedged into the rocks at the bottom, and the friction made it impossible to pull Bethany any higher. I finally managed to work it up over the top, so I could pull it up unencumbered. Of course, when it cleared the sapling, a loop of slack came into it that gave Bethany more terror, banged her against the face of the cliff, and almost plucked me off the ledge.

After that, it was just a matter of hauling upward, hand over hand, faintly hearing Bethany, now getting hoarse with it, shrieking and begging me not to drop her. I expect she thought the whole business was some refinement of the games that Derwood had played with her for a day.

After I'd gained fifty feet or so, I had to stop. The skin was going from my hands, and if I lost it, I wouldn't be able to pull Bethany up any more. Also, I was already exhausted, gasping and quivering with fatigue. I put a foot on the loop of slack I'd won, held the rope in one hand, and wiggled the other arm out of my shirt. When I had both hands free, I wrapped my bloody palms in the sleeves of the shirt, and started hauling again.

After I'd gone through three more cycles of hauling and

resting - terrified that I would have a heart attack, or faint, and kill Bethany - I allowed myself to look over the edge. She was still more than a hundred feet down. I hadn't even managed to pull her back to where she was before Derwood let her fall. The thought of Derwood made me glance for the first time at the far end of the ledge. He and Suellen were gone.

I don't know how long it took me to get her the rest of the way up. When the strength left my arms and would not come back with any amount of rest, I took another turn around my waist and backed to the far corner of the ledge, snubbed the rope on a boulder, and slowly worked my way back to the edge, working forward within the loop that contained me. For each of those trips, which took possibly ten minutes to accomplish because of the terror that I would slip off the ledge myself, I gained a net of perhaps ten feet. Eventually, sunlight slanted onto the ledge, and I understood that it was now past noon, since the ledge was on the west face of Honeyman Bald. But I had no idea how long Suellen and I had taken to creep up here along Flat Creek, how long we'd delayed at Apostle House, even how long we'd spent talking to Derwood. There didn't seem to be any content to this day except hauling on the rope, listening to Bethany's terrorized voice, hauling anew. At some point, I realized that she was just below the ledge, and I staggered to the edge to keep from jamming her hands against it.

I looked down at her, and said, "Honey, it's Daddy. It's OK, Beffie. I've got you." She looked at me without comprehension and began to scream again.

I found that it was impossible to lift Bethany over the edge, something I could have done easily a day ago. Now I simply hadn't the strength. And Bethany was incapable of helping me. Her eyes were wide open, staring at me with no recognition. I talked to her, I pleaded with her to reach for the edge and pull herself up, even a little, enough to keep me from scraping her forearms across the sharp lip of rock. She only kept screaming, in a voice that was no more than a croak.

In the end, with my body shaking with the spasms of fatigue that precede collapse, there was nothing for it but to back away from the lip, dragging her arms across it. I suppose it was God's mercy that only one of them broke in the process. When she was safe on the ledge, I staggered toward her in utter exhaustion and experienced another mercy, in that I didn't get close enough to the edge to fall over, myself, when I passed out.

23.

When I opened my eyes, Bethany looked at me, and said in Lee's voice,

Right through grade school and junior high, Tim and I were pretty good friends, in a latent sort of way. And around that friendship there was an indelible tint of forbiddenness, and - I don't know. Soap and giggling and mercurochrome and wetness and mild pain. Nothing much came of it, though, until in the ninth grade, we got registered by our mommas in Miz Conley's Studio of Social Skills.

"For God's sake, Lee. Haven't you been paying any attention at all? Do you know what's going on, that I'm unconscious to listen to this crap? Shut up! Go away! I don't give a rat's - "

You used to care, Hap. You're killing me, not caring.

Her face began to pucker inward, racing through the old age she never lived, her hair greying and thinning. I could see three or four fractures reaching around from the crushed back of her skull.

"Stop this, Lee. Listen to me. Bethany almost died today. She's lying next to me right now, hurt, frightened out of her mind. I just can't stop to listen to that tale now, honey. Really. I promise, though - "

She brightened a little.

What?

On Honeyman Bald

It came to me that these appearances, her apparent immortality, could have survived her as a burst of energy that she'd managed, or bargained for, after she and DB disappeared into the sea of fog. That she had sent it up to me while she fell, the radio operator inside the doomed Titanic transmitting even as the hull disappeared into the Atlantic, as the wall of ice water rushed through the steel coffin, slamming doors open one after another. And that what she had achieved might be finite, not immortal, and coming to an end. And besides, if I were honest, part of what was killing me about Lee was that she sacrificed herself not just for Bethany, but for all of us. She laid down her life to save mine. I reached out to touch her cheek. It was cold and wet.

"All right, Lee," I said, as gently as I could. "I promise I will listen when I've got Bethany taken care of. You can tell me all about handsome Timmy, and whatever it was that possessed you about him, and I will listen and try to understand. Now really, Lee, run along and rest. Bethany will die right here if I don't get her to a doctor."

I woke when the westering sun hit my face. Two or three sun-warmed flies droned around Bethany's mouth; beyond that lay the silence of gentle air and great height.

There was not a chance in hell that I could swing myself and Bethany around that sapling to get back to Apostle House. And besides, what would I find when I got there? I was a rag, a walking corpse, no match for Derwood. Suellen would have to escape or endure him as best she could. "I can put up with a little discomfort," she said. I had to admire that.

I stumbled to the other end of the ledge, and there found its continuation through a rockfall into a marshy little backthrown meadow that led me to the woods at the fringe of Honeyman Bald. I had found Derwood's path of escape, and probably the path DB followed to ambush us at the clifftop. I went back to pick up Bethany, and found her unconscious, breathing heavily, her broken forearm purple and swollen.

"That's good, Beffie," I said. "You just pass out and stay passed. The less you know about this the better. We've got a little walking to do now, and it's going to take some time. C'mere, let Daddy have you."

The only way I could lift her was to sit her up, and then kneel on the ground next to her and get my shoulder under her waist and slowly stand up, bracing myself with a hand against the rock wall at the back of the ledge. When I had her more or less balanced, I started walking.

When I got to the top of Honeyman Bald, I tried to orient myself. The village of Hahnemann straddled a pass on the northeast flank of the mountain, and that's the way I headed, trying to give Apostle House a generous berth. It was a lot of staggering and floundering downhill, and the second time I tripped on a dead branch, I dropped Bethany in a little stream and sprawled beside her.

It didn't look like Flat Creek, though I couldn't be sure. There were no tracks in its mud. I decided to hope it would join Flat Creek somewhere short of the French Broad River, or the Atlantic, or that it would cross the road through Hahnemann in a recognizable way. At least, following it, I would be going downhill, and in a way that I could accurately retrace my steps if I had to. The thought almost made me vomit.

When I knelt to pick up Bethany again, I noticed for the first time that she was wearing nothing but a flannel shirt, pretty much the duplicate of the kind Derwood wore. That seemed intolerable. I unbuttoned it and worked it carefully over the broken arm, and threw it in the creek, and then I stripped down myself and donated my underwear - sweatsoaked and clammy - and shirt. Bethany's skin was covered with welts, and her face was bruised and swollen. Damn him, damn him!

I tore a rag from my shirt and dipped it in the little stream to sponge her face, murmuring skinned-knee comforts, promising her through cramped lips that Derwood would pay abundantly for what he had done to her. Bethany did not wake up, which I welcomed still. I wiped my own brow, and threw the rag away.

Another half hour of creek slog and bank scramble brought me to the road, though not by the dumpster and car; evidently the little creek we'd followed joined Flat Creek farther down beyond the road. As I looked up and down the road, trying to figure which way to follow it, I heard a high and gassy scream behind me. I put Bethany down and turned to face the sound. It seemed impossible that I could drag myself the mile back to Apostle House; tenfold impossible that I could rescue Suellen from what was happening to her. A hundred times unthinkable that I could hear her scream and turn my back, leaving her to it. I started up the creek bed, sniveling with exhaustion.

Before I managed twenty steps, the scream came again, directly overhead. A hawk, trying to unnerve meadow mice and rabbits into bolting from cover. Not Suellen. Thank God. Not Suellen, this time. I recovered Bethany and carried her to the road.

In another stumbling half hour - during which the sun sank into the trees and not one car came in either direction -

On Honeyman Bald

I saw the dumpster. My car was still there, unbelievably. I'd thought it would be stolen, vandalized, or rusted to oblivion. The key was in my pocket, folded inside Tim Summerton's love note. I unlocked, and laid Bethany on the back seat. She was still unconscious, pale, and breathing hard. I sat behind the wheel and wept.

After some time, I started the engine and began wondering if it would be a good idea, or even possible in this bashed-up wreck, to drive her all the way back to Gabbro before I got her to a doctor. I was dithering about that when I saw someone in the side mirror, walking up the road toward me. It was too skinny to be Derwood, so I rolled down the window to ask about a local hospital.

"Hey," I called. "Excuse me?"

"Ya, me too," Suellen said. She opened the back door and knelt next to Bethany. "Nice going, getting her back by yourself. It killed me to leave you with her."

24.

She looked like any backwoods girl who'd been roughed up by her boy friend or her father. She had a split lip and a black eye. The engine died while I gaped at her, not knowing whether to laugh or scream.

"Wha?"

"You said it."

"No, but how the hell did you get away?"

She turned on the dome light so she could look at Bethany. She winced when she saw the broken wrist. "Oh," she whispered. "Oh, my God, poor Beffie." She lifted Bethany and slid under her to cradle her head. In the driving mirror, her face looked like Wet's had when he saw the physical evidence of Suellen's rape.

"It was him that was glad to get away," she said. "I wish I hadn't let him."

"I can't believe it," I said, and I couldn't. "He was twice as big as you, and - "

"Not twice as shifty, though." She sighed. "Soon as you were occupied with Bethany, he hauled me back to Apostle House, telling me how much he was gonna improve me. Asked me wasn't I ashamed of myself, how could I do these unnatural deeds he'd seen me 'locked in,' how he put it."

She laughed, tightly. "I saw right away where his head was. I told him he was right, I was ashamed of myself all the time, but I was only flesh and blood, and if he only knew how delicious it was ..."

On Honeyman Bald

She picked up Bethany's head and began to stroke it. "I asked him if he'd like to hear another kind of story. He said no right away, and he started hitting me. But he kept coming back to it. After a while, it was obvious he was waiting for me to start."

"You told him stories?"

"Love secrets of the Lesbians, you bet. Certain kind of older guy, they don't necessarily get much out of the actual experience. On the other hand, they can get turned on, just from talking. I just figured that'd be easier on me than letting him get turned on his way, which he was set up to do."

"Holy shit. Scheherazade."

"Like that. Difference was, I wanted him to get turned on."

"Why?"

She snorted. "How else was I gonna get him to untie me so I could use the knife? Sheesh."

I started the engine again. It sounded like a car that has been driven by fools for forty years. "You tried to kill him?"

"Huh uh. If I had, he'd be dead. I waited until he was on me, giving me the business. I kept talking to him, and while I was making up more stories, I pulled the knife out of my sock and rearranged him some."

I turned and stared at her. "You ... My God. Did he scream, about an hour ago?"

"Like a pig. You want the gory details? He's hurting pretty bad, mostly in places that were the cause of a lot of his trouble, and I don't think he'll be bothering girls for a while. Part of what took me so long was cleaning myself up. Can we go?"

The car rattled and died before we were through

Hahnemann. Nothing I could think of would make it start again.

"Shit," I said. "This can't be real. You see any sign of help around here?"

Suellen craned toward the rear. "Only lights I can see are back at the church. Shit, we can't be hanging around here. Somebody's going to know about Derwood, and here we are with a couple of beat-up women and a knife."

"Well, so what? That's his lookout, seems to me."

"Yeah? You don't know much about country folks, do you?"

I did. If Derwood was a hero in these parts, anybody who tangled with him or brought a charge against him would be suspect, not he.

"Stay with Bethany. If you see a cop of any kind, even a sheriff, flag him down. But lose the knife first."

"Just did that."

"Good. I'm going back to the church, and see if we can find somebody that actually owns a telephone."

"Don't get your hopes up. See any poles?"

I stopped before I went in the Hahnemann Charismatic Testimony Chapel, and tried to smooth my appearance some. It was a lost cause. I was smudged, distraught, half-dressed and staggering with hunger and fatigue. I opened the door on dim light, a scattering of worshippers at prayer, and the Reverend Cloyd Hunnimon at work.

I suppose I expected a prosperously robed televangelist with a pinky ring and comb tracks. Hunnimon was skinny and sour-looking, dressed in work clothes, with a grey brush cut and a rattlesnake around his neck. The snake noticed me in the darkness of the entrance and turned a yellow stare on me. No one else did. Cloyd Hunnimon began to sing.

"A-amazing Grace," he sang, in a reedy hiss that seemed to come as much from the snake as from him. "How sweet the sound."

He turned to lift the snake toward the spotlit cross that was the only illumination in the place. The snake looped around to keep an eye on me.

"How *sweet* that sound, brothers and sisters. It has saved a wretch like me, and many another. There is a wretch come into God's house just now, a stranger who stands in need, who is hurt and hungry and in the prison of his steely heart. When saw we such a one?"

"Jesus and the apostles!" shouted the twenty or so communicants.

"And did we minister unto them?"

"Yea!" It seemed less enthusiastic.

"We did, or did not, according to the capacities of our hearts. Speak, stranger." He turned toward me, and so did all the rest. A collection of Appalachian faces stared at me, like so many leather masks. I drew a shaky breath.

"I apologize for interrupting your service - "

"*You* are our service, brother. What is your need?"

"I have a badly injured girl outside, my daughter. My car is broken down, and I need a lift to the hospital."

Silence.

"Just for her. I was hoping there was a hospital in Bryson City. Or a clinic?"

One of the worshipers spoke up. "Nearest hospital's Asheville. How bad hurt is she?"

I started to cry, then, something I never used to do. "She's got a broken arm. She's been beaten up and raped, and she's been unconscious for two or three hours."

On Honeyman Bald

Cloyd Hunnimon walked down the aisle toward me, and he and his snake fixing unblinking stares on me. "Did you do these things, brother?" His voice was nonjudgemental to a point just short of accusation. The snake's tongue flickered at me. I stared back. Of course, I thought. That must happen all the time.

"No."

He relaxed. "But you know who did."

"I certainly do. Der-"

Hunnimon's hand shot out to cover my mouth, and the snake reared and buzzed. "Stop. Do not cast accusations in the Lord's house. Show me the girl."

For God's sake, a faith healer. "Sir, thank you. If no one here can get us to a doctor, I'll try one of the other houses. I don't mean to interrupt your worship."

"Everyone in town is right here at church, brother. Don't waste her time, which may be short. Where is she?"

I didn't have the strength to fight him. "Come on."

At the car, I introduced Suellen as Bethany's sister. Cloyd Hunnimon gave her a narrow look, and bent over Bethany. Bethany was wet with sweat, and her eyes were open, but not seeing. Hunnimon backed out of the car.

"Take her up and follow me."

Suellen and I exchanged a look, and she shrugged. What choice do we have? We made a basket of our arms and worked Bethany onto it. Bethany's head lolled against my shoulder, conscious but utterly without strength. Her breathing quickened, and she felt hot and damp.

Cloyd Hunnimon led us down the driveway past the church, and to a little cluster of trailers, parked under the trees. One of them was lit, and he knocked on its door.

"Sister 'Licia," he called, in that reedy voice. The snake

lifted its head.

An answer came from within the trailer, and footsteps. The door opened on what I took at first to be a child. But Sister 'Licia was an old, old woman, past the age where age makes any difference. She might have stood four feet eight in her prime, and she was bent and crippled a foot short of that. She took us in at a glance that slanted from waist height.

"Bring her in."

We did. I started to tell Sister 'Licia about Bethany's mistreatment, and she shook her head and held up a translucent hand. She made a short gesture at a couch that stood against the back wall of the little space, and we let Bethany down on it. Reverend Hunnimon brought a knitted blanket and laid it over her shoulders. Sister 'Licia's knotted fingers set the blanket aside and unbuttoned the shirt, which she gently removed and handed to me without a word, and pulled down the underpants.

"Her wrist," I began. Sister 'Licia swatted toward me with that frail hand, and I shut up. While she was at it, she waved the Reverend away toward the back of the trailer. He retreated hastily and began running water and clanking pots. When Suellen saw what Derwood had accomplished, she turned away with a tight little groan of anguish. Sister 'Licia spared her a glance, and turned back to Bethany. Bethany stared over her shoulder.

"Little sister," Sister 'Licia said, in a voice as soft as wheat. "Little sister, look at me."

Slowly, Bethany's face focused on her. She said, "Oh," and began a hoarse sobbing, her voice deep and alien. Sister 'Licia nodded. "I know," she whispered. "I know. It's done with. Daddy and sister are here now."

Bethany looked puzzled, but the sobbing slowed.

On Honeyman Bald

Suellen and I knelt by the couch. "Beffie," we said more or less together. Neither of us knew how to go on. But Sister 'Licia whispered to her for a solid half-hour, at one point in which Cloyd Hunnimon came forward with a mug that smelled suspiciously of pussyflower tea. Suellen and I matched glances over that, and Suellen shrugged and tipped her head toward Bethany. Look at her. Wouldn't a sedative be the right thing? I nodded. When she'd sipped a little of the tea, Bethany drew a breath and fell back against the couch. Her breathing evened and slowed, and the hunted look faded a little. Sister 'Licia nodded, and turned to us.

"This little girl has been to Hell," she said. "I would gladly to say to Hell and back, but she's a long way from back. I can't fix that arm. Fella down the road could. Cloyd?"

Cloyd Hunnimon spun obediently and left the trailer. I heard his footsteps running - *running!* - into the darkness outside. I started to cry again. Sister 'Licia, evidently one to husband her speech, tipped her head toward the steaming pot of tea, and turned to Suellen. I went and found a mug. When I had filled it, Suellen was crouched on the floor of the trailer with Sister 'Licia's hands on either side of her head, Sister 'Licia's mouth at her ear. The whisper was as faint as breath. Suellen nodded from time to time, and whispered something back. Sister 'Licia then waved at me to turn my back, and I heard Suellen's tee shirt slipping over her head. By the time she was looked at and reassembled, Cloyd Hunnimon was back with a big, bluff-looking guy in Oshkosh overalls who held an old-fashioned black leather bag. He squeezed into the trailer with the rest of us and picked up Bethany's arm in a huge paw. Bethany squeaked with pain and tightened her face.

"Woe," the doctor said. "Whoa now, baby. We'll set this

right for you." He turned to us. "Might need a shot, and a speck more room, though."

Sister 'Licia's all-directing hand shooed excess personnel out the door. But as we stood in the chill under the trees, the doc popped his head through the door.

"Sister? Little girl's asking for you, and I might could use somebody to help hold her still."

Suellen went back in, and I turned to Cloyd Hunnimon and the snake.

"Reverend, I just don't know what to say, where to start. You folks are just about … "

He waved it off. "When saw we you an-hungered or sick or in prison?" he asked, rhetorically enough. "Couldn't face ourselves in the mirror, we didn't respond when a stranger comes through. You could be Jesus himself in disguise. Where'd we be if we sent Him off still sick and in trouble?"

"Let me set your mind at rest," I said. "You're doing this one for practice. But even the doc, making a house call."

He chuckled a little. "He's used to that. Hard to get cows into a clinic."

"Cows? He's a vet?"

"Course. Think we'd have a MD up here? Jake's a doctor, all right, and he can fix that arm good as new. Just don't bring your girl to him for ladies' complaints."

I turned to the trailer in time to hear a short yell from Bethany.

"That'll be the bone settin into place, I expect," Cloyd said. "Hard to do that without having it sting some."

By the time the vet had finished, and taken his tiny fee, it was after midnight. We were grounded and immobile in Hahnemann, North Carolina, which may have the most thoroughly Christian population this side of the Vatican, but lacked a motel.

It was a done deal of course that Bethany would spend the rest of the night on Sister 'Licia's couch. She lay there now, unconscious again but benevolently so, dressed in a flannel nightie that accomodated her splinted wrist, her eyes closed and blue-shadowed. I thanked Reverend Cloyd and Sister 'Licia again in words blurred by fatigue, and started toward the road to bed down in the car.

"C'mon, Suellen. I'm about dead, and I expect you are too."

"Ya."

"Scuse me, folks," Reverend Cloyd said. "What was you planning to do now?"

"Sleep in the car," I said. "We've done it before."

"Sir," he said. He and the unsleeping rattlesnake gave me hard looks. "You have been through a terrible, terrible day, so I will say this as gently and pleasantly as I can. This young woman is no more your daughter than I am. I would be tempting the inescapable, infallible, and hair-trigger judgment of the Lord of Hosts if I were to countenance the two of you passing the night in each other's company. I will not be party to it. Bethany's sleeping now, and out of danger. Sister 'Licia will fix Suellen a pallet on the floor by her, and she will sleep there. You may sleep in your car if you insist, but in fact there is a perfectly good bed in the next trailer but one, which is presently unoccupied. Let me go and see to it."

Suellen and I exchanged glances. The corner of her mouth curled, and she disappeared into Sister 'Licia's trailer with an exhausted little twitch of her butt where no one but I could see it. Reverend Cloyd emerged and started to usher me toward a dark shape fifty feet away in the trees.

On Honeyman Bald

"Reverend," I said. "I can't tell whether to be insulted at your suspicions, or to thank you for the overestimation of the danger I pose to anyone. We accept your arrangement with .... with yet another...."

I gave up and let him lead me away.

The empty trailer was an Airstream, still on its tires and ready to roll. It was musty but clean. So was the bed; it had sheets on it, with Smurfs gamboling from one end to the other. Reverend Cloyd prowled about, rocking the Airstream on its springs as he opened windows, flicked lights on and off and flushed the toilet. I was starting to fish in my pocket for a tip when he put out a hand and wished me good night. Be of good cheer, he said. You are among friends.

As he stepped down into the grass outside the door, he and the snake leaned back to whisper to me.

"Brother," he said. "It wasn't you I was thinking was the danger. Sleep well, now."

*   *

You promised.

I groaned, and buried my face in the Smurfs.

"All right," I said. "For God's sake, keep it short."

Lee's Tale Concluded

Miz Conley's was a sort of cotillion school for fairly well-off white children. I think it didn't fold until around 1980 maybe. You went there, and the boys learned to dress right and bow, and ask girls if they were having a good time. Girls learned to say, yes, thank you, and to help boys not be embarrassed at the horror of it. You didn't have dates, but you danced with who was written on these little cards in Miz Conley's old-fashioned handwriting. The fall class graduated with a Christmas dance, and the spring one in June, to more or less coincide with the end of school. I was in the spring one, and so was Tim.

When the graduation dance came along, my folks let me pick out my own dress for it from the Penney's catalogue. The one I chose was meant to be both demure and sophisticated; a high-necked, sleeveless, steel blue little number that turned out to be made of some extremely satiny, pliant miracle fabric. The miracle was, when you put it on, you could see just about every rib and pimple and underwear seam standing up in what my mother called bas relief under the shiny fabric. She went right back downtown and bought me a cotton slip to wear under it, to sort of smooth me out.

The dress was a big success. The basement of the Country Club was as hot as Araby, and the boys in their suits and the girls who'd bet on crinolines were sweating like pigs. But I stayed pretty cool, which helped deal with getting asked twenty times if I was having a good time. I danced in turn with every boy there, and the last dance on my card was with Tim Summerton.

Now, one of the bad boys in the class had brought some kind of tasteless cheap liquor and spiked the punch, which may also have led to my going into the Ladies' and taking off my slip before the last dance. I stuffed it into the trash can, and checked out the effect. Good enough, and much cooler, but now my bra was in bas-relief, and it looked ugly. I scrapped it. One of my girl friends about fainted when she saw how that looked. It's a new look, I told her, called bra relief. Without the slip there was a great big panty line, and I was ready to shed them too, but that was farther than I could go. For one thing, I was afraid maybe individual hairs might show up under that thin and clingy dress.

When Tim came up to me, and bowed, and asked if I was having a good time, I sipped my punch and said, You bet I am, Timmy, but not half as good as I'm about to. He blushed, which pleased the hell out of me. He had pomaded his hair down shiny and tight and dressed up like Tiny Tim, to make fun of Miz Conley and her old-timey ideas. I thought that was about the funniest, most daring, most heroic thing I had about ever seen. It fit with my pointy little nipples in a flapperish, '20's kind of way.

Our dance was a waltz, and we stumbled through it stiff-leggedly, and then the band - which I think sort of misunderstood what was called for - went into "Good Night, Sweetheart." I snuggled up to him and let my head fall on his shoulder, under the brim of his Tiny Tim hat. His neck seemed to smell like soap and apple butter. And in about three bars of "Good Night Sweetheart" I could feel him - through that all-transmitting dress - getting a very serious hard on.

"Is that the little pink thing you showed me one time?" I whispered, drunk as a doorknob.

I could feel the heat of embarrassment on his cheek, where my forehead was near it. But Tim Summerton was not the boy to let a girl get the best of him. "Growed some since then," he claimed.

"Quite a bit, just the last couple minutes," I whispered. "You wont to go somewhere and let me see?"

I found myself with a dry mouth, the echo of a snore in my ear, and an erection without a destination.

"Thank you, Lee. I don't think I can take any more just

now."

We stayed apart from each other after that dance and met later, across the road from our houses, where there's some dunes along the edge of Lake St. Luke. My mother found us again, this time with the Gabbro County Sheriff. We were passed out under a magnolia, after a night that left my virginity more or less intact, but not my virtue or my cotillion dress. Tim disappeared the next day, and I did not see him for more than twenty years. I found out later that his father had shipped him off to Culver-Stockton on the afternoon Greyhound, to make a better soldier of him.

"You poor thing."

I cried for a few days, maybe ten hours of it without stopping, and then off and on. I got over it, as we all do with these things.

"Not totally, evidently."

It was more the humiliation, than losing Timmy. See, Hap, this is what I been trying to tell you. Love is a miracle, when you look at what it comes out of.

She was her old self here, her hair black and spangled with stars, her face fresh and alive and young. Maybe as young as that girl in her flapperish cocktail dress, except that she was in front of a blackboard, tapping today's lesson with a piece of chalk.

Love is a miracle when you look at what it comes out of.

For some reason, she went back and underlined the "what".

"Love? You're a mile ahead of me, Lee. When we get this business settled, do remind me to tell you what's happened to Bethany today."

That would be just fine, Hap. I have to go now, though.

On Honeyman Bald

The family that cries together ....

It was as out of date as a radio jingle. I waved her off.

But she winked and flowed into me in a burst of sexual sweetness. The residue she left was the stars from her hair. They glimmered and faded one by one, until I was back with the Smurfs.

The Airstream was as dark as a coal mine. I lay there, aching, barely able to roll over. When I could think, the first thing I thought of was not Lee, not Bethany, but Derwood Barnes Cather. Where was he? Badly hurt, dying, dead? Or superficially wounded in a way that would let a panicked girl flee without bothering to give him a physical exam and verifying the result of her knifework. Suddenly it seemed to me imperative that we know. If he was more or less functional, or could soon become so, then we were far from being finished with him. He had stalked and brutalized Bethany to avenge DB's death. To take what seemed to fit Suellen's account best, if he were mutilated but alive, he was in deep criminal jeopardy in regard to Bethany and Suellen. And me, for that matter. Would he not be far more dangerous yet, looking to eliminate the threat of criminal prosecution?

The woods outside my window were alive with the sounds of wilderness. Of skulkers and predators and of victims who crept forth under the thin and clingy cover of darkness to attempt a little business - food, sex, a drink of water - without being dismembered and bloodily eaten. The latch on my door, and on that of Sister 'Licia, where Bethany and Suellen slept vulnerable and easily taken: were they reliable? Were they even locked?

On Honeyman Bald

I rolled over, and the Airstream creaked as I slammed my head onto the pillow. Nonsense, I said. Even if Derwood is only superficially wounded, look where he's hurting. He's not going to come out in the middle of the night. If he's alive, he's up to his ass in Darvocet.

Some time after that - I do not know if a minute or an hour, but still in the dark pit of night - the latch snapped open, and the Airstream creaked and tilted doorwards.

25.

I gave myself less than a second of disbelief, and lifted the covers as silently as I could so I could roll onto the floor. My heart banged so hard I could see my pulse at the edge of vision. I tried with no success to remember where anything useful as a weapon might be, even my clothes to use as a garrote. I hated the thought of facing Derwood - goddam Derwood, why couldn't he leave us alone? - naked and unarmed. I began to grope on the floor for a shoe.

"Hap?"

I pulled the sheet over myself and collapsed onto the pillow. "Holy shit, Suellen."

She was a wavering shadow in front of the window. "Can I p - please - "

"God damn it, you about gave me a coronary."

The shadow sank to the floor. "Don't be mad. I've got to talk to you. Please don't be mad."

"You know, that's just exactly what your - " I managed not to say it. It was, though. Don't be mad, her late mother had said, and had proceeded to slip into bed with me and give me the one truly repentant occasion ... Well, that's not true either; I've done a lot of regrettable things. But getting myself boffed by Trudi Ransom will always be at the top of the list. I found the switch on the little bedside lamp and turned it on.

Suellen was crouched by the front door, and I have never seen anyone look more downcast.

On Honeyman Bald

"Turn it off," she sniffled, ducking even lower. "If the Rev sees me here, he'll shit."

I turned it off. "What is it, Suellen?"

"Beffie ..." She began crying again, wretchedly.

Fear dashed against the back of my mouth. I jumped out of bed and shook her. "What? Is Bethany worse?"

"No, no. She's the same, I guess. She's still sleeping. But I haven't slept a bit. Hap, Jesus, this is all my fault, all of it." She collapsed onto my knees, making me pretty aware that they, and everything connected to them, were naked. I picked her up and walked her toward the bed, pausing to toga myself in Smurfs before I sat down.

"Not hardly," I said. "I'd say the fault lies exactly a hundred percent with Derwood, don't you think?"

"He's ... I don't know. Maybe." She wiped her nose on the sheet. "See, he's like a wild animal, and anybody with any brains stays out of the way, and keeps people they love out of the way. I let Beffie go out there in the dark after you when I knew damn well he was around. I should have gone with her, I should have checked if she found you, or if she was OK. I fucking went back to bed. And then ..."

She pounded the mattress. "And <u>then</u>, Jesus, I just had to have lunch. If we hadn't pulled off, we'd have missed that accident, and got here practically a whole day sooner. That afternoon, instead of the next morning. Maybe before she broke down, maybe before she got so, so ..."

Suellen broke down herself. "So damaged," she wailed.

I looked at her, and dark as it was, I was beginning to see things. I groped a hand to her cheek.

"Suellen, you can beat yourself up like this, or you can keep the blame where it belongs, which is on the guy who actually did it. He's not a wild animal, he's a human being, and he's as guilty as he can be."

"Why did he pick on her? I could have handled him, but Bethany is ... She's not tough, Hap. I could have handled him."

"And you're feeling bad because it was her this time and not you?"

"I could have handled him. I handled it when DB ... when he did that."

I took her face in my hands, and wiped the tears away. I opened my mouth to tell her that survivors should not feel guilty, and it came to me that words would never convince anyone of that, who believed otherwise. I stroked her hair, trying to convey by that, that I didn't share her view of it. Try it yourself some time.

After a few seconds of that, she sighed. "I'm sorry," she said. "I shouldn't have come here."

"I'm glad you did." It sounded phony and formal the instant I said it.

She stood. "No you're not, Hap. I give you the creeps. You wish the hell I'd get out of Bethany's life. You want her to marry a guy and have babies. Hell, I don't blame you. Lee felt the same way." She flipped a hand. "Who wouldn't?"

"Well," I said. "You don't, evidently."

"Oh, well, you know, there's where you're wrong. If that would make Beffie happy, that's what I want. And maybe it would."

"But?"

She collapsed against me, crying so abjectly that it was no more than a whisper. And so was her voice. "But I love her so much."

I held her then, stroking her and soothing, but crying myself. Knowing, really knowing at last that Lee was gone forever; leaving me hurting, angry about the hurt, and guilty about the anger. Knowing that I would have either a strange new family or no family at all, on the sad trajectory to the Rest Home dumping ground.

"Well," I said at last. "There's something we have in common. Love is a miracle, when you look at what it comes out of."

I raised her chin to look her in the eye, and gritted my teeth. I still don't have to say it, I thought. But I said it. "I'll tell you what. You're very young, both of you, though I admit, in your case you've had your share of tough luck and hard knocks. Anyway, if Bethany feels the same about you, and if you two still want to make a go of it together, then you have my blessing. Not that you asked for it."

That brought on the tears again. "No, but I wanted it. God, more than you can possibly believe. You are a dear, wonderful man, Hap. Thank you. Oh, God, thank you." She threw an arm and a leg over me, clamped herself close, kissed me hard, and let her head drop on the pillow. In five seconds, she was snoring.

Love secrets of the Lesbians. One of them is, if you crawl into a guy's bed half-naked, he will shortly abandon the bed. I grumped myself into my trousers and found a soft spot on the shag carpet up front. In five seconds, it felt like a waterbed.

*   *

Luckily, dawn in the Smokies is deafening with birdsong. Suellen and I woke at about the same time, in light so pale and thin you were not sure it was not fog, or imagination.

"Is this Smurfs?"

"Yup."

"You were sleeping on actual Smurf sheets, and you let me have them? You didn't have to do that."

"Actually, I did. It wasn't the Smurfs, though."

"Oh." She smiled shyly. "I get it. Jeez, I'm so sorry, Hap. That wasn't very nice."

"You know what was nice? Somebody needing held again. But I tell you what, you better get dressed and scram, or - "

"Yee, shit, the hair-trigger judgment of the Lord of Hosts. I'm gone."

*   *

After Suellen crept back to her pallet, I sat in fuddlement on the Smurf bed, and wondered what to do next.

Derwood.

I would have to go back up to Apostle House and see what I could learn from what was there; fondly hoping I would find his bloodless corpse. I recalled tales of that, of men bleeding to death from a minor - or sometimes not so minor - cut to the sexual apparatus. Wonderful, and what a fitting end that would be. I considered bringing Bethany up to see it.

The gnashing of my teeth got me fully awake. I dressed and stepped out into the shrill dawn. The grass was a carpet of dew, bearing narrow footprints that led from my door to Sister 'Licia's. I walked over them, and then stood irresolute. Silly to knock and wake them, I thought; but the latch clattered, and Suellen came out looking scrubbed and cheerful.

"She's still sleeping," she whispered. "I can't tell how she's doing."

"We better be ready for her to take a while to get over this," I said. "She's traumatized in more ways than I want to think about."

"Ya, that fucking Derwood. I can't believe I let him get away. I should have killed him right then."

"Well," I said. "I think we're damned lucky you got away. But I'm going - "

I broke off because Sister 'Licia appeared then, not from within the trailer but from the woods behind it. Her walk was slow, and over her arm she held a wicker basket covered by a dishcloth. The cloth was stained with something pinkish. Blood, sure, or just as easily berry juice. She glanced at the trail of footprints connecting the two trailers, nodded, and entered her own without comment.

"Yee," Suellen whispered.

"Shit," I agreed. "Go in and see if Beffie's awake, and ask Sister 'Licia what about moving her today. I have a feeling they'll be glad enough for us to go."

Apostle House stood silent in the morning light. The sight of it made me sick with rage. Now I would, for a third time - fourth, counting our initiation as bacon on the hoof - have to creep into it, not knowing, of any breath I drew, whether there would be another after it. I wished, again, that I'd brought the Glock. Not bothering to reflect that I'd have had to bring it with me to Confession on the way up to visit Bethany and Suellen. I would really, seriously, have to go home to Gabbro for a change of clothes one of these days.

The thought of walking into the house I'd shared with

On Honeyman Bald

Lee made invading Apostle House trivial. I opened the door and went in, Suellen's knife in hand, heart pounding in a what-the-hell kind of way.

The place was quiet again. The silence of abandonment, concealment, or death? I got no answer from the cold ash of the fireplace, the tipped-over furniture, the books scattered on the floor like broken birds. Was this wreckage from Suellen's struggle with Derwood, or from some other? I pictured Derwood staggering around his house in a welter of blood and rage, flipping heavy chairs like matchsticks, and so forth. Trouble was, the end of that scene should be Derwood's corpse, picturesquely sprawled or abjectly huddled. Missing.

Missing, too, from the back corridor. Where Bethany had been held prisoner, I found the rest of her clothing, along with items - souvenirs and apparatus - that I will not corrupt this file by describing. I took what was hers, and left the rest.

In the bedroom, no sprawled corpse, but blood, some bloody towels, and drawers pulled open from which more towels and sheets drooled, some of them with bloody handprints on them. All right, so he'd been hurt badly enough to bleed quite a lot, but not too badly to minister to himself. Blackly as I hated Derwood, my scrotum winced at the thought. I'm not sure I wouldn't have preferred a clean shot to the heart.

A sprinkling of blood led down the corridor to the tool room, and again it was a knife-clutching creep, silence, and anticlimax. No ambush, no corpse. No drops of blood beyond the tool room or on the ledge at the back. The little tree by which Derwood swung himself around the rocky prominence at the end of the ledge was bent far over, ruined for its purpose of allowing access to the far ledge. I could not remember if that had happened when I used it to break Bethany's fall. I let myself consider hopefully whether I might have weakened it enough to drop Derwood into space when he tried to flee Suellen. I peered as far as I could, but the gravel bar at the foot of the cliff was hidden in foliage. To check it out, I would have to hike the hundred stories down there and look.

No way. Not only a probable waste of time and an effort that could well be beyond me, but I was not going to visit Lee's landing place, now or ever. If Derwood was there, beginning to rot in the sun, well, fine. But I would proceed on the assumption that he was not, that he was no more than superficially wounded, now mending, in hiding and bent on revenge.

As I left Apostle House for the last time, I indulged myself a little. I used Suellen's knife to slash Derwood's portrait to ribbons.

Back at Sister 'Licia's, I found Bethany awake but not doing well. Her broken wrist, and all the numerous physical insults Derwood had administered were hurting, competing for what attention she could spare from the consciousness of degradation and humiliation he'd worked on her. She was impervious to pussyflower tea and unresponsive to anyone but Suellen. At some point in the morning, a local appeared with Reverend Cloyd, wiping his hands on a greasy rag, and announced that my car was now running.

"Weren't but outa gas," he said. "I put in a gallon, 'll get you down to Bryson to fill 'er up."

I blushed, and dug a five out of my wallet that he reached for, then glanced at Reverend Cloyd, and waved off. So I walked him back down toward the car, and slipped him the fiver under the Rev's radar. I pulled the car around the back of the Charismatic Testimony Chapel so we'd have a shorter carry getting Bethany to it. I was followed in by a Swain County Sheriff's Patrol.

The guy who got out of it was a sour-looking deputy, fiftyish and hard-shaven, with tight pink facial skin and a greying mustache. His uniform fit him better a few years back, I'd have bet. He nodded at me and cocked his head.

"Understand they was a complaint here. Little girl got herself raped?"

"I wouldn't have put it quite that way," I said. "A man abducted my daughter from her home and brought her out here and abused and raped her, yes. He damn near killed her, and I don't know if she'll ever get over it."

He nodded. "Know who the fella was?"

I experienced a tiny dash of shrewdness: make him say the name. "He lives about a mile up toward the top of Honeyman Bald," I said. "Heavyset guy, with a long pigtail. Goes around preaching Christian conservation, something like that."

The deputy - L. Cornwell, by his name plate - pulled out a little spiral-bound notebook and wrote all that down, but didn't rise to the bait. "Where's he at now?"

"I couldn't say. He - " I decided to keep Suellen out of this until we could see where the wind blew. "After he was finished with her, he left her hanging off the cliff up there, in a very dangerous situation. He took off while I pulled Bethany back onto the ledge."

L. Cornwell cocked his head again, like a dog recognizing the term "supper" in the middle of a sermon about the Eucharist.

"Expect I need to sit down with the young lady in

question. Bethany was it?"

"Yes. I don't know if she's in any condition to be interviewed, but we can try."

Inside the cramped trailer, Bethany answered his questions, which were none too gently put, in faint monosyllables. Yes, she'd been abducted. From home. In Carrboro.

"That where you're from, sir?"

"We're from - Bethany grew up in Gabbro. She's living in Carrboro now."

"By'rself?"

"With me," Suellen said, grudgingly. "We share an apartment."

L. Cornwell gave Suellen an up-and-down look, and turned back to Bethany. "Now then, little lady," he said. "Did you - "

"Don't call her that," Suellen said, her voice hard and flat.

Cornwell repeated the once-over on Suellen, who rose abruptly and absented herself, looking murder over her shoulder. It bounced off, and Cornwell turned back to Bethany.

"Did you recognize the fella?"

"Yes," she whispered.

"Knew him from somewheres?"

"Derwood Cather." She ducked her head and shuddered. "Derwood Barnes Cather."

Cornwell sighed, and asked Bethany how she could be sure.

"He introduced himself. His picture is on the back of his book. It was him."

"Uh huh. Y'understand, this is a very serious allegation,

little - ma'am. You'd have to testify to it in court, if we was to go ahead and press charges."

Bethany buried her face in her hands. "Whatever."

"Wait a minute," I said. "She might not be able to do that for a while. Maybe a long time. I can testify just as well."

"You saw him rape your daughter?"

"No, thank God. I saw him dangling her off the edge of Honeyman Bald when he was finished with her."

He shook his head regretfully. "Sounds like reckless endangerment, for sure. 'Fraid we'll need the little lady's testimony, to make rape stick. And even then, sir, I gotta tell you."

Cornwell flipped shut his notebook and looked out the window. "Not that I agree with it necessarily, not at all. A jury out here, they're like to think first off the lady brought it on herself, about any kind of rape trial. Seen it time and again, cases that'd just make you sick. You might want to think hard, before you put this little girl in court, let a lawyer start askin her about what was she wearing, did she flirt with the defendant, was she a virgin before this alleged incident, what was the exact nature of her domestic relationship with that other young lady, I don't know what all."

Bethany raised her head and glared at him. "I don't give a shit," she said. "You can ask me whatever you want about anything." She started to stand, and immediately turned white and sat again. "Anything."

Cornwell nodded. "All right, ma'am. You walk me through it, beginning to end, and then I expect you better let your daddy get you home and to a doctor, before too much more time goes by. Sir, I'm going to take Bethany's story here, and it might be just's well if you and the other lady was to absent yourselves. Leave me a contact number."

On Honeyman Bald

Outside, the Reverend Cloyd Hunnimon was in murmured conversation with Sister 'Licia, which broke off at my approach. It was a murmurous day for Cloyd; he spent quite a time leaning on the door of L. Cornwell's cruiser after Cornwell came out of Sister 'Licia's trailer, discussing I could not overhear what.

We brought Bethany out and got her situated on the back seat. When Cornwell pulled off, we had a chance to thank Cloyd and Sister 'Licia again, in the most heartfelt manner we could muster. The snake was absent, which I regretted; I had come to think of him as a straight shooter. In fact, maybe it was my own bad reaction to this string of disasters, but I was overjoyed to see the last of them as we rattled and shimmied down the gravel road to Bryson City

Bethany's resolve to do anything to bring Derwood to justice didn't last. During the long and mostly silent drive back to the lowlands, she slept on the back seat, rousing once or twice to limp on Suellen's arm into rest-area pit stops, from which they both emerged white and tight-lipped. By the time we were past Greensboro, the gravitation of a black hole couldn't have dragged her back to the Smokies.

In somewhat the same spirit, I didn't bother to suggest taking Bethany back to Carrboro. I wanted her at home in Gabbro in the house where she grew up, looked after by the doctor who'd tended her since she hit adolescence. And nobody questioned that it would mean setting up housekeeping with Suellen too. Some things are just too complicated to settle by talking.

When we got home, I announced a laundry and bath rotation and let people sort themselves out as they wished. Suellen carried Bethany upstairs to her old room, and spent the night curled in a chair next to her.

*   *

I spent the first week in Gabbro boxing up Lee's things - something I had been unable to do after she died, and now was unable to live without doing, as fast and as thoroughly as I could. I sold our bed and bought a new one, and painted the walls a guy sort of color called "Balsa" by the Duron folks. The notion of growing old in the surroundings of my cuckolded marriage with Lee was humiliating, and I made no secret of getting the place spiffed up to sell.

I got no great opposition from Bethany and Suellen, who had troubles of their own and only wanted privacy in which to tackle them. I think what they wanted, and I was not about to grant, was that they should inhabit the "master suite" (a large bedroom and bath) upstairs, and that I should move into one of the kiddie rooms. I had promised to bless their union, if they chose to call it that; not to house it.

Still, it seemed evident that Bethany needed a devoted and full-time ... partner, I guess, if she was ever to recover from what Derwood had done to her. You can hear my teeth gritting here, I expect. Eventually, I grasped the nettlesome issue and remodeled the back wing downstairs, which consisted of a screened porch, a mud room, and the guest room that once was Taylor's. I called up Chavis Baley, the sexton of Gabbro Presbyterian and a wonderful architect-contractor-carpenter as long as you didn't expect him to make any serious decisions on his own; and he helped me turn it into a sort of mother-in-law suite with a pleasant bedroom, a study, and bath. The whole business set me back a couple of thousand dollars and took the rest of October and part of November.

Suellen spent the time in Carrboro, giving notice on her job and wangling her way out of the lease with Horace. When it was finished and Chavis was well out of range - though he is so completely backwoods and fundamentalist that I doubt it would ever have occurred to him that he was creating living arrangements for what he would have seen as an abomination - she moved in.

I had hoped that the change would be good for Bethany, who had spent most of the construction time in bed in her old room upstairs, curled in a ball of lethargy. When it came time to move in with Suellen, she was wan and listless about the whole business. I could see Suellen was hurt by it, though she was too tough to show anything. But Bethany had no joy in it, or in company, or in study, or in taking Covington for walks in the autumn sunlight; or in anything else anyone could think of.

And no appetite. She faded and skinnied almost hourly. Her doctor tried this and that, even herbal remedies he'd learned from a half-Lumbee great-aunt, and finally booked her for a series of tests at Duke. The very name was a lead sinker in my belly. The tests took place over a stretch around the middle of November, and involved leaving Gabbro every morning at five to make a 7:30 check-in at the Duke Medical Center. I knew the way by broken heart. When that was over with, we had the pleasure of waiting a week for results, all of which of course came back, as they always do, negative. Bethany suffered from nothing but the effects of rape, brokenness, and fasting. But then, as Suellen and I sat at the kitchen table wondering whether a Thanksgiving meal would be just too horrible to endure, or might bring Bethany out of her slough, the phone rang. Suellen got it, and called

On Honeyman Bald

Bethany, who loitered palely in and spoke four or five monosyllables before handing the phone to me.

"It's Doctor MacFell," she said. "He wants to see me again."

I took the phone in dread. "Hap Maryland."

"Bill MacFell, Hap. I got a call from the folks at Duke, recommending I do another simple test on Bethie. She's set to have the cast off her arm tomorrow, and I'll do this other at the same time if that's OK."

Hell, why not. The day before Thanksgiving; with any luck, we could replicate last year's ghastly celebration.

"Is it - could you give me some idea what we're up against here?"

He sighed. "Better not at this point, Hap. No call to upset you for what might be nothing. I can promise you one thing, though. It's a simple procedure we can do and get the answer in about no time. No need to interfere with your holiday plans."

Oh, of course not. Tell you what, you med students out there. If you ever encounter a patient you hate with all your heart, and you want to give him as much hell as you can manage consistent with the Hippocratic Oath, tell him there's no call to upset him for what might be nothing, and let him wait a day. Patients, if you want to put your family through the Ninth Wringer of Hell, come out of your conference with the doctor and ask to be driven straight to Saint Ann's Catholic church, and there spend an hour kneeling in the Mary chapel, without saying a medical word to anyone. Decline to discuss your health.

Suellen, who had completely devoted herself to Bethany through the whole business, called me on my cell phone that night after she had Bethany tucked in.

On Honeyman Bald

"Hap, my God, I'm going out of my skull. Can we talk?"

"I have to walk over to Chavis's and pay him. Want to come along?"

"See you in the back."

I stirred Covington out of the comfy sofa she'd made her own in the living room, and we walked toward the Lumbee hamlet of Baleys Cross under a sky full of November stars. Covington, now a dozen years old, carried out none of the zig-zag investigations she'd done in her youth, and was content to waddle along, a childless matron who'd figured life out. Suellen was all over the place, scooping up rocks and green walnuts from the roadside and hurling them into the ticking dark.

"Honest to God, Hap, I say I can't stand another thing, and then something ten times as bad comes along. Now this, this <u>wasting</u> business. And she won't say anything about it. It's got to be, I don't know. Cancer. Leukemia. Lou Gehrig's Disease. Permanent hyperclinical depression. God, I can't stand it. How can you be so calm?"

"Me? I'm dying."

She was quiet for a while, and then said, tightly, "I get it. Older guys don't let on, do they?"

A string of one-liners presented themselves on themes of age, gender, and sexual preference. Choosing among them gave me time to cool down. "Maybe that's it. Remember, I went through this a year ago."

Suellen was smart enough to be a little contrite. "I know. I'm sorry. That whole business was mostly before I knew you or Lee, except as this sick president that everybody worshiped. I expect it was hell for you."

"I don't like to think about it, particularly now. Maybe it was about what this is for you, except I guess that I'm older and had twenty good years with her. Both of those cut both ways. And now, ... Jesus."

And I realized that it was almost impossible for me to remember clearly the pain of Lee's illness. The business with Tim Summerton had cauterized not only my twenty years of headlong bliss with her, but most of the horror and sorrow of losing her. I hated the bastard almost as much for that as for the other. When we got to Chavis' house, Suellen hung back in the shadows, not ready to come out - as it used to be innocently called - even to such a humble corner of Gabbro society as this. She was silent on the walk back; when Covington began not keeping up with us, she scooped her up and stroked her fiercely, and in the end carried her all the way back. People as young as Suellen and Bethany have only the crudest of tools with which to govern themselves and their lives, and infinitely greater forces with which to contend. No wonder they do dumb things.

Bethany came to the Thanksgiving table looking better than she'd looked for weeks. She was nicely dressed but pale, and I don't think she topped 90 pounds. She led the family - if that is what we were - in a prayer of thanksgiving for her deceased mother, and then rose and made the following sober speech:

"Daddy, Suellen, I have something to say that I know will upset you. I hate that, because I love you both. It seems impossible that it's been only one year, exactly, since Mom had her first surgery. It kills me that she's not here to help me now. But I want you to know that this is something I've suspected for a while now, and Doctor MacFell confirmed it for me yesterday. I'm going to need your love and support more than I could have imagined."

On Honeyman Bald

Under the table, Suellen's shaking fingers dug into my knee. Her eyes were lowered, like one waiting for punishment.

Bethany took a sip of water and smiled at us like Joan of Arc on her way to the stake. "I wont to make this short, so here's the deal. I'm pregnant. I'm going to have the baby, and, boy or girl, I'm going to name it Lee. I sure hope nobody will try and talk me out of it."

26.

If it is possible to soar with the angels and then fall with the damned in the space of two seconds, Suellen and I achieved it - Suellen, with her famously lively apprehension, in half the time it took me.

"Beffie! That's ... oh, my God, no, that's horrible. You're going to have Derwood's - "

"Stop!" Bethany clapped her hands to her ears. "No one is to mention that name in my presence, now or ever. He does not exist. The baby I am going to have is my baby and no one else's. He or she will have Mom's first name and my last name. Lee Morgan. Get used to it."

Hey, nothing easier, from my point of view. Lee Morgan was Lee's name when I first knew her, and when I delivered Bethany in the heat and dust and uproar of a country fox hunt. It's the name I courted her by. But I'll tell you, the notion of nursing Bethany through a pregnancy so she could deliver the unmentionable man's bastard child Lee Morgan, a child got on that hard-won little girl by rape and brutality, hit me hard. And compared to Suellen, I was blasé. She celebrated her prospective parenthood by gaping at Bethany, starting a half-dozen times, with knit brow and open palm, to explain to her how quixotic and crazy she was being, each time to be silenced by Bethany's immovable unwillingness to discuss, to hear any talk whatsoever of Derwood, to hear anything at all. In the end, Suellen shocked me - and, I think, Bethany - by bursting into tears and leaving the table.

We stared after her, and Bethany looked down at her plate, dropping tears into her thawed turkey.

"Seriously, Beffie - " I started.

"Oh, shit, I knew it. You too? You think you can talk me out of this, that I've prayed and agonized over for weeks?"

"Weeks?"

"You think this was some big surprise? I've known I was pregnant since the morning I woke up at Sister 'Licia's. I just was waiting for the official word, so fucking Suellen would believe it too."

Don't call her that to other people, I thought. If I ever say to someone, fucking Lee was jerking me around all those years, something in me will start to rot. I shouldn't even say it to myself.

"Give her a little time to get used to the idea," I said finally. "Hell, give me a little time. Give yourself a little more time, Beffie. You have no obligation to give birth to - to that guy's baby."

"Pronouns, labels, codes and abstractions are as bad as the name. Do not refer to it. This is _my_ baby, and mine alone. Are you suggesting I might be the kind of mother to kill my baby?"

"Oh, gosh, Bethany," I sighed. "If you think of it that way, of course not. But honey, that's the thing. It's not a baby yet. It's just..." I tossed a hand. "An idea. A possible baby. It has no consciousness yet, or personality. It wouldn't even suffer."

"_Even_ suffer? You don't get it, daddy. You never get it. This idea is going to be a baby that will grow up loved and happy, and be a child and a new person with problems and love and suffering and happiness all mixed together. Can't you see that? Don't you see what a miracle love is, when you look at what it comes out of?"

*   *

Lee was wearing a yellow rubber raincoat. Water streamed down it, though I never saw rain or any other source.

We always knew Beffie was a smart little girl. It's a pleasure to hear that about her.

"Where did she get that line?"

Line?

"About what a miracle love is. Does she see you too?"

That's not something I can really talk about much.

"Thank you, Jacob Marley."

Well, you said it to Suellen, and she talks to Bethany. There's a perfectly natural explanation.

"All right. In case you should happen to drop in on her, do you think you could talk her out of this business about bringing Derwood's baby to term?"

Please don't mention his name.

"Right, right, Jesus. Sorry." I really was sorry. Lee's signal - if that's what it was - was starting to deteriorate again, and Derwood's name made her pull the hood of the raincoat over her head. I could hardly see her face.

"Stop, Lee. I really am sorry. I haven't seen you for weeks. I was afraid you were ..."

What?

"I don't know. Gone. Dried up."

She smiled and the water evaporated from her raincoat.

On Honeyman Bald

The family that cries together, dries together.

She undid the old-fashioned metal clips in the front and tossed it aside. Naked, perfect, she melted into me, leaving the smell of yellow rubber on my skin.

*   *

After that day, Suellen gave up on her attempts to change Bethany's mind, at least in my presence. All through the Christmas run-up that every year snaps at Thanksgiving's heels, she acted as if the announcement had never been made, and spoke of everything else, or of nothing. I know she mentioned it to Wet, because he called me about it.

"The hell's going on down there, hotshot?"

"Where do you want me to start?"

He snorted. "We could begin with the cozy family you're apparently headin, but I give up on that long since with Suellen, knowing how far I can push her, which isn't much. On that score, I figure she'll get tired of nowhere and nothing jobs and go back to school, and if this partnering stuff survives that, it'll crack up over the baby thing, which is what I actually called about. Is she nuts?"

I thought so, but I bristled at having to defend her to Wet. "I take it you are referring to my daughter Bethany."

"That's the one, yeah. Name slipped my mind."

"And your question was?"

"Why in God's name is she set on carryin that rat bastard's bastard baby to term? Good Christ, you'd think she couldn't get rid a it fast enough. That's no big - "

"I'm glad you didn't mention the name. It's taboo here. The whole episode is. She refers to the bastard as 'it' when there isn't any choice. As in, 'Please do not name it.' "

On Honeyman Bald

Wet was silent for a moment. "You thought about getting her some help?"

"Wet, I just about think of nothing else. The two counselors we have here in Gabbro bounced off of her, and one of them apparently violated confidence, because all of a sudden people are looking at me funny and crossing the street. My so-called consultant business has gone about to zero. Of course, that might more likely be the lesbian relationship with what's-her-name."

"I know, name slipped your mind, touché. Listen, hotshot. You and me were never cut out to be in-laws in the best of times, like if Taylor'd ended up with Suellen. I don't know even then if I coulda rallied around, brought shower presents, played Grampa. Damn it, this is just goddamn ridiculous. We're talkin about a kid that's no blood relative of Suellen's or either of us, and fathered by a fuckin - " He coughed and it turned into a hacking cascade. Wet never got all the way healthy after his pneumonia; or at least he hadn't yet, three months on. By the time he ran down, and got his breath back, he'd cooled off.

"Never mind," he said. "I know you good enough to know you've tried everything you can think of to talk her outa it, and you're too stubborn to admit it to me. They need any cash?"

"Good of you, Gramps, but I think not at this point. For one thing, believe it or not, I recognize that Suellen has no legal or moral obligation to act as, uh, parent in this. All the less for you. Why don't you think about coming down for Christmas? We're expecting a cross-burning on our lawn, might be kind of cheerful and traditional."

Christmas was one of the most bizarre and painful

family observances any of us had ever endured. Just for starts, Suellen had never celebrated Christmas under her mother's rule, and Wet hadn't been the one to bring it up when he inherited her seven years ago. She'd sung all those hymns enough to know them by heart, but she'd never once sung Silent Night because the Resurrection Angels didn't operate in the winter. Bethany took personally every reference to pregnant virgins, and sniffled her way through "Wonderful Life" and the Alastair Sim "Christmas Carol," leaving Suellen out in the cold. I had to leave the room during Marley's visit to Scrooge, the melancholy tune of "Joe Hill" meandering through my head.

And then, Bethany and I were ripped to shreds by remembering last Christmas, when we'd spent almost every waking moment in agony over Lee as she went through the hell of her first round of chemotherapy, and we tried to pretend that it was just a good old-time family Christmas, and not a shaky miracle that was maybe the last we would have before what we then innocently believed to be The Worst happened. Well, that worst went ahead and happened, followed by two or three others, much worse; and here we were again.

Still, Wet Parsonage showed up on Christmas eve with a big grin and an armload of packages. He was faking it, and everybody could see that, and gave him all the hotter hugs for it. Wet had probably gone from snickering about homosexuals to despising them as he grew from high school into manhood. I know I did. And as a long-time cop, he'd probably given them more than his share of grief. Now that it was a fact in his life, he could have boycotted the Suellen-Bethany liaison, or sniped at it, and he didn't. He made an effort, in fact. The biggest of his boxes contained a pair of luxurious bath towels monogrammed Hers and Hers. Not such a hit was the $25 gift certificate at the Lambda Leather Boutique at Cross Creek Mall; and it went downhill from there.

Still, nobody burned a cross on our lawn. What we got instead was another visit from the Ministerial Alliance, the same gang of four who'd prayed over Lee to such good effect a year earlier. I may have been a little short with Sam Wainwright when he called, because I suspected what they were up to this time was not so much doing anything they could for us, but looking for a chance to wag a finger at our ... God in Heaven, must I call it a "life style?" In any case, their call gave Suellen a chance to scram, which she took, along with Wet. Bethany - pale, still skinny but starting to pooch a little bit - opted to stay and hear them out. I am convinced that she only did it because she wasn't willing to be discussed behind her back, nor to leave me to deal with them. I was grateful for that.

They came in trying not to look... I don't know. Not to look all too ministerial, I guess. You could tell they'd agreed ahead of time to be loving and reasonable; at least not to let the word "abomination" cross their lips in the first five minutes. In they filed, Sam Wainwright followed by Catholic Father Conor, AME Zion Reverend Farnell Hastie, and skinny Pentecostalist pastor Plummer Baley shyly bringing up the rear. Bethany kicked off the fun by offering eggnog, which they declined, though Sam Wainwright and Father Conor clearly regretted it.

Sam took first licks.

"Hap, Bethany, it is so good to see y'all again. We have missed you sorely at the church. Bethany, honey, it grieved my heart when I heard the terrible things that - "

On Honeyman Bald

"I don't think about them, Sam. Truly. If you want to spare me further grief, you won't ask me to."

Well, maybe we should cut this short by letting that exchange represent the whole painful half-hour of the four of them ministering away, and Bethany pretty much refusing to be ministered unto. Farnell Hastie raised the issue of what she planned to do about, what he understood - here the barest glance at Bethany's new waistline - that she was expecting, as a result of her ordeal. It was as clear as air that he was itching to hand her the 800 number for Planned Parenthood, but couldn't with Father Conor there. Father Conor talked of adoption, and Bethany gave him a modified version of what she'd answered me on the issue: Why on earth would she want to give her baby to strangers?

That skated us close to the thin ice of the Abominable Household. Sam spoke softly, reasonably, about every child's right to and need for a man to call Daddy. He remarked on how lucky Bethany had been to get me in that role, when her own Daddy had passed untimely while Lee was carrying her. Well, Bethany said, little Lee might not have a daddy, but (s)he would have the best of Grampas, two of them in fact.

And that brought an almost audible groan from the Ministerial Alliance. Father Conor, a little behind the curve on gossip, looked surprised and asked who the other grandfather might be. There was a moment of silence before Bethany said, "Why, Wet Parsonage."

"Bethany considers herself committed to a young woman who is the ward of a Fayetteville policeman," I explained.

Father Conor looked as if I'd said Bethany wanted to marry a right whale. "Bethany, I have to tell you that the Church - that no religious body in the state of North Carolina or any of its faiths would for a moment countenance such an arrangement."

"Well," Bethany sighed. And her face toughened. "Well, then I guess countenancing is just one of the things we'll have to learn to do without."

There was more talking, if not much more saying. But as they were going, Plummer Baley lagged behind, and spoke up for almost the first time. "Miss, I won't pretend to hardly even understand how you're thinking or where your heart lies, much less know what sort of countenance to give it. But I will say this. Folks at Indian Girl Swamp Pentecostal Tabernacle do have considerable experience of not being countenanced. You ever looking for a church home, you give us a call."

Tears sprang to Bethany's eyes, and she gave him a quick and unavoidable kiss, leaving a little wet place on his cheek. He was following the other three down the front walk, scrubbing at it with a rumpled hankie, when the phone rang.

"Leonard Cornwell, Swain County Sheriff's Office, Mr. Maryland. Thought you'd like to know we apprehended Derwood Cather last night. We'll hold him long enough for whoever wants, to come out here and identify him and swear out a complaint."

OK, here's the story of that fiasco in a nutshell. Bethany's mental armor against what had happened was to refuse to think about it. Only the fact that she didn't take the season of virgin birth literally, kept her from denying that it had ever happened. The very notion of going out to Swain County to be confronted with Derwood in order to lodge a complaint of rape against him put her in a state that it took Suellen and me a sleepless night to settle her down from.

On Honeyman Bald

Toward dawn, she fell asleep, and so did we. And some time after lunch on a balmy Epiphany afternoon, she sat with us on the side porch, rocking gently on the old metal glider and sipping lemonade.

"I do apologize for my behavior of last night," she said. "But I also hope that I have heard the last of any notion of going out there to face it again."

It was Bethany's notion that Suellen and I represented complainants enough to settle "it," that our identification was more than sufficient, and that she was in too delicate a state to make the trip. Her counselor at Tri-County Mental Health backed her up on that. Suellen said, well, there was no way she was going out there and leave Bethany here alone. Besides which, it had already occurred to me that getting Suellen and her knife into the picture might lead to incalculable complications. Was Derwood entitled to redress for the attack on his manhood? Probably not, but I was no lawyer, and had no idea what would strike a Swain County grand jury as justifiable. In the end, I made the trip alone.

I was placed in a witness room, facing a one-way mirror, and a bunch of guys were brought in, in wheelchairs. They were all stoutish, older guys of the country type, but only one of them was Derwood Barnes Cather, and I was all too glad to identify him.

"That's him. Second from the left. That's the guy who kidnaped and raped my daughter, and stood by while his so-called son raped her friend."

"Very well, sir," the Swain County DA said. "Where's the young ladies?"

Well, they were unavailable and unwilling to testify.

Did I witness either incident?

No, I did not.

Exactly what did I witness?

I told him about Derwood's abduction of Bethany from Carrboro.

"You're saying she went with him unwillingly?"

"Of course that's what I'm saying."

"Well, see, only she can testify as to that. I can't go in there with your opinion on it, for a woman that's of age."

So I cut to Derwood's chucking Bethany off the ledge, dangling her over a thousand-foot drop. I told him about the condition Bethany was in when I finally got her back onto the ledge.

"He agrees that he went a little too far in that, trying to give her a thrill in the course of what he claims was consensual rough sex, with a young lady that was smitten with him during a scholarly visit to Chapel Hill. I must say, I'm surprised and disappointed in him for that."

"Why? He's a fraud and a liar who'll say anything."

"I meant about kinky sex with a young coed. Why would he lie about that?"

"To keep you from believing the truth, which was worse. I can't believe what I'm hearing here. It was nothing of the sort."

"Well, sir, we'd have to have the young lady's testimony on that point."

"Surely you don't believe that stuff about consensual?"

"What I believe is not a basis for an indictment. For that, you have to have evidence."

So I told him about what Wet and I had found in the graveyard.

"His story on that is that those are scattered bones he'd found over the years, in the woods. Been a lot of folks killed out here, going back to the Civil War and beyond. Soldiers, drunks, lost hikers, skiers that broke something and froze to death, got tore up and scattered by foxes and such. He recovered what he could in each case, and gave it a Christian burial. I will say it was derelict of him not to report his finds to the authorities."

"And every one of those foxes hid the skull."

"Sir?"

"Dental work. You have no way to identify any of those anonymous bodies, I bet."

He got a little huffy at a civilian teaching him his job. "As it happens, one of them does include a partial skull, though without teeth. That's not so unusual. I've got to tell you, sir, I have no inclination to go into court with a case I'm not sure I can win. That would include just about everything you've been talking about here, and certainly any kind of rape indictment where the alleged victims won't testify."

"I see. What can we nail the bastard on, based on what I've told you? That you'd feel you could successfully prosecute?"

The DA leaned back in his chair and gave me a cold look. "Hard to know what a jury'll do, in't it? When the defendant is well known in the jurisdiction and the accuser in't."

"Known for pulling this kind of stuff? Murder, rape, cannibalism... Jesus, you guys know what kind of man he is."

"We do know a little bit, sir. Not as much as we know about some, being this is the first time he's been in trouble. Doc Cather is known for keeping to himself, except for acts of charity and sacrifice such as springing for a eye operation on a fella's little girl, got her sight back. He done that out of the royalties he gets on these books. His banker, what shouldn't have, gave me to understand that set him back two years worth of book royalties and speaking fees. He adopted that young punk from Tennessee that was nothing but heartbreak and trouble to him, and stuck by him through thick and thin. Tore him up fit to die, when DB took that fall. I understand your wife was involved in that as well, for which you have my condolences."

The DA shook his head. "His tithes amount to just under half the annual budget of that little church up there't Hahnemann, where he lives, which I do know about from personal experience, being married to the volunteer treasurer. Jaycees give him Swain County Man of the Year, two years running. Regard to your daughter, if she won't testify, I'd think reckless endangerment is about as much as I'm likely to get a conviction on, and it would be based entirely on your eyewitness but uncorroborated testimony. You want to press that?"

"Reckless endangerment."

"Yes, sir."

"And what is the likely penalty for a first offense of reckless endangerment by this saintly man?"

The DA let me see that he was choosing to ignore the sarcasm. "Ninety days, up to a year if it was aggravated, which I believe I could get to stick. He'd be out in six months."

"Wonderful. He can come to the baby shower."

So I went through with it. I won't clutter this tale by narrating the trial. It gave me two more near-fruitless drives from Gabbro to Swain County. The courtroom was packed with Hahnemannians, including the Reverend Cloyd Hunnimon and Sister 'Licia. I could not get mad at them when they gave me sorrowful looks aplenty at what I was saying about their neighbor. I owed them too much. The whole business was a farce whose sole satisfaction was being allowed to watch a baggy-pantsed Derwood Barnes Cather spraddle in and out of the courtroom on the arm of a deputy, keeping his legs as far apart as he could manage. Neither his defense lawyer nor the DA asked him about it, mercifully. Reverend Cloyd and Jake the veterinarian testified truthfully about the condition Bethany was in when they found her, after her spell of being recklessly endangered. I left as soon as I could and drove myself back to Gabbro. Deputy Cornwell called in a week and told us Derwood had been found guilty and drawn a six month sentence. You see why I tend to bypass the cops when I get into these messes?

27.

After a warm Christmas, we had the coldest, rainiest January in the archives of the Gabbro weather bureau. Which, truthfully, amounted to a sequence of 9th grade General Science classes at Gabbro Middle School keeping records of what they saw out the window and on the roof of the gym, in a spotty tradition dating from 1937. Still, it was raw and nasty, and calculated to bring us all down with cabin fever.

None more so than prospective - what? Auntie? Co-Mom? Call her what you like - Suellen Ransom, who was finally too proud to keep taking my charity, and went back to college for the spring term, and took a half-time job maintaining the guinea pig and white rat colonies for the Biology Department so she could contribute something to the finances. After Bethany got past her spell of morning sickness, she pitched in and pretty much ran the house, doing most of the cooking, cleaning, and laundry, while I scoured the region for consulting jobs.

A week or two after Christmas, I got a sorrowing letter from Sam Wainwright, on behalf of the Ministerial Alliance, begging me to lead my young women away from what he called their "wrong-headed apostasy." Suellen got some stick-on letters and a scrap of lumber out of the garage, whose ends she rusticked in the biology department's wood shop, spelled out "APOSTATE HOUSE" on it, and put it up over the porch. Bethany ignored it at first, and then took it down, amended it to read "A PROSTRATE HOUSE" and stuck it over the doorway into their wing. A week or so later, Suellen peeled off the second R and stuck the remainder over my bedroom door.

Sounds a little jolly, maybe. It didn't feel so. Each of us was in her or his own world most of the time, each had one grounds or another for exasperation with both the others. Some of us had several. Suellen, the lifelong bird of passage, had a particularly rough time of it, watching Bethany swell through that raw and bitter February toward a birth that Suellen considered a fatheaded and monstrous mistake, and whose issue would have no claim on her loyalty and patience.

Hell, she was a good-looking twenty-nothing who'd lived free and rough most of her life. I won't string this out; she started staying out late, coming home smelling of beer and good times. Bethany was forgiving, then tight-lipped about it, and there was in the end a row. Both women looked to me to referee, and I did what I could. But Suellen saw it as clearly as any of us.

"Look, Hap," she said to me one night at the grim end of February, while we wrestled the trash out to the curb in a sleety drizzle. "This pregnancy is ruining the whole deal. We're about past the time now when she could have gotten an abortion, so I guess we're in for it. What do you see my obligations are here?"

"If you have to ask - "

"All right. I agree, but look. I'm not married to Bethany, that's impossible and uncountenanced. All I do is love her. I'm not related to her baby. And by God, I despise the kid's father, and the process by which she got the kid." Suellen whomped a bag of mixed recycle into the bin, and slammed the lid. "And my opinion on any of that counts about as much as Covington's."

"Mine, too. I just don't see what else we can try. And as long as she's my daughter - "

"Which she isn't."

"That was a helpful remark. I was there when she was born, and I married her mother when she was seven. I raised her and I love her as much as I loved my own daughter."

"You think I don't? Here's the deal, though. I already hate her kid. I would make a lousy Mommy to it, and I love her too much to make her try to deal with that. If she won't get an abortion, then I will have to remove myself, if only to protect the kid."

I was a little surprised to find myself dismayed. "I see. And when are you planning to acquaint her with this piece of news?"

Suellen crouched on the sidewalk and started to cry. "As soon as I can get up the guts to, God damn it. It'll kill her, and me too."

I squatted next to her for a moment, and not one helpful thing came to me that I could say. And besides, while I was still hunkered there, awkwardly patting Suellen's shoulder and wondering how I was going to get Bethany through this, Bethany opened the front door and peered out at us.

"You guys all right? Daddy, phone."

I was glad of the diversion for as long as it took me to shuck off my slicker and take the phone.

"Hap? Tim Summerton here. Look, I got some things I need to talk over with you. I hate to impose, but I'm kind of up against it. Would it be OK if I dropped over?"

What Tim had besides breathtaking gall, was the

product of his first year trying to be a college president: a botched-up agenda for the Board of Trustees and a bogged-down and feckless search for an Admissions Director to replace the one Lee had held against better offers by force of personality, and who had gone to Wake Forest for twice the salary in the second month of the Summerton administration. Some of Tim's problems may remotely have arisen in things that Lee and I understood but never wrote down, but some were so much of his own doing that I had to wonder if he was up to his job. I will give him this: he had each problem written out, with lists of possible solutions, on a yellow legal pad. None of the solutions looked sensible to me, no matter how neatly they were arrayed.

When at length I had talked him through as much of it as I could stomach, I started shuffling him out of there. I actually had the door open when Bethany came through the living room, ready for bed in one of my old painting shirts, barefoot and scrubbed. When she saw who was there, she turned away and headed for the back of the house.

"Hey there, Beffie," Tim called. "Don't run off."

Bethany flung a hand in the air and ran down the hallway. I think I heard a gritted-off sob. When I turned back to Tim, he was just palpably ogling her legs and the flash of cotton panties under the shirt.

"She's upset, poor thing," Tim smiled. "I swear she's the image of her beautiful momma."

I didn't let myself think twice. I planted my feet and slapped him hard enough to make him stagger over Covington and sprawl on the floor. The legal pad and file folders flapped against the walls like trapped pigeons. It was a very satisfactory result from a simple slap.

He pulled himself up on the door jamb and looked at

me like he was trying to decide whether to hit back, press charges, or beg forgiveness. Well, it certainly wasn't forgiveness. He adopted a responsible and manly tone. "Hap?" he asked. "What the heck was that about?"

"Keep your mouth and your self out of my family, Summerton. Who the fuck do you think you are?"

Injured innocence. "Me? I'm just about Lee's oldest friend, is who. I think I'm entitled to mourn her as much as anyone. As much as you, truth of it."

"I think you have funny ideas about what you're entitled to, Tim. Can we leave it at that?"

He got mad, at last. "No, I don't think so, Hap. I don't think we can leave it at that. Lee and I had something special until you came along."

"Something special, was it, you fucking sneak? I just bet. What, weekends at the Holiday Inn Fort Bragg?"

He looked perplexed. "I don't know what that's supposed to mean, unless you're telling me a vice president has more money to spend than a professor. Good for you. The fact is, Lee was always perfectly happy to take in a movie downtown and go dutch on the Dairy Queen, until you came along."

"I *came along*? I was married to her, you idiot. That's an arrangement people have, that's supposed to mean other people stay away."

He put on a sulky look. "I'm talking about before you were married, before you came to Gabbro. Lee and I were very good friends, and I think in time she would have - " He waved a hand. "Never mind, let it go. She broke my heart, when she dumped me. She knew that, and she went ahead and did it anyhow, because you came along with your broken heart and your cute little boy and your big, fat salary."

On Honeyman Bald

I snorted. "Noble of you even yet, how you sneer at her when she's dead. I wish you'd been half that noble while she was alive."

He put replaced sulkiness with patience. "What the fuck are you talking about, Hap?"

The creased and smudged love note had never left my pocket since Bethany gave it to me back in September. I pulled it out and handed it to Tim. "That," I said. "And probably dozens more like it that Lee remembered to throw away. Shall I read it to you? From memory? 'My God, you are still magic. Your taste is on my...' "

Tim looked at that note, and I swear, his hair stood on end. Scrooge cannot have shown Marley a paler countenance. Gotcha, I thought, you guilty son of a bitch.

I was reaching for the door to kick him the hell out of Lee's house for good, when he looked up at me with fierce hilarity in his eyes.

"Oh, my God, Hap. Oh, my God, I can't believe this. Where in heaven's name did you find this?" He was chuckling and slapping the note, shaking his head, reading it over and over. "By God, the jealous Pantaloon finds the smoking gun."

"I'll show you a smoking gun if I ever see you here again. Now, will you for God's sake, get out, before - "

"Wait, Hap. Wait. Look at this handwriting, and look here, at my handwriting. Look at all the same to you?"

I looked, reluctantly. Why, no, there was not the least resemblance. The mash note was a loopy, immature scrawl, and Tim's working papers were written in a hand so neat and italic as to reek of calligraphy. His handwriting was another thing about Tim Summerton, as a matter of fact, that had always set my teeth on edge. Why hadn't I remembered that? But there you go; the jealous mind is pretty much no mind at all.

"My God, Tim," I said, my mind spinning down the track of who Lee's secret lover could have been, if not this cockatoo. "I guess I owe you a big apology. Now, Jesus, I don't know what to think. I'm sorry I hit you, and I guess I'm sorry I disillusioned you about Lee. Apparently, what she had going was with somebody else."

Tim put a manly and steadying hand on my shoulder. I could feel the exercise callouses on his fingers through my tee shirt. "Listen to me, you poor bastard, and see if you can understand this. I wrote that note, all right. I wrote it the night before I got shipped off to military school, when Lee and I were in the 9th grade."

He grinned, and chucked me under the chin. "Close call, though, Sherlock. We were a pretty hot item in those days."

*   *

"I guess I owe you an apology," I said. She was grey and indistinct.

Don't apologize.

"No, really. He explained about the note."

What note?

The doofy dead. "Well, that one that Bethany ... the one about, he can't wait to taste you again, all that. The one he wrote you before he got sent to military school."

She looked worried, said nothing. She had begun to degrade again, taking on the color of the fog around her. A tear gleamed and she faded quickly until she became no more than a location, a place that was Lee but that, if I ever took my eyes from it, I would never find again. I felt the wind of falling. Her voice came from the grey place like static from Samarra.

No, you were right. Bethany was right.

She said something else, that started with "The family," but I couldn't make out the punch line. Her voice became as contentless and indistinct as the fog, as the slight singing in my ears.

*   *

I came down to breakfast on a Sunday in mid-March. Bethany was on a blanket outside the back door, in lotus position, squarely facing the rising sun, the first sun we'd had in weeks. Covington was lying on the blanket, catching the slanting early rays, and rose when she heard my step in the kitchen. I didn't intrude on Bethany, but let Covington in to supervise egg-scrambling.

When I had a satisfactory pan full, I dealt myself a plate, and cleared my throat in Bethany's direction. She raised a peremptory hand and inhaled substantially.

"Quiet," she said. "I'll come in directly."

I took her bathrobe from the back of a kitchen chair and hung it on the doorknob, and dashed salsa on my eggs. Covington scratched at the screen, and I let her out. Bethany ignored her, and sat stock-still. She'd pivoted slightly to follow the sun's southward climb.

I'd had a cup of coffee and the sports section when Bethany came in, sun-blinded, banging her shin on a chair and knotting the belt over her paunch.

"Ow," she said. "You wont to think about going to church?" She was shivering a little.

Nothing could have sounded less fun than the pointed

nonstares and the broken-off conversations that would have met our saunter into Gabbro Pres. "What, as penance? Who'd have us?"

"Pentecostal Tabernacle."

"Oof. You're kidding, right?"

"Why would I kid about that?"

"You sound like your mother. Is this something that came to you out there while you were staring at the sun?"

"No. It came to me in the middle of the night. I was cleansing just now."

I got up and poured myself more coffee. "Well, thank you for being willing to say that, Bethany. Cleansing?"

"Listen, Daddy. I'm not a hundred percent crazy. And I'm not trying to fool myself about where this baby came from. He's half me and half - well, half bad. Or he would be if I didn't do something about it."

She cupped her hands around the paunch and got on a transcending sort of look. "I've done this from the very moment I decided to have this baby. He'll be my baby, and only mine, so ever since he was just a little ball of cells, I've visualized all the badness melting away from him. All the blackness and hatred and hurt that ... that came into me then, I'm seeing it in every cell and tissue and organ while they're growing, and I'm cleaning it out, right down to the molecules. Sunlight helps."

"Uh huh. You let the sunlight come in through your eyes, and - "

"For as long as I can stand it. Daddy, I knew you'd get it. It wasn't hard at first, but it's getting harder, now he's got so big and complicated. I can see him though, and I know he's as clean and healthy as anything. Just, I have to keep after it, now he's starting to get a real brain and a heart.

That's the hard part, it's so full of wrinkles and complications."

"Isn't it, though." I flipped a hand. "Beffie, anybody in town would say you're as crazy as a loon. I'd say it too if you weren't my girl. But sometimes, well, you do make sense. OK, let's see what the Pentecostals are like. Heck, tongues of fire ought to be purifying as anything, right?"

There are two Pentecostal Holiness Chapels in Gabbro, but the one Bethany had in mind was Pastor Plummer Baley's, half of it cantilevered on thin air over Indian Girl Swamp because it was a Baley church, and it's rare indeed for a Baley operation to actually own enough real estate to put a church on. We sat in the last pew, because that's all the room there was, and anyhow, I figured it would give us a fighting chance to get on solid ground when the whole mess collapsed into the swamp under the stomping of a gang of Pentecostals.

But in fact, things were pretty mild. No snakes, for example, which put them a notch more High-Church than Cloyd Hunnimon. I later learned that it was the Wednesday night Fire Services where most of the speaking in tongues happened. What we got was some pretty recognizable Bible readings, four or five heartfelt a capella hymns - you don't dare bring an organ or a piano into a church that's built on air - sung from the heart and without nuance or vibrato by maybe a hundred reedy Baleyesque voices; and a sermon from Reverend Plummer Baley delivered, I swear, straight at flushed and soft-eyed Bethany. It was about what he called the fullness of God's knowledge and power.

He started by picking up a bud that was stuck into a pop bottle on the pulpit, and asking the children in the front row what it was, and what it was going to do. A flower, they agreed, or would be as soon as it opened.

"Think so, do you? Well, whose hand made this pretty thing?"

"God's," piped the kids.

"You bet. Let's open 'er up, shall we?" He started to pick at the folded petals.

"Stop," a sallow girl in the front row yelled. "You'll wrack it."

Plummer affected to be frustrated. "Yeah? How we supposed to get it open, then?"

A chunky guy in overalls stood up. "God'll take care of it," he claimed, and sat down, looking surprised at himself.

Plummer smiled at him scornfully. "You tellin me, brother, that Jehovah the all-powerful, the God of Abraham and Jacob and the Lord and Ruler of all the worlds and planets of the universe, He whose mighty Word sets worlds in motion, has got the time to stop by here at Indian Girl Swamp in the State of North Carolina and open up a flower for us?"

The farmer looked abashed, so Plummer helped him out. "Why, sure he does. I'd sure have gall to think I could do it, wouldn't I? I'd just ruin it, like our little sister told me just now. God will open this flower, in His good time. But now looka here, they's a little midge settled on it, looking for a meal, I expect."

He held the bottle up. Nehi cream soda, it said. "Everybody see that? Looks like a little black dot, I expect, from more'n a couple feet away. The whole creature isn't but a smidgen. And its feet and wings, why they're so small even I can't see 'em. Who gave them tiny wings permission to buzz that midge in here?"

On Honeyman Bald

Nobody's needed, I thought. That's the problem with bugs, isn't it? But not in Plummer Baley's world.

"Why, God done. God made and remains fully aware of that bug, and He is present in the tiny muscles that flap its wings, in all the cells of its body, yes, and of all the myriad midges and bees and mosquitos in this entire swamp and every other swamp and meadow and backyard in this state, and all the states of this and every other nation on every planet in the overflowing and ever-expanding universe, yes! I *tell* you, that if there are midges on Mars or on any planet that circles the tiniest speck of starlight we can see, God is there to know each stroke of every wing. He made and knows them all, every molecule and atom, every electron and quark, and infinite levels below that."

Quarks, I thought. Pentecostal Divinity schools have changed some.

"Even as," Plummer's voice dropped, "He knows the thoughts and desires of all creatures great and small on all those worlds and on this one. Every thought of all our brothers and sisters across the great Earth, from sea to sea and pole to pole, including the United States, North Carolina, Gabbro County, and right here in this rickety Tabernacle. He knows the beating of our hearts and the flickering webs of calculation, fear and hope inside every skull in this church. And always has, brothers and sisters. Before thou wert, I AM, he tells us. Through all time, from the awesome and terrific Bang that started it, to this Sunday morning and onward to the End whose shapes and terrors we cannot guess; past, present and future a single great Plan that is the story of all Creation."

He left the pulpit, bright-eyed and puffing a little, and walked down the aisle to stand in the very center of the congregation. People pivoted to watch him, maybe wondering if he was fixing to explain about the quarks.

"Now, then," he whispered to them. "Is there any power on earth or in this great universe who is strong enough to stand against that mighty Plan? Who do you think could subvert it, who could possibly have the power it would take to ruin and bring to nothing God's infinite and detailed knowledge of the past and future of every atom, and every thought of every living thing in Creation? Another and greater God?" He opened his arms. "The devil? But we know that there is no greater God, and the Devil's powers are as nothing against Him."

Plummer Baley's voice began to rise again. "Not the Devil, not the feeble scheming of governors and legislatures, not the horrendous power of the hurricane, the leviathans of the deep nor the irresistible voices of earthquake, fire, and flood, not even the all-engulfing black hole at the center of the vast and silent Milky Way can oppose Him. Nobody and nothing in all Creation; except," he said, crouching and whispering again, "just you and I can, brothers and sisters. You and I. That's why He given us freedom and the knowledge of good and evil. Any one of us can snap our fingers at God's mighty plan for us. All we need is the infernal gall to do it."

Plummer stood for a moment, shaking his head at the notion of that infernal gall. Then he raised his shoulders, hands outstretched. "Shall we? Or shall we fall on our knees in awe-struck gratitude that the Great Architect of all Creation bothers himself to know about you and me, to love us and to plan for us?"

Silence. Plummer Baley stood at the center of a hundred parishioners. God and the Devil, dreams and fears

On Honeyman Bald

flickered and wheeled like galaxies behind their eyes. Bethany breathed in a little shakily; slid her hand over mine and squeezed. But the sallow little girl in the front got restless and turned to look at the pulpit.

"Looka *there*, Momma," she squealed.

And in the Nehi bottle stood a full-blown and virginal daffodil.

28.

It was not long after that, that Plummer Baley began to call on Bethany, at first for pastoral purposes; though it was not too much longer after that, that Bethany began to - oh, well, slick herself up a little before Plummer would arrive. Brush her hair, change into a formal maternity top rather than the bagged-out sweatshirts she generally made do with. It didn't escape Suellen's notice, and after Plummer's second or third visit, I heard a rumbling snarl in the driveway one Saturday at the end of April. It was Suellen, straddling a Kandy-blue Kawasaki.

"Holy cats," I said, when she clomped in the back door. "Where'd that come from?"

She didn't pause on her way to the Prostrate House wing. "Tuition money. Where's Beffie?"

I had to tell her that Beffie was out, though I didn't add that it was Plummer Baley's creaky Beetle that had flivved her off in the direction of the Historic Gabbro Days parade and street fair. I didn't have to. Suellen, victimized again by her lively apprehension, snarled something I didn't catch, and slammed the door of her room. I took the Intelligencer and my coffee out to the Kawasaki. It was hot and ticking. Its speedometer went up to 150. When Suellen reappeared in a half hour, there was a faint smudge on her cheek, and her hair was wetly combed into a roadworthy ponytail.

"Can't have been three weeks after Reverend Baxter disappeared, mom figured out for me I was pregnant, and put me on the Fayetteville bus. Nothing's gone all that wonderful since then, would you say?"

"I never could figure out - OK, I know, nobody deserves how she died - why you always praised and defended your mother. That was just brutal."

Silence. "So I wouldn't have to face up to what a shit she was. It was on that bus I figured out I was in Hell." She laughed, and set about tying her massive duffel on the back of the Kawasaki with bungee cords. "Poor me, huh? Hell, if I'm there, you must be too."

"Has anything happened in the last year that would tend to bear that out?"

"Right. Well, if that's what this is, then there's nothing to lose, right? So I'm not putting up with any crap. If Bethany wants to have the baby, and footsy around with that preacher kid, why, fine. That's Hell, for you. But as far as I'm concerned, I'll take it on my own terms. Give her my love."

She kicked the Kawasaki to life. "I just wish it didn't have to hurt so much. Bye."

I think I have mentioned that sound travels pretty freely in Gabbro, City Without a Skyscraper. I heard the Kawasaki blat all the way until she turned the corner of Church and College, on her way to the bypass. For as long as I could hear it, it sounded pissed off and sorrowful.

Bethany was pretty crushed about Suellen's taking off, but it wasn't long before she was agreeing with me that it's what had been in the cards, that Suellen could not have been expected to take on parental responsibility for a baby whose very existence infuriated her. And in fact, Bethany didn't have much emotional capacity left over to mourn Suellen, after what she'd been through. For that matter, I was never convinced that she'd made a big emotional investment in Suellen in the first place; I think stubborn unwillingness to be talked out of it had played a bigger role than she would ever have admitted. I certainly saw few, if any, little tokens of affection between them after the short honeymoon in Carrboro. In a couple of weeks, she was talking about converting Suellen's room to a nursery.

*   *

And that's what we were doing on a Monday morning in June when I found the packet of letters from Tim Summerton to Lee. They were bundled in rubber bands on the back of a linen-closet shelf where I'd gone looking for the other side of a duct that was supposed to feed clean and allergen-free air to the baby, as soon as I figured out how to mount the filter unit. They were modern, explicit, and written in Tim Summerton's irritatingly perfect, grown-up hand.

The first one in the stack was shy and formal, and dated ten years ago. It charmingly spoke of ancient history - the junior high prom, for example - and proposed lunch. As they progressed, he quit dating them, maybe to compromise their usefulness as evidence. Still, I recognized some of the events referred to over the years, when there was anything in them but the bliss of her embrace, the textures of her skin. The last spoke of weekending at Lake Junaluska over Labor Day. Lee had come home from a college administrators' meeting at Junaluska with the first of the headaches that announced the tumor. I thought at the time, she was working too hard, or maybe suffering from the cotton defoliant that plagues Gabbro in the fall. She was tired, grateful and affectionate when I put her to bed with an alcohol rub.

And guilty as hell. Oh, God, I cannot stand the thought

that she was trysting with Tim Summerton behind my back and just as slyly slipping forth to mate with Death, while Tim kept his secret and showed the world a manly face, and while stupid, superficial, complacent me thought myself blessed, oh, the happiest man in a five-state region, the lucky hubby of a world-class immortal beloved. When my absence to investigate the vent stretched on long enough, Bethany came looking for me. She found me on the floor of the closet.

"Daddy, are you - Oh, my God! Oh, Daddy, stop. Put it down. Give it to me."

I handed her the Glock, having discovered that actually killing yourself requires more volition than I could summon.

"Daddy, what is it?" She collapsed in tears against me. "Don't leave me now, Daddy. Whatever it is, I love you, I love you so much, don't ever scare me like that. What is it?" She clamped herself to me, weeping as if I had really gone through with it.

"OK, Beffie. I won't. Evidently, I don't have the guts or energy for it."

"What is it?"

"What is it? I'm almost sixty years old, I've never been anything but a goddamn fool my whole life. I'm about to start the part of my life everyone dreads who makes it this far. I just thought I'd cut to the chase."

"But, Daddy, why now?"

I handed her the pack of love notes. She read the first line or two of a couple of them, and then put them down to fold herself against me.

"I thought I told you about that."

"You did. I thought it was a false alarm. That note you gave me in Carrboro was from junior high."

She didn't say anything. I pulled back to look at her.

"You knew better, didn't you? Did you catch them or something?"

"Nothing like that. I could just tell."

She could tell, but she couldn't tell me. She sighed, and worked herself into a more comfortable cuddle. The bulge of her belly fit nicely into my lap. "I think she was fixing to give that old note to Tim, sort of for old time's sake. It was like he got under her radar, or something. She loved you with all her heart."

"Maybe not exactly all, Beffie." I sighed. "It's all right. I've already been through this back in September, so it's not exactly a horrible shock. Thank you for loving me. Please take those letters and burn them, and then keep me away from fucking Tim Summerton for a while."

And - Jesus, how's this for boneheaded persistence in the face of Hell - we went back to fixing up Bethany's baby's nursery. For a baby got by rape and destined to bear the name of a lying, scheming adulteress.

A postcard came from Suellen on the fifteenth of June, while Bethany was downtown, picking up supplies for her impending maternity. It was a Smokies panorama. If you were really imaginative, you could convince yourself that a pale smudge on the extreme left was Honeyman Bald. "Thinking of you," was the message. I chucked it on the hall table and went to pick up the phone.

"Sir, this is Plummer Baley speaking. I, ah...well..."

"I'm sorry, Bethany's out at the moment. I'll tell her you called."

"No sir, wait. It was you I wished to speak to, sir, if you would be so kind."

"Well, sure, Plummer. What's up?"

On Honeyman Bald

"Sir, as you know, I have been much taken with the company of your daughter Bethany."

I smiled. "Well, Plummer, I believe the feeling is at least a bit mutual. Bethany and I were both just blown away by your daffodil."

"Yes sir. Kind of a cheap trick, I'm afraid. I rehearsed it. Or I guess God and I did ..." There followed a silence long enough to become awkward.

"Plummer?"

Sigh. "Sir, this is being quite difficult over the telephone. Would you be available for a brief conversation in - oh, maybe a half hour?"

"All right. If Bethany comes back, shall I tell her you're coming?"

"Please don't."

Fine, I thought. He's going to explain how he can't keep company with a pregnant girl any more, and ask me to break it to Bethany. Damned if I will. When he rang the doorbell, I led him out to a pair of tree-shaded deck chairs Lee and I used to sit in, sharing wine and the *Intelligencer* on soft summer evenings. Back when I believed in her. Plummer sat in the one she had used, and scooted himself forward to look at me with unparalleled earnestness.

"Sir, I probably don't have to explain to you that a Pastor of a little church doesn't hardly make enough from it to live on."

"Mm-hmm." Much less run around with women.

"I do have other resources. I am partners in a woodworking business with my uncle, Mr. Chavis Baley, and we are turning a decent income from that."

"Chavis is a wonderful craftsman. I never thought he'd have the nerve to go into business for himself."

He brightened up. "I take care of that side. I get the contracts, and he does most of the skill work. Right now, we have more jobs lined up than we can get to for six months, and some of them are substantial. The Pentecostal Chapel in Bozlee - "

I stopped him with a palm. "Hold it. Very interesting. Is there a point you might be getting to?"

He blushed. "Yes sir, there is. I just wanted to let you know that I have more resources than might appear."

"Resources," I nodded. "Good."

"Yes sir. What I'm saying is, I could support her in a decent way."

"Support Bethany?"

"Yes sir. If you was to do me the honor of allowing me to propose it to her."

"You're asking my permission to propose marriage to my daughter, is that it?"

"Yes sir. That's it." He looked as hopeless and flustered as anyone I've ever seen.

"What ever happened to Hey, babe, what say we throw in together, share the rent?"

He stared at me. "Sir, surely you don't see me as that sort of man. I would never have the gall to look you in the ... Oh, really, sir."

"Just kidding. Seriously, you surprise me, Mr. Baley. You can't help being aware that Bethany is expecting."

"Of course. She has told me all about that, and how she is dealing with it. I must say, sir, it is one of the first things that attracted me to her."

"The fact that she's pregnant?"

"No, the way she's coping with it. She is not taking any of the numerous easy ways out, from abortion to bitterness, rationalization, or ... well, insanity would not be out of the question. She is facing squarely into her situation and making the best of it. I admire that more than I can say. I would be honored to serve as father to her child."

I looked at him, and shook my head, and clapped him on the shoulder. It was as skinny and solid as a pipe fence. "Mr. Baley, you are quite a fellow yourself. You have my permission to discuss marriage with Bethany. Don't be so long getting to the point with her, though."

"Don't you worry. That won't be half is tough as this was."

Oh, yeah? Bethany pulled in the driveway just then, swerved, and ground the transmission of the car over one of the painted rocks that line it. There was a ripping sound, and several quarts of oil gushed onto the grass.

Bethany stuck her head out the window and yelled, "Daddy, Plummer, help. I'm having contractions."

I turned to Plummer. "Here we go, kid. Can you take her to the hospital? Looks like our car is out of commission."

"I walked over here. Let's call the EMT's."

"Go help her. I'll call."

I ran in the kitchen and dialed 911 - Gabbro having just installed that Twentieth Century amenity - and looked out the window while it rang a dozen times. Plummer had Bethany in one of the deck chairs, and was patting her hand and talking to her. She was looking at him like he was crazy. 911 picked up, and I gave her the particulars. She promised an ambulance "just as quick as we can get there, sir."

I hung up and dashed into the yard. Plummer was down on one knee next to the deck chair.

"Miss Morgan," he said, a little breathlessly - though hell, what did he have to be puffing about? "I wish to ask you to do me the profound honor of being my wife."

"Aiee!" Bethany huffed. "Just a ... just a second. Aghh! Oof. You what?"

"I said, Will you marry me? Please?"

Bethany looked at him sorrowfully. "That's very kind of you, Plummer. But I'm very damaged goods. You don't want to ... and anyhow, I'm a little busy right now." She turned to me. "Daddy, I got to admit, I dawdled over this a little. I think maybe I was having my first contractions when I left this morning. It didn't feel like the books said. I thought I was just a little stiff from painting the nursery."

"Good Christ. How long has this been going on?"

"A couple of hours. Don't yell at me."

"I'm not, I'm not. Your mother did the same thing when you were on the way, cripes. I suppose you get it from her."

Plummer asserted himself. "I am not being kind. I am proposing marriage, and one surely does not do that out of kindness, for gosh sake." I had to smile a little. He could have done a lot worse than to sound like Jimmy Stewart.

He put his hands on either side of her face and glared at her. "Do I look like I'm being kind?"

"Well," Bethany said, thoughtfully. "Actually, yes, you do. I will think about it, Plummer. I'm very flattered. It's very kind - it's very good of you to offer."

"Flattered. That's what people say when they're trying to be nice."

She grabbed his head in turn. "Do I look like I'm being nice? Just, right now, I have to say I'm a little.... Ngnnnh! Where the hell's that ambulance?"

Bethany began to pant, and Plummer turned to me. "Get a washcloth or something, and a nightie for Bethany.

Bethany, with all respect, I'm afraid you will have to get those shorts off."

I went, because it didn't seem like a bad idea. Boil water, and lots of it, fast. God, not that. Please just get us to Gabbro General, OK?

I retrieved Bethany's nightie from her room, and I heard tires in the driveway as I pulled a clean washcloth out of the linen closet. Thank God, the ambulance. I took a second to dampen the washcloth, and went back out. I knew something was wrong the minute I opened the back door. No flashers, no heavy diesel sound, no squawky voices from the radio. No ambulance. Nothing in the drive but a dusty pickup truck, and Derwood Barnes Cather.

I started to go back to call 911, and realized I already had, and I couldn't afford to leave Bethany alone with him long enough to do it again. I ran toward Cather, screaming with rage.

"Jesus Christ, Cather, why aren't you in jail? What the hell are you doing here?"

He held up an arm. "I served my sentence. I got wind of little Beffie's pregnancy on my release, and came here to see what I could do to help."

"Help? You can detonate, you fucking felon. You can disappear from the almighty register of Creation and never be mentioned or thought of again until the last syllable ... Agh! The fucking gall! Go away, and don't come back." I was beside myself with rage, and from that vantage point counseled keeping some perspective. The main thing was getting Bethany to the hospital, not wasting time tearing Derwood Cather's heart out. I turned my back on him.

But Derwood wasn't having ostracism. "I regret alarming your daughter. Perhaps I had no business acceding to intimate relations with her. What passed between us, however, was consensual. Now I am here to face up to my responsibilities as the child's father, and to ask her in turn to acknowledge me by naming the baby after the son you all killed."

He turned to Bethany. "You hear that? I ask that you name the child DB Cather Morgan. You know in your heart, it was never a matter of rape. You cannot refuse me."

Bethany looked as if she were face to face with the Prince of Darkness. She was as pale as paper, lathered in sweat, and shaking. She drew herself together, and spoke through gritted teeth for as long as she could.

"Murderer, bastard, rapist. You have nothing whatever to do with this baby. It has taken nine months, but I have purged every last drop - Nnngh! Ah! Shit!"

Plummer dropped to his knees beside her and held her hand as if, hell, nothing was going on but childbirth. "There, love. There, my sweet. Pant, now, and we're going to have to get these clothes off."

Bethany started struggling out of her shorts, and Plummer stood up to screen the sight from Derwood.

"Sir, I don't know who you are, but I want you to leave. We're busy here, and Bethany pretty clearly wants nothing - "

"Sonny, I don't know who you are, either, but I'll tell you who I am. I'm the father of the baby that's about to join us, and I got a right to be here."

Plummer swelled up. He looked like it would take about three of him to add up to Derwood, as much as jail had diminished Derwood. "You heard me, sir. Get out. Bethany wants nothing to do with you. I know what you did to her. Shame on you, and get the hell out of here."

On Honeyman Bald

Derwood's lip curled. His fists clenched, and he looked like he was about to break the little preacher in half. He reached for Plummer's neck, and I lunged forward to help, too late. There was a flashing and complicated blur of arms and bodies, and suddenly Derwood was sprawling against the hood of his truck with blood streaming from his nose. It took him some time to get past the pain and surprise, which Plummer used to resume ministering to Bethany, keeping an eye on Derwood as he pulled Bethany's underwear off and got her into the nightie.

Derwood crouched and began to advance on Plummer when a snarling roar came from behind him, and the Kandy blue Kawasaki streaked into the drive, skidding sideways on the gravel and bouncing off one of the painted rocks. It reared, swayed, straightened, and came at us, screaming like an F-16. When it was close enough, Suellen launched herself at Derwood and knocked him ass over teakettle into the camellias.

I have to say, Derwood handled himself well at first against this new threat, but Suellen was too strong and quick for him, and at the end of it he was on his knees with both arms behind him in hammerlocks, and Suellen's forearm across his windpipe.

"OK, shithead," she snarled. "Time to finish up on you. This guy bothering you, lady?"

"Holy shit, Suellen," Bethany said. "Where have you been all this time? Plummer was doing fine. You think you can just - Nnnagh! Owwwah, shit!" She dropped the nightie and and gripped her thighs, panting and sweating. A little bloody fluid ran from her. Suellen stared at it and turned putty-colored. Her eyes rolled back, and she fell onto Derwood.

On Honeyman Bald

Derwood shook her off, and rounded on Plummer with a hook that would have decapitated him if it had landed. Plummer stepped inside it and past Derwood, and the next thing I knew Derwood was down in the camellias again, and this time he stayed down. Plummer picked the washcloth out of my hand and started to bathe Bethany's face.

I heard tires on the gravel of the drive, and turned wearily to face the next intrusion. Glory be, it was the EMT's, flashers and all. We looked like the last scene of Hamlet, and I guess I don't blame them for doing a little triage. They glanced at Bethany and rightly classed her as "In labor, birth not imminent." Suellen was coming around by the time somebody knelt by her, and she whacked the little vial of whatever he had under he nose, sending it to bounce off Derwood's windshield. It was Derwood himself that got their attention. After a minimum of vital-signs stuff, they loaded him on one cot in the ambulance and Bethany on the other, and took off. Plummer and Suellen and I trailed along in Derwood's truck.

On the way to Gabbro General, Suellen said she'd realized as she went west out I-40 that Derwood's sentence would be running out any day, so she detoured to Bryson City to see if she could get a chance to kill him and disappear for good. She said it that casually, and Plummer boggled a little.

"You have to know Suellen and what she's been through," I said. "Go on."

She got a job waitressing at the Courthouse Cafe, and kept her ears open. One of the other waitresses worshipped Derwood, and confided his release date. On that day, which was this very morning, in he walked, bold as brass, and almost spotted Suellen before she could duck back into the kitchen. Before she knew it, he'd borrowed the waitress' truck and disappeared. It took Suellen a while to catch up with him, and she followed him across North Carolina, waiting for him to take a pit stop so she could, as she put it, slit his throat in peace.

"It was me that had to take a break, in the end," she said. "I damn near didn't get there in time."

"Right, Wonder Woman," I said. "Thank God you got there in time to faint at the sight of childbirth."

Suellen snorted and blushed. "Well, shit," she said. "It's a scary sight." She punched Plummer in the arm. "Not too scary for you, though, Ace."

Plummer looked serene. "I had some experience with gut shots and sucking wounds in the SEALs," he said. "This wasn't that bad. Sir, if you would be good enough to drop me at the AME Zion Church, there is an errand I must run. I will join you at the hospital."

"Don't be long," I said. "You'll miss the rest of the fun."

Suellen looked after him as he ran up the steps of True Foundation AME Zion. "Shit," she said. "That little squirt was a SEAL? That's the toughest kind of cutthroat, hardass guy there is."

"Seems like Reverend Plummer's got some depths to him," I said. "Sorry for the pun."

"Sorry pun."

When we got to Gabbro General, they were waiting for insurance information before they could decide what kind of room to put Bethany into. Apparently there'd been no hesitation about Derwood; he was in a ward, surrounded by monitors. The tentative diagnosis was stroke. We got Bethany through the admission nightmare and settled. Contractions were coming pretty thick and fast by the time Plummer Baley stuck his head in.

"Sir, Miss," he addressed us. "If I could have just a moment alone with Bethany now."

I wasn't about to deny Plummer Baley a damn thing. We stepped into the hall, and Plummer shut the door after us. He didn't get all the privacy he wanted, though, because a nurse came in to have a good look at Bethany's cervix, and left the door ajar when she went out. That let us hear a concluding murmur from Plummer, followed by "Nnnggh -ss" from Bethany.

"Sorry," Plummer said. "Was that...?" He couldn't bring himself to put words in her mouth.

"Yes," Bethany panted. "You dope. Yes, yes."

Plummer stuck his head out and beckoned us in, and disappeared for a moment. When he came back, Reverend Farnell Hastie was with him, gowned and masked like the rest of us.

Farnell looked mildly around the assembled celebrants, which now included an obstetrician and a nurse swabbing Bethany's business end with a disinfectant mop. He smiled gently and opened a well-worn book. "Dearly beloved," he began.

And when everything had been said, interspersed with groans and pants from Bethany and instructions from the doctor, he concluded, "I now pronounce you husband and wife." He peeked toward the messy business at Bethany's crotch, and added, "And family, any second now I expect." He beamed over his mask at Plummer. "You may kiss the bride, but I guess keep the mask on."

But while that was going on, Bethany gave an exhausted whoop, and Lee Morgan Baley slid slickly from her. There was the suspenseful moment of silence, then the quavering first gasp of air and the treble yawp of outrage. And Suellen fainted again.

29.

Bethany and Plummer live in a house that Plummer and his Uncle Chavis remodeled out of a tobacco barn about a mile from our house. It has running water, electricity, plumbing, and high-speed Internet access, which is handy for Bethany, since she can take courses from Chapel Hill while she nurses. She is majoring in Finance now, and serves as treasurer of Baley Construction in her spare time. She seems as happy as it is reasonable for anyone to be.

I would have to say, unreliable source that I am, that her cleansing exercises worked. Little Lee slept through the night at six weeks, and is sunny and adorable by day. She shows not a trace otherwise of her paternity, not even a Y chromosome. She looks, therefore, just like Bethany, which is also to say, like her grandmother Lee. The Adulterous One. The one whom, if I had the character and self-control Bethany has, maybe I could purge from myself and my sleep as thoroughly as Bethany banished Derwood Barnes Cather.

Suellen has gradually gotten her mind around a distant-Auntie sort of role, into which she has not been able to prevent a measure of fondness from creeping. She still lives in the Apostate Feminists' Wing of my house. There are those - and they include half of the population of Gabbro County - who consider it a scandal. It has probably cost me some consultation jobs, and I have not even the consolation of gratuitous sex to show for it.

On the other hand, her companionship is worth ten

times the lost fees. Bethany, for all her nearness, for all the welcoming smiles and hugs when I visit, is gone from my life for good and all, the motherly center of a family of her own. At least for now, Suellen seems as comfortable, and as comforted, in the arrangement as I. We respect each other's combat readiness.

From time to time we sit out in the sling chairs and share the Gabbro *Intelligencer* and a bottle of pinot grigio while the seventeen-year locusts trill. When she's feeling particularly mellow, I razz her about male bonding.

The poor old *Intelligencer* still sorely misses Faye Bynum's stern hand. Once a week or so, Bethany or Suellen or I will drop by Faye's bedside and chat, or bring her something from the New York *Times*. Faye's recovery is being slow, and I wonder whether she'll ever pick up her duties again. She has given up on asking for cyanide, though the place is as smelly and frazzled and chaotic as ever. She has begun to write a weekly column featuring denizens of the Total Care Wing who manage to stay human in spite of it.

The number-banging man in the wheelchair made it to nine-nine-nine a couple of weeks ago, and got stuck there. Yesterday, when Suellen and I were there to visit Faye, his cheeks were wet, and his banging lacked all conviction. As we left, Suellen slipped in to whisper in his ear. He stopped, and assumed the expression of an explorer on a new and infinite shore. "Honey," he said. "You're an angel. Thank you so much." And he went back to it with fresh zeal. "Ten-oh-oh," he bellowed. "Ten-oh-oh."

Suellen turned to leave, and her grin froze. She backed away, holding her hand out toward me in a beckoning gesture.

"Holy shit," she whispered to me. "Look who's in there

with him."

It was Derwood, of course. While we stood gaping at him, one of his eyes flew open and glared at the ceiling before it slowly pivoted to look at us, frozen to the spot.

Derwood was a pitiful sight. He was shrunken and half-mad looking, the part of him that wasn't already dead . An intravenous line dripped liquid into the arm on his good side, while the other lay flaccid and helpless on the blanket. The eye looked at us for long seconds, and then the working half of his face leered into a ghastly smile. The number banger started up through the next thousand.

"My deliverer cometh," Derwood muttered. "Thank the Almighty Lord of the Universe, you've come at last."

"C'mon, Hap." Suellen plucked at my jacket. "Let's get the hell out of here."

"No!" Derwood tried to yell, and got as far as a croak. "Wait. Save me, for God's sake, man. It's so easy."

"Ten-oh-two," bellowed his roommate joyously. "Ten-oh-two."

Derwood tilted his head at the IV. "I never did anything to anyone as bad as this, I'm going mad here. I'm begging you. Pull that IV apart and let a good big bubble of air into it, put it back together. I'll be dead before you're out the door, and they won't find out till morning. God damn it, man, look at me."

His good arm plucked the blanket back, and I got a look at what Suellen's knife had done. It wasn't something I could contemplate for more than a quarter-second. Derwood looked at me with tears pouring from his good eye. "How long would you want to live with that?" He tossed his eye at Suellen. "You fucking her now? Keep her away from knives, and don't turn your back. Can't you have pity on a man that'll never fuck again?"

Suellen yanked me toward the door. "Pity?" I said to Derwood. "You want it now, do you? Too bad you didn't have it when it meant something. No, lie there, you fuckless bastard, until you rot, which I hope it takes years. Sleep well."

I let Suellen pull me out the door while Derwood howled his despair and rage, and the number-banger moved up to Ten-oh-three. Suellen was blazing, and so was I. It seemed to me that we had found the perfect punishment for Derwood, a nothing that was beyond all the somethings - beyond all the humiliation, pain and death - we could ever have administered. But when we got to the street, I stopped.

Ten-oh-three, Oh, ten-oh-three. As I am now, so you must be.

"Go on ahead," I said. "I'll catch up with you."

Suellen started to protest, and then half-smiled. "Softie."

When we were back home, she brought me an Urquell and settled into the other sling chair. "How'd it go?"

"Wonderful," I said. "I just killed a man. It went wonderful."

I looked at the beer as if she'd brought me a bizarre new kind of shampoo. "When I opened the IV, instead of air going in, he started to bleed out of it. He's loaded with anticoagulants for the stroke of course, so he just emptied out like ..." I waved an arm, drained of metaphor. "Like a hot water bottle. When we saw how it was going to go, he asked me to pull the curtain across, so he'd have time to die before anybody spotted it from the hall. And he still couldn't let me go."

I held the beer up to the sunset, and put it down in the grass. "All these punk kids he raised to be model citizens. They all put in some time helping him cut lady hikers out of the herd so he could wow them with wilderness poetry and get them into bed. They picked carefully for women who wouldn't be traced to them, in case they had to insist. You'd be amazed, he said, how many people take off for a hike in the woods without telling anybody where they're going. And you had it exactly right; DB got out of line, getting to you before Derwood got his licks. He was scared as hell of DB, by the way. He'd been wearing a Kevlar vest around him for months."

"Oh, for shit's sake. That's how I could see him get shot, and it never touched him."

"Bruised him pretty badly, he claimed."

High in the golden air, two or three swifts hacked away at the bug problem. I watched them circle and shear a hundred yards up, chittering about the big crawlers in the sling chairs. "Stupid bastard kept trying to get me to say it wasn't his fault about you, Suellen. And all the time, the number guy is banging away and he's draining, and the lake of blood is filling up the room. Like all anybody is, is just this great bag of blood that, if you aren't careful, you'll rip it and leave a mess. And then what difference does it make, whose fault anything is? It's just a cleanup job. God, why aren't we more careful with each other?"

Suellen came and knelt in the grass next to me. "That's all _he_ was. It doesn't mean that's all anybody is. You did him a big favor."

"Right." I turned away so she wouldn't see the tears. "I

told him he wasn't that bad a poet, all in all. Could you do that favor for me, when I ask? Tell me one last lie? But maybe not quite so messy."

"I'll be there, Hap."

I nodded, and remembered how much I loved Bethany and her baby. "Don't hold your breath. But don't get out of touch."

*   *

I won't defend myself, Lee said. It was something I chose to do. I did love you with all my heart, but I chose to fool around with Tim. I didn't even like him all that much. I just....

"Did you let him tell you how you hurt him, when I came to Gabbro? Was that a piece of it?"

I guess nobody's as wonderful as the people that love them think they are, are they? Or maybe they can't bear living up to the worship. First Tim, then Terry, and then you. I could tell myself it was for old times' sake, that some part of me was still the flapper who seduced Tiny Tim. Maybe that was the truth. I chose it freely, if the choice was otherwise never to fall.

Terry Morgan was Lee's first husband, Bethany's father. "Bethany thinks Tim got under your radar. Whatever that's supposed to mean."

You never really get over the first one you love with your whole body. I don't know. What do I know is, I only loved you, Hap. I loved you so much, we were so perfect, maybe I had to spoil it so I could bear it. Please, please forgive me.

I reached out to her, and my hand passed through her. Always before, she had been solid, at least up to the point where she would merge into me.

"Don't worry," I said. "I loved you too. I forgive you,

On Honeyman Bald

Lee. Please forgive me for thinking ill of you. You know - "
The moment I began to say it, her voice joined mine, word
for word – *"I will love you just the same until there is no more
world for anyone."*

Saying it made it true, though maybe it had not been,
before that. Her face became distinct and shining, the stars
came back to her hair. *I knew it,* she said. *You see what a
miracle love is, when you look at what it comes out of ?* She
began to cry, and I held her close, crying too. Not so much
for the loss of her, as for joy at the years that we had. I began
to feel the wind of her falling. She drew back and looked at
me as if she could never get her fill.

The family that cries together ....

"Dies together?" I was weightless now like her, joined
in the fear and the rapture of free fall.

Flies together.

She reached for me and we merged. For the rest of my
life on this earth, that falling has never left me.